Armand Cabasson was born in 1970. He works as a psychiatrist in northern France. *Wolf Hunt* is the second *Grande Armée* murder investigation, featuring Quentin Margont, set in the Napoleonic Wars. It was awarded the 2005 Napoleonic Foundation Fiction Prize. Armand Cabasson is a member of the Souvenir Napoléonien and has used his extensive research to create a vivid portrait of the Napoleonic campaigns. *The Officer's Prey* is the first in the Quentin Margont series.

Isabel Reid studied History and French at Oxford university and has lived in France and Geneva. Her most recent translations are *Murder on the Eiffel Tower* and *The Père-Lachaise Mystery* (with Lorenza Garcia), both by Claude Izner.

Praise for the Officer's Prey

'. . . vivid portrayal of the Grande Armée . . . worth reading'
Literary Review

'. . . with vivid scenes of battle and military life . . . Cabasson's atmospheric novel makes a splendid war epic . . .'
Sunday Telegraph

'Cabasson skilfully weaves an intriguing mystery into a rich historical background.' *Mail on Sunday*

WOLF HUNT

Also by Armand Cabasson

The Officer's Prey

WOLF HUNT

ARMAND CABASSON

Translated from the French by Isabel Reid

GALLIC BOOKS

First published in France as *Chasse au loup*

First published in Great Britain in 2008 by Gallic Books,
134 Lots Road, London SW10 0RJ
This edition published in 2011 by Gallic Books

A CIP record for this book is available from the British Library

ISBN 978-1-906040-83-3

Typeset in Fournier MT by SX Composing DTP, Rayleigh, Essex
Printed and bound by CPI Bookmarque, Croydon, CR0 4TD

2 4 6 8 10 9 7 5 3 1

CHAPTER 1

IT had happened five years ago, in 1804, but to Lukas Relmyer those five years seemed no more than a minute. He stopped on the last step, momentarily paralysed, and had to force himself to go forward into the cellar. From the outside, the ruins of the farm had not changed, but in here the ceiling had deteriorated, collapsing in places. Relmyer wandered into the middle, avoiding the rays of sunshine as if he feared they might scorch him. He touched a large prominent stone. Like last time. Suddenly his hand seemed to him changed, more fragile, hesitating between childhood and maturity. An adolescent's hand. Lukas Relmyer had difficulty breathing. He thought he heard a scraping behind him. He turned round sharply, although he knew that the noise had occurred five years ago and was long since silenced. He could almost see Franz, pressed against the cellar wall, on tiptoes, trying to loosen a stone. Franz was smiling, but he was only a memory, a lie. Or a ghost perhaps.

'It almost moved, Lukas!'

How many times had Franz said that? Sweat glued his hair to his forehead. He had been at it for hours, but still he smiled. Truly, he had never lost heart. Of the two of them, he had been the more determined. But Franz had collapsed. His body had struck the roughly paved ground. Relmyer had hurried over to help him. He had taken Franz in his arms, shaking him and shouting his name. By that time neither of them had eaten or drunk anything for two days. The man who had locked them up there had not returned. They had wondered what on earth he wanted. To abduct them? To punish them as a joke? To let them die of starvation? Or worse? Relmyer had lain Franz down and taken his place, using a cut stone to scratch away at the mortar. His palm bled, and his fingers, from rubbing against the wall. They were trying to widen a crack that allowed a sliver of light through, proof that the ceiling of the cellar was just above ground level.

'Is everything all right, Lieutenant?' asked a voice outside.

Lukas Relmyer was disorientated by this sudden reminder of the present, but immediately he forgot the outside world again. Around the ruins three French hussars were on the lookout, their muskets at the ready. They anxiously scanned the surrounding forest. The horses whinnied and snorted – did they sense something? It would not be easy to see danger coming in the impenetrable tangle of trunks, branches, thickets and shadows.

The trooper who had spoken went up to his officer to say quietly to him, 'If we stay, the Austrians will discover us and cut our throats. We could just leave the lieutenant here. After all, since he's so gifted with his sabre, he doesn't need us to protect him: he will be able to follow us back to Vienna on his own.'

'Go and tell him that yourself, Pegrichut . . .'

But the soldier had not dared. His lieutenant had seemed so agitated when they had arrived . . . It was best to keep your distance from men like that. Some duellists made free with their blades and would run you through for a minor transgression.

Relmyer came to stand by the opening, opposite the steps. The sun fell across his face. He had remembered the opening as being very high. But not any longer, simply because he had grown. It seemed so narrow! He would have liked to go out through it, but his adult body would not fit. He looked at the spot where Franz had lain. They had succeeded in dislodging the damned stone. As it fell heavily, their spirits had lightened. The sky had been revealed. Four neighbouring stones had rapidly followed the first. After that it had been so much easier. Relmyer had pulled himself up and edged forward, the sides of the hole scraping his ribs. Once outside he had begun to laugh, to cry and to thank the Lord. A bursting forth of emotions. But fear had rapidly taken the upper hand again. The man who had imprisoned them could return at any moment. And Franz would never be able to join him up here. Emptied of all energy, he had continued to lie on the ground. He was unable to stand up any more, so how could he find the strength needed to haul himself up here? Relmyer had understood that he would not succeed if he tried to pull his companion out. The deprivations and the exertion had weakened him to the point where he was not even sure of being able to muster the strength to get out again himself if he went back down into the cellar. So Franz had stayed there, stretched out, exhausted, while Relmyer extended his arm to him from outside. The memory was so vivid that today Relmyer almost put out his hand towards the wall, even though his eyes showed him that no one lay against it. After all, memories can be as vivid as what you can see.

He had left Franz, promising him that he would come back with help. But when he had kept his word, some hours later, his friend was no longer there. Franz's body had been discovered the next day, in another part of the forest. Today Relmyer had come back again. He had not found Franz lying there, of course, even if he secretly hoped for that absurd miracle. Past and present, adolescence and adulthood, past dangers and threats to come: all were muddled together in the melting pot of that dilapidated cellar.

Lukas Relmyer knelt down opposite the wall and mouthed, 'I'm going to find whoever did this to us, Franz. I promise you that. I promise for both of us.'

Although the words were silent, his determination was very real.

Relmyer stood up. Just before leaving he took out of his pocket a tin soldier he had bought in Vienna. He put the toy – an officer wearing a tricorne – in the centre of the hole through which he had escaped five years earlier. The figurine was small but, in the slanting rays of the sun, it cast a long shadow on the ground, brandishing a sword menacingly above its head.

CHAPTER 2

FOR the French soldiers, 21 May 1809 signified the end of the world, or so it seemed. That day a hundred thousand Austrians attacked Napoleon, who could only muster twenty-five thousand combatants in response. The rest of his army – some fifty thousand men – was stranded on the west bank of the Danube or on the Isle of Lobau, in the middle of the river, waiting to cross. The Austrians had destroyed all the bridges so the French pontoniers had built temporary ones – a large bridge, almost half a mile long, linking the west bank to the large Isle of Lobau, and a little one, just a hundred and ten yards long, linking the island to the east bank. The enemy kept sabotaging these structures, which then had to be repaired. Upriver, the Austrians would push flaming barges, rafts piled with stones, tree trunks, and even toppled windmills into the river. These were caught up by the current, which had been swelled by thawing snow, and would then damage the piers of the bridges or take out pieces of makeshift platform.

The French on the east bank were assaulted on all sides by hordes of Austrians. The village of Aspern constituted the left flank of the French army and Essling the right. In the plains between the two villages the cavalries of the two camps mingled.

Towards six o'clock that evening Archduke Charles, Commander-in-Chief of the Austrian army, gave the order for the village of Aspern to be taken at any price. He even took to the battlefield himself, prepared to risk his own life in order to encourage his soldiers. So the French, who had captured Aspern, then lost it, then taken it again, several times, saw streams of Austrians once more pouring into the bombarded, burnt-out village. Aspern was defended solely by the Legrand Division. The enemy attacked from the north and north-west with the Fresnel, Vogelsang, Ulm and Nostitz Divisions, while from the west and south-west, the Kottulinsky and Vincent Divisions mounted the assault. Finally, in the south, in the Gemeinde Au, a dense forest, the Nordmann Division haphazardly fought the remains of Molitor's division in the hope of taking the village from the rear. A few hours previously Archduke Charles had also been there to galvanise his troops. But now they wandered about in the thickets, their attack stymied by the trees and by the French. Aspern had become nothing more than a pea that enormous Austrian jaws were attempting to crush.

Captain Quentin Margont, leaning against a barrel, tried to make sense of the situation. Around him, soldiers in his battalion were firing off salvoes, sheltered behind a makeshift barricade blocking one of the two main streets of the village of Aspern. A bric-a-brac of carts and furniture was all that they could find to keep the Austrians at bay. The enemy attacks had been relentless since early afternoon, but this time it seemed as if the whole of Austria were marching in their direction. Line after line of infantry hurried towards them in waves.

A French aide-de-camp arrived at the gallop. He had been commanded to pass on orders from headquarters, and was desperately looking for the general of the division. But the more the Austrians advanced, the more his resolve wavered. Was there no such general? Not even a general for the brigade? A colonel, surely? When the first bullet whistled past his ear, he told himself that he would settle for a captain. He approached Margont, leaning well forward on his lathered horse.

'Hold firm! The 18th Infantry Regiment of the Line is on its way to help you! Pass the message on to your general.'

'But that's us – we are the 18th Regiment!' protested Margont.

The aide-de-camp blinked. 'You are? So you don't belong to Molitor's division then? Well, that won't do at all – you shouldn't even be here! You must go and assist Molitor!'

'But that's impossible . . .'

'Well, those are the orders, Captain!'

'We don't even know where Molitor's division is!'

'I don't either, but that's your problem. Transmit my message to your colonel.'

'But look, you have to understand, we can't just leave, and we need reinforcements immediately!'

'You are the reinforcements! The reinforcements for General Molitor!'

This ridiculous dialogue came about because the aide-de-camp, frightened at having to come to this scene of carnage, had delayed in carrying out his mission. He had received his orders half an hour ago and they were no longer valid, superseded by others delivered by another messenger. Margont, however, like all the subaltern officers, was unaware of this.

'We don't give a damn about your Molitor! Where's our

back-up, for God's sake? And why is the rest of the army taking so long to reach us?'

'There are no bridges left, the Austrians have destroyed them all! Go and assist General Molitor!'

With that, the aide-de-camp turned tail and fled, his horse speeding off at full gallop.

'No bridges left?' repeated Margont, dazedly.

His old friend Sergeant Lefine slipped along the barricade until he reached the captain, without ever exposing even the smallest part of his body.

'What's happening with the bridges? What does that mean, "No bridges left"?'

The deafening sound of firing interrupted every conversation. Second Lieutenant Piquebois, who had only heard every third word of the conversation, exclaimed: 'Excellent! Molitor is on the way with reinforcements!'

This happy news was received with cries of joy. The Austrian battalions, in their helmets, white coats and breeches, progressed in dense lines, like a tempestuous snowstorm in springtime. Bullets plundered their ranks, carpeting the streets with injured men, who crawled to the sides to avoid being trampled. The officers wore dark greatcoats and belts made of gold cloth. They brandished their swords so that they could be seen by their men and to exhort them to keep advancing.

Between the smoke from the weapons and the smoke from the fires, visibility was decreasing rapidly. Men were firing blindly. A first Austrian battalion came to break through the barricade that Margont was defending. The soldiers riddled each other with gunfire, standing within a few paces of each other. The white coats fell, again and again, but others came to replace them. The air was heavy with the smell of burnt powder. Lefine, who was standing near Margont, shouted something to him, but all Margont could hear were cries of rage or pain and the rattling of the explosions hammering against his eardrums.

'What did you say?'

'. . . lost!'

Margont knew how the rest of the sentence went. The French were falling back in disarray, hotly pursued by the Austrians. Every house had been turned into a bastion, and from the windows people were pelting the assailants. The church and its perimeter wall acted as a fortress. The French were sheltering behind sections of wall and the ruins of houses destroyed by the artillery. Some even crouched behind gravestones in the village cemetery, and piles of horse manure . . . A corporal collapsed in front of Margont.

'These idiots are killing as many of our men as they are Austrians!'

He grabbed Lefine by the sleeve and knocked loudly against the door of a stone building.

'France! France!' he thundered, knocking fit to break his fist.

They couldn't retreat any further. The mass of withdrawing soldiers clogged the streets, and bullets were raining down on the panicking dark blue mêlée. Lieutenant Saber arrived at a run, forced a passage, stepped through a window and edged his way to the middle of the crush of muskets pointed at the Austrians. A moment later, he opened the door to his friends.

'What would you have done if I hadn't been here . . . ?'

Margont shoved him forward so that he could take cover, only to be jostled himself from behind by Lefine and other frightened soldiers.

The Austrian advance slowed, then stopped altogether. The determined resistance of the French had somewhat dented their confidence. Margont climbed to the first floor. He forced his way through the injured and the shooters to get to a skylight. Every window in the street was bristling with muskets, which were crushing the Austrians with their fire power. Were they winning? Were they losing? The situation was increasingly unclear. Before Margont's very eyes, the building opposite collapsed to the ground with its crowd of defenders. All that could be seen of it now were dancing flames and twirling tendrils of black smoke dotted with orange sparks. The aide-de-camp whom he had been conversing with earlier was galloping back towards them, but his horse turned tail almost immediately at the sound of the explosion. The sight of the building collapsing terrified him.

'They make everything jump!' cried a voice, referring to the cannon the Austrians had installed in the part of Aspern they controlled, and which they used to bombard the French point-blank. The French, decimated and discouraged, withdrew, houses collapsing in their path.

The minute Napoleon heard that Aspern was lost, he ordered its immediate recapture. If Aspern fell, the plains where his centre was concentrated would become indefensible. The French would have control only of the village of Essling, which would find itself encircled, and would also fall. The Emperor's line of defence was like a row of dominoes. If one stronghold fell, all the others would automatically follow suit. It was all or nothing. Aspern-plains-Essling or the very bottom of the Danube.

Margont hurried towards the back, trying to restore some order amongst the crush of survivors. No one understood what was going on except the very highest ranks – and even they were not absolutely sure . . . He saw French troops milling about in the south of the village. Which ones and what they were doing he had not the faintest idea. The blue lines were spread out in the fields and the meadows as if on a training exercise. Were they not even going to launch another assault on this pile of stones and embers? Officers were giving signals to the survivors of Aspern to hasten their retreat.

'I agree, let's get on with it,' fumed Lefine. 'You don't just hang about waiting to be killed, that makes no sense.'

They barely had time to get into line formation. A general – was it Molitor? No, it was another general whom Margont did not know – drew his sword and pointed it at Aspern's steeple, which was still standing but riddled with holes made by round shot, its roof caved in and smoking, a laughable spike.

'Advance!'

This counterattack, led by the Carra Saint-Cyr Division (which had just got across the river before the collapse of the bridge) and by the remains of the Legrand Division, was effective. The French drove back the white coats or trapped them in the gutted houses. The Austrians took their revenge by counterattacking in turn.

Finally the sky began to darken. No reinforcements had arrived, but night would bring relief – surely the fighting was not going to continue in darkness? The French were now losing house after house. On the Danube, the repaired bridge, repeatedly damaged by the skiffs the Austrians sent downriver, collapsed once again, hurling the troops of the 2nd Regiment of Cuirassiers into the brine where they sank like stones.

Finally the intensity of combat diminished. Margont, overjoyed at having survived, walked towards Lefine, to celebrate with him. He was so relieved and happy that, without thinking, he passed in front of the breach in a wall. A sharp report rang out. Instinctively Margont dived for cover. He was not sure he had been hit because he had strained his muscles so much that he hurt all over. Lefine's face was distorted in terror. Margont followed his friend's gaze and looked at his side. A dark stain was spreading there.

'I can't believe I did that,' said Margont, as he lay carefully down.

CHAPTER 3

MARGONT spent an interminable amount of time lying by the Danube in the company of a mass of other wounded. Groans and entreaties mingled with the deep rumbling of cannon fire. Medical orderlies, far too few of them, ran from casualty to casualty. One very young orderly regarded Margont with disdain and, without even taking the time to examine his wound, announced: 'It's nothing.' Another, however, looked horrified whenever he passed him. Finally a small boat brought a handful of *voltigeurs* overburdened with munitions, a pathetic reinforcement, and left with several lucky patients, one of whom was Margont.

Napoleon had planned to cross the Danube very quickly. He had not believed that the Austrians could hold out against his army and had thought they would withdraw. The totally unexpected turn of events generated utter confusion. Lobau was acting as a stopping-off point for the divisions who found themselves stranded, and also as a temporary hospital. Soldiers accumulated on the island like grains of wheat in a granary. A hundred thousand Austrian soldiers still firmly held the east bank of the Danube, while Vienna, whose population was hostile to the French, lay on the west bank. Only yesterday Napoleon had controlled most of Europe, and now his empire appeared to have been reduced to the Isle of Lobau, two and a half miles long by two and a half miles wide.

Margont was treated by an orderly who was well-intentioned but intimidated by the officer's rank. He apologised as he clumsily pricked Margont's skin again and again. The wound was superficial; the bullet had only grazed his side, biting into the flesh without piercing his abdomen. Gangrene was what Margont was worried about. Was it going to devour his body like rot in an apple? He spent the night in a terrible state of anxiety.

The next day, at four in the morning, the battle resumed.

The groaning multitude of casualties on Lobau increased, spreading like a tide of agony. Medical orderlies and volunteers offered them pails of water that they refilled from the Danube. Not the best drink, but there was nothing else. More French and Badois arrived, bleeding.

One of the newly arrived sergeants, with as many slashes as an old patched shirt, propped himself up on one elbow and loudly proclaimed: 'We've come from Aspern, troops! We recaptured that damned village! Long live Marshal Masséna!'

This news was greeted with cries of 'Long live Masséna!' and 'Long live the Emperor!' Margont thought of Lefine, Saber and Piquebois. Were they still wandering around amongst the heaped ruins, suffocated by the smoke, and fighting the Austrians bullet for bullet? Or had the regiment been relieved, was it resting at the rear, in reserve? Perhaps his friends were lying broken, in a boat, their hands trailing in the water, drifting . . .

News and rumours continued to spread, and became more and more exaggerated. Aspern and Essling had been attacked again, and lost, or almost, then retaken, nearly . . . And in the plains separating the two villages, the killing continued as ever. Meanwhile the bridges had been repaired again and soldiers swarmed over them. Boats continued to cross to and fro, so weighed down with casualties that they became dangerously flooded. A major from the 57th of the Line was brought in, along with some cuirassiers furious at having been stopped in the middle of a charge.

'Silence for the major!' shouted a quartermaster sergeant.

'Yes, listen to the major!' echoed the cavalrymen.

The officer was placed in the shadow of a willow tree and the soldiers fell silent. His thigh was bleeding but he paid no attention to that and focused on his audience.

'The Emperor is crushing the Austrian centre!' he announced vigorously.

An explosion of 'Hurrah!' and 'Long live the Emperor!' followed. In fact the major, intoxicated by finding himself propelled into the limelight, had made his declaration more convincing than the attack he had participated in warranted. While the casualties on Lobau rejoiced at the demise of the Austrian army, in reality that army's artillery was destroying the ranks of their attackers, and even the French cavalry, called in to back up the ranks, could not defeat them decisively. But it was true that the extreme aggression of an adversary far inferior to them in number had shaken the Austrians' confidence and had forced them to exercise caution and moderate their hotheadedness.

Margont spotted Jean-Quenin Brémond, an old childhood friend. Brémond had reddish light brown hair and large side whiskers. Despite his boundless energy, he radiated calm. He indicated which of the wounded were to be operated on as soon as possible, teaching an orderly in passing how to tie bandages more securely and requisitioning the more able-bodied to help out the others . . . His practised eye picked out Margont immediately. He turned pale and strode rapidly over to examine the wound.

'It's not serious.'

Margont breathed a sigh of relief.

'But even so, there is still the risk of gangrene.'

'I know, Jean-Quenin. I'll change my bandages when they're dirty and I'll make sure that I eat properly. Have you treated anyone we know?'

'No. But that doesn't mean anything. There are wounded all over the place.'

'And here come even more!' cried several soldiers.

The Danube swept away the remains of the little bridge, which had just collapsed again. Pontoniers and infantry, carried away on the current, waved their arms frantically. While the thousands of soldiers of Marshal Davout's III Corps found themselves trapped on the island, Napoleon fulminated on the east bank, searching for reinforcements to sustain his attack on the Austrian centre.

'It's going increasingly badly for the citizen emperor,' said Brémond worriedly.

He had been a revolutionary from the outset and did not approve of the transition from republic to empire, even though the Empire did respect several of the fundamental principles of the Revolution. So from time to time the medical officer referred to Napoleon as 'the citizen emperor' because he considered that all citizens were perfectly equal. To him, being emperor was a job like any other, and more important than 'emperor' was the word 'citizen'. Nothing annoyed him as much as people who used the term in an ironic or pejorative fashion, to insult their servants. He came across people like that more and more often, republicans who were not prepared to make any concessions. If he had been a colonel, a 'citizen colonel', Napoleon would probably have entrusted him with the garrison of a town. A far-off town and a small garrison. But as he was a doctor, he could at least speak freely about bandages and amputated limbs.

Margont had a more complex point of view. Aged nine in 1789, he had become immediately impassioned by the revolution, understanding only a minuscule part of what was happening, and imagining the rest. Twenty years later, like Jean-Quenin, he was a humanist and a republican but his opinion of Napoleon was slightly different. Monarchies and empires, Austrian, Prussian or English . . . they had all brought war to the French Republic, and its product, the French Empire. Mostly because this empire did not believe in aristocracy by right of blood, and accorded everyone the same rights. The proponents of each of these models, monarchy and republic, wanted to eradicate the other model in order to mould the world in their own image. Now France found itself truly isolated in this struggle. The only other republic lay all the way across the Atlantic, in the United States of America. Who should one support? There were really only two possibilities. Either Napoleon, the military genius who, although he had transformed the Republic into a 'republican-inspired empire', defended some of the core principles of the Revolution with his thundering victories. Or one could support a government – but made up of whom? – that would not be able to stay in power when faced with enemy armies, at which point a French king would rise again, extracted from some unknown dusty prison cell. A king that the European monarchies would hasten to install on a throne in Paris before arguing about who should control the strings of this puppet monarch. Margont therefore served the Emperor because there was no choice. To him, ideas were more powerful than men. Whether people marched crying 'Long live the Republic!' as he had done, or 'Long live the Emperor!' did not matter; they all carried with them the ideals of the Revolution: liberty, equality, respect for everyone . . . And these notions infected those they were fighting. If republican ideals did not triumph immediately, they would win out in the end. The question was what would happen until then. For war followed war without respite, year upon year . . .

'Since your wound is superficial, you can make yourself useful,' said Brémond. 'I think there's someone you should meet.'

The medical officer pointed, but all Margont could see were the wounded and suffering.

'She's Austrian but she speaks good French.'

Margont spotted her. She was wearing an ivory-coloured dress with bloodstains at the foot, like a deathly hem.

Many women chose to follow the army although it was forbidden if they were not actually employed by it. Canteen workers and supervisors, laundresses, young bourgeois girls dreaming of adventure, society women, Austrian women who fell in love for the duration of a campaign, prostitutes: these distressing times rendered them all equal, all in the same boat. The sentries tried to prevent them from reaching Lobau, but in the general confusion several had, in spite of everything, managed to get there. These women searched for their husbands or lovers amongst the sufferers, praying all the while that they were not there, offering water and trying to get information . . . Stationing themselves on the south side of the island, where the prisoners and wounded were sent, they were far enough from the fighting not to be exposed to any danger. The front line was in fact four miles to the north-east and could not be seen because of the woods covering the island and the banks of the Danube. It was possible to tell where it was only because of the thunderous noise, and the plumes of smoke that filled the sky.

'She's looking for a missing boy,' explained Brémond. 'In all this chaos everyone laughs at her questions. If an officer were to accompany her, some of the soldiers might be a little more courteous, and her search would be much more effective.'

'I'll go and help her.'

Margont stood up, grimacing: an invisible beast was devouring his side. But helping out whenever possible came naturally to these two men. The reality of war had failed to poison their humanist spirit. They did not view the woman as an enemy. Their adversaries were the kings, and those who supported them. As fervent republicans, they wished to liberate the Austrian people from the monarch's stronghold.

'But be careful!' added Jean-Quenin Brémond. 'Don't start leaping about, forgetting about your injury.'

Margont nodded meekly.

'Yes, yes, I know. Good doctors see bad patients everywhere!'

As he approached the young woman, Margont scrutinised her without her noticing. She was undeniably charming. Her brown hair emphasised her pale complexion, and her face, with its narrow nose, fine eyebrows and delicate features, attracted many glances. But as well as her enchanting appearance, she also gave a disconcerting impression, perhaps false, of both strength and fragility. This paradox, infuriating, like a jumble of knots impossible to unravel, made a profound impression on Margont. He asked himself if he was the only one who felt it. She was going up to Austrians as well as French, shuddering at the horror of their injuries, asking them something, but they all, invariably, shook their heads. She stopped for a while, undecided, in front of a soldier of the Landwehr, the Austrian military service, whose head was no more than a bundle of bandages, his grey uniform an amalgam of shredded linen. As he appeared to be deaf to her questions – or perhaps he was dead – she had to make do with examining his hands and then she moved away. She repeated the same sentences, sometimes in German, sometimes in lightly accented French.

'I'm looking for a young Austrian, Wilhelm Gurtz. He's sixteen years old, blond and quite well built. He may have signed up for the Austrian army, so he might be here somewhere.'

She spoke with composure despite the sight of all the martyred bodies and the weight of the looks she was receiving. Margont was struck by a feeling of consternation tinged with jealousy. He had been injured, but no woman had seen fit to seek him out. The Austrian girl disappeared into a wood where there were more injured men than trees. A cuirassier motioned her over. His mouth was bleeding, coating his red moustache with scarlet foam.

'He's lucky to have such a concerned sister!'

The Austrian girl shook her head. 'I'm only a friend. He has no family, he's an orphan.'

'I'm an orphan too!' cried a *voltigeur* with bandaged hands. 'But I don't have a friend looking for me!'

Margont appeared at that moment. He bowed courteously. 'Mademoiselle, allow me to introduce myself – Captain Margont, of the 18th Infantry Regiment of the Line. Perhaps you would accept my assistance in your search?'

The young woman suppressed a smile – how chivalrous. She gazed at him briefly, trying to decide whether she could trust him.

'That's very kind. My name's Luise Mitterburg. Do you know where there are other prisoners or wounded?'

Everywhere, Margont almost replied.

'Let's follow the river,' he said.

The abandoned *voltigeur* watched them moving away. He felt he had paid his dues – he was too often sent to the front line for his liking – was he not due something in return?

'Beautiful girls for the officers, wenches for the soldiers and misfortune for the *voltigeurs*,' he concluded.

There were two people accompanying Luise: a scowling old woman dressed in black and an aged servant. Luise oscillated between discouragement and determination.

'I spent part of my childhood in an orphanage,' she explained spontaneously. 'I'm very attached to it, even though I had the good fortune to be adopted. One of the orphans, Wilhelm Gurtz, an adolescent, disappeared three days ago. We're looking everywhere for him. Perhaps he took it into his head to join one of the regiments as a volunteer. We absolutely must find him.'

Her voice faltered on the last sentence. But her eyes remained dry.

Margont asked, 'What does he look like, your—'

'Quite plump, with chubby cheeks – he eats out of loneliness and despair. Straw-blond hair, thickset, bandy-legged, and he walks slowly. He has very blue eyes, and he seems young for his age. A regiment probably wouldn't take him . . . oh, what am I saying, of course they would! Regiments accept everyone. Soon battalions will be made up of children and old people.'

It was already a bit like that, in fact. As for a lower age limit, there were child-soldiers as young as ten, platoon members as young as fourteen, and combatants as young as sixteen.

'So what do you suggest, Captain?'

'The prisoners are gathered—'

'I've already been there.'

Margont found her habit of interrupting him irritating but rather seductive.

'Why do you keep looking in that direction?' she asked, indicating Aspern.

Although the ruins of the village were hidden by the woods surrounding it, fat columns of smoke, either white or black, signalled its presence. The Austrian woman was obviously observant.

'I was there yesterday,' replied Margont. 'That's where I was injured. My friends are probably still there. As everything has been destroyed, I'm wondering what is still burning.'

'Even when war has ravaged everything, it must still burn the cinders.'

Luise leant against a tree. Her face was filmed with perspiration. The heat was crushing, and the sight of the wounded made the atmosphere even more suffocating. 'I'll never find him. The war has plunged the world into chaos – who will care about an orphan?'

'Me,' retorted Margont.

She laughed, perhaps mockingly – he could not tell.

'Why?'

Margont hesitated, then said more than he would have liked. 'Because at a certain stage of my childhood, I also found myself more or less an orphan.'

Either he had said too much or too little. Luise, however, unnerved him by replying: 'That doesn't surprise me. I had guessed as much.'

She paled and, forgetting about Margont, went over to a greying man who was wandering amongst the injured, trying to avoid looking at them. With his eyes reddened by crying and his black clothes, he looked like a crow of ill omen. When he saw her, he shook his head sadly. 'He's dead,' he announced in German. 'It's not the war, he was murdered.'

'That's what we were afraid of, isn't it?' she answered with surprising calm.

'Some French soldiers are guarding his remains. They asked me a great many questions and they don't want to let us have the body. They think he was a spy or a partisan. And even worse, they're exhibiting his body near Ebersdorf.'

'Their military failure is making them aggressive and stupid. They—'

She stopped, realising that Margont might understand German. A good thought, but a little late . . . She turned towards him and, tilting her head slightly to one side, said courteously in French: 'I've just been told that Wilhelm has been found. Near here. Alas, he . . .' She found it hard to continue.

Margont spared her the necessity. 'I speak your language.'

Far from being embarrassed by that announcement, Luise went on: 'It's a very great sadness for us not to be able to bury the boy in consecrated ground. I know that I'm taking advantage, but perhaps, since you're an officer, you would be able to help us sort out the misunderstanding by explaining things to the high command of your army. We only want to learn what happened and to offer him a decent burial. Please . . .'

She was trying to coax him by acting the weak young girl at a loss. But Margont felt certain that she was neither weak nor at a loss and he told himself to refuse, then gave in without knowing why. 'I'll do whatever I can.'

'Thank you, thank you so much,' she hastened to accept his offer.

Margont rejoined Jean-Quenin Brémond, cursing himself. The woman had manipulated him! And what on earth would he say to 'the high command'? Yes, she had definitely taken advantage of him, but what was worse was that he had capitulated to her in full knowledge of what she was doing.

Besides, the word 'murder' had been used. That was serious, and unforeseen.

He asked Brémond to write him a safe-conduct, so that he would not be taken for a deserter. A bullet had nearly punctured his stomach – no need to risk dozens of others, delivered by the firing squad.

'I won't be long,' he explained. 'I don't think I'm in a condition to fight, but I can move about . . .'

Jean-Quenin Brémond agreed. 'Stop feeling guilty: you're in no state to rejoin your company. In any case, the bridge linking us to the Austrian side has been destroyed again. And when it's repaired our field marshals will prefer to use it to let through the regiments who haven't fought yet, rather than a raggle-taggle band of cripples who don't even know where their battalions are.'

Jean-Quenin hated all the administrative formalities that the army was so fond of. He took malicious pleasure in rendering them ridiculous by conforming to them to the letter. He therefore scribbled an illegible note charging Margont with searching the surrounding area in order to find requisitions for the Army Medical Service: linen to make into lint, food, spirits . . .

'Don't think that just because your injury is mild, you can do whatever you like,' he added.

Seeing that Margont was no longer listening to him, he tapped his friend's wound. Margont paled in a convincing demonstration of Brémond's point.

'So, don't over-exert yourself. I'll lend you one of my horses; you will tire yourself less.'

Margont thanked him warmly and mounted the horse that, spooked by the increasingly loud shots of the artillery, snorted and pawed the ground.

The man who had found Wilhelm was called Bergen and he taught in the orphanage where the adolescent had lived. He convinced Luise Mitterburg not to come with them.

She and the two servants followed them only as far as the western bank, using the large bridge, which the pontoniers were shoring up as quickly as possible, while anticipating another tree to destroy it again. As soon as she arrived on the other side of the river, the young Austrian walked rapidly away. She was finally realising what the news she had just been given meant. She was still managing to hold back her grief, but for how much longer? She did not want Margont to see her crying. She disappeared into a crowd of women. Racked with worry, they assailed her with questions but she had no answers for them.

CHAPTER 4

ELEVEN bodies were laid out by the side of the road linking Vienna to the village of Ebersdorf. In the heat of the sun, their nauseous emanations filled the air. Three men were lacerated, striped with wide gashes – the vehement work of hussars was evident. Some had no apparent wounds and seemed to contemplate the sky with their staring eyes. Almost all were wearing the grey greatcoat with red cuffs of the militia. The French army, finding itself well advanced into enemy territory, wanted to protect its rear, particularly its lines of communication. This meant that certain officers were pitiless with spies, both the civilians who organised ambushes and the soldiers who fought for the enemy.

Bergen indicated Wilhelm. A bullet had struck him in the middle of the chest. His green jacket was stained with dried blood. Margont noticed the most striking feature last, as if his soul had at first rendered him blind to the 'detail'. The adolescent had been mutilated. His smile had been extended from ear to ear, with a knife. He looked as if he were roaring with demonic, absurd, atrocious laughter and this impression was so real and lifelike that it seemed to give the lie to his death. Yet, already the body was decomposing. Margont looked away.

A second lieutenant was standing guard with two sentries. Recognising Bergen, he came to stand opposite Margont's horse, saluted him and immediately declared: 'No deal. The remains of partisans and rebels must be left exposed as a deterrent to others!'

With his triangular face and vituperative tone, he looked like a viper who had just been disturbed.

'Captain Margont, 18th of the Line, Ledru Brigade, Legrand Division. The next of kin wish to recover the body of the boy with the mutilated face.'

'First they'll have to walk over mine!' the second lieutenant retorted at once.

Margont almost felt like doing that. All he would have to do was launch his horse forward . . .

Bergen intervened. 'I am one of the young man's teachers. I assure you he never did anyone any harm. He was an orphan! Don't you think he's suffered enough in life without having to endure this punishment after death?'

The officer's eyes widened. 'You want an orphan? As the war proverb says, "One orphan lost, ten thousand found!" If they listened to me, they would display the body of an enemy in every street in Vienna and a gallows in the square of every conquered village.'

Any entreaty would simply bounce off such an entrenched view. Margont, making an effort to remain polite, asked, 'Who gave the order? To whom can I go, to—'

The eyes of the second lieutenant blazed. They were persisting in wanting to steal one of his corpses! He was hatching them like eggs.

'The 18th of the Line has not been charged with ensuring the security of the area! You have no authority on this subject. If we don't subdue the Austrian civilians now, in two weeks' time, they will slit open your stomach and piss in it while you sleep!'

He had fought in the Spanish campaign. There the two sides had outbid each other in atrocity. Frenchmen were found burnt alive, scalded, nailed to trees, emasculated, enucleated, dismembered, crucified . . . On their side, the French soldiers burnt villages said to be partisan and meted out bloody reprisals . . . The officer had returned alive from the Spanish quagmire but his soul and part of his reason had had to stay there, ensnared in a vision of horror.

'I also fought in Spain,' Margont told him.

The second lieutenant blinked, stupefied to find himself exposed in this way. His lips moved but his voice did not follow. Margont helped him out.

'In any case, the body we wish to take away is decomposing. Better that his next of kin bury him now, rather than you having to do it later, in the sun.'

The junior officer stiffened. 'Of course, obviously.'

'How was he killed?'

'He was caught by a patrol two days before the battle, during the night. He must have tried to rejoin the Austrian army with an accomplice. They were discovered somewhere in the woods near the Danube, not far from Vienna.'

'Was his companion arrested or killed?'

Regret showed in the face of the second lieutenant. 'Alas, he managed to escape. The soldiers were too far away, it was night-time . . . And it was already pretty good to have caught one of them. The other just had time to fire once before disappearing.'

'It wasn't a patrol that was responsible for that boy's death.

Look closely at his jacket: there are burn marks all round his wound. Someone shot him point-blank.'

The officer went at once to examine the body, worried by this discordant fact. Then he stood up, reassured.

'Well, in my opinion, it was his accomplice who killed him. Either accidentally – he panicked and it was dark – or so that he wouldn't denounce him if he was captured. Many Austrians left their mothers, wives and children in Vienna, he would have been worried about eventual reprisals—'

'And the mutilation? How do you explain that?'

The second lieutenant shrugged. 'Perhaps it was a soldier from one of the detachments whose friend had been killed by the partisans. War drives people mad. As for mutilation of corpses, I've seen worse . . .'

Margont did not doubt it. The man had become deaf to the horror of war because he had heard its cries of agony for so long. He had become accustomed to 'all that'. For him, this abomination was no more than an anecdote, a momentary distraction in a dismal day of sentry duty. Although he did not know it, he was as dead as the corpses he guarded. The second lieutenant turned to Bergen.

'Go ahead, take him. I'll make an exception for a veteran officer of the Spanish campaign.'

The Austrian nodded. 'Thank you, Officer. God will reward you.'

'If your God exists, the settlement of accounts between the good I've done and the bad I've done will send me straight to hell, even if I were to let you leave with all eleven corpses.'

'There were only two?' queried Margont.

'According to what I was told, yes. But the country is crawling with vermin. Enemy soldiers skirt round the front to the north or to the south, and cross the Danube in boats or at fords or by the remaining bridges. Then they hide in the forests and harass us. Don't go adventuring for any reason in the countryside without a strong escort, Captain. Otherwise the air you breathe through your nose will leave you through the gash in your throat.'

The second lieutenant spoke animatedly. His eyes, although exhausted, with black rings under them, were always alert. He probably woke every night brutally brandishing a pistol at his phantoms.

He added: 'But tell me, what did this young Austrian do to be so popular? The day before yesterday two hussars from the 8th Regiment came to ask me about him. They were sent by a lieutenant, one Relmyer. Is he a friend of yours?'

At that name, Bergen's eyes widened. Having been mournful and resigned, he became extremely talkative. No one could make out his mixture of French and Austrian. He had to repeat himself more calmly. He was so emotional his voice trembled.

'Did you say Relmyer? I know a Relmyer, I know him very well – Lukas Relmyer. He's one of my old pupils. We haven't seen him for years. Did you say a hussar came? An Austrian hussar?'

The second lieutenant raised his eyes heavenwards. 'Don't be stupid. If your Relmyer had been an Austrian hussar, I would have shot his two sidekicks on sight!'

'If this Relmyer sent cavalrymen to find out about Wilhelm, it must be him,' concluded Bergen to himself.

Bergen and Margont decided to go back and see Luise Mitterburg. Bergen would then try to borrow a wagon in the village of Ebersdorf to transport Wilhelm's body back.

On the way, Margont asked: 'You mentioned murder earlier when you announced the boy was dead. What makes you think it was a crime?'

'It's an old story, which concerns only the Austrians. But I don't think Wilhelm was killed and disfigured by one of your patrols.'

Bergen appeared ill at ease, defensive. The question had upset him so much that he completely changed the subject. 'Relmyer's back! Mademoiselle Mitterburg is going to be so happy!' he exclaimed.

Margont experienced this sentence like a blow to the stomach. 'Are they . . . engaged?'

'No, Captain. He's her adoptive brother, as it were.'

Bergen told Luise Mitterburg what had happened. She was overcome by emotion at the news that Relmyer had returned. She questioned Bergen relentlessly. Where was Lukas? How long had he been in Austria? Why had he not come to see her? How dare he serve in the French army? Why the devil had he chosen to join the bellicose, brave but wild hussars? And there were further interrogations that Margont could not even understand because the young woman was talking so fast. Finally she turned to him.

'I don't know how to thank you. Or rather I do. Here, take my address. I live with my adoptive family.'

Margont took the paper she held out to him and looked at the awkward handwriting. She had written the lines in pencil, leaning on the palm of her hand.

'You will always be welcome,' she added. 'I have another favour to ask you. I know, it's becoming a habit. I'm always being told off for it. I think it's to do with having been abandoned. I have the feeling of having suffered an irreparable injustice and sometimes have a tendency to think that all the world owes me something, that people must help me, me more than anyone else, because I've suffered more than normal. Out of compassion. If you were queuing for food you would give up your place to the invalid behind you, wouldn't you? But in any case, as you have no doubt foreseen, I would like you to go and find Lukas Relmyer for me. It seems he is serving in the 8th Hussars. I want you to tell him that I absolutely must see him. In exchange, I swear to you I will similarly devote myself to helping you if you ask me a favour in return. What's more, I will ensure that you are invited to parties . . . Viennese balls are a unique pleasure! You're here now anyway, and it will be better than killing each other. That's not what I meant . . . The war, of course, that's another thing altogether . . .'

Finally she interrupted her long discourse. She had spoken without interruption, so keen to stifle Margont's reservations with a torrent of arguments, that she had lost the thread of what she was saying and tripped herself up.

'I accept, Mademoiselle. I will go and find Relmyer, as soon as the fighting stops.'

Luise Mitterburg thanked him profusely.

Margont hurried to cross the large bridge before it collapsed again. Was he in love with the Austrian girl, he asked himself. He could not tell. He did not believe in love at first sight; it was too inexplicable, too sudden. Certainly, she had some sort of hold over him. He felt there was a reason for it, but he could not express it clearly. He told himself that once he had succeeded in discovering the secret, the charm would dissipate and he would be free from her influence.

Margont slept for several hours, weakened by loss of blood. The wounded were perishing en masse, for lack of care. Others were still arriving and were laid down between the corpses and the dying. What few surgeons there were continually amputated limbs, which were piled into wagons and transported far from sight.

Towards two o'clock, the air was rent by the deafening roar of artillery fire. The soldiers sat up, if they had the strength, narrowing their eyes in the direction of the fighting, trying to guess the cause of the racket. They learned that the Austrians had placed in battery, in the front line of their centre, two hundred cannon – two hundred! – and were firing relentlessly on the troops of General Oudinot, who had barely eighty. Shortly afterwards, the little bridge was repaired once more, but no reinforcements could get through because of the stream of injured and panicked deserters fleeing onto the Isle of Lobau. By the time some order had been restored, the bridge had collapsed again.

Finally, a little after three o'clock, Archduke Charles, short of ammunition and worried about Austrian losses, gave up crushing the French, who were resisting with an energy born of despair. His adversaries were beaten even if they were not annihilated, and he judged the result satisfactory and put a stop to the attacks. Napoleon therefore immediately ordered that the east bank should be abandoned and his troops fell back onto Lobau and to the west bank. Each army had lost twenty thousand men, killed, wounded or taken prisoner. Napoleon had been vigorously driven back and so had just suffered his first personal military reverse. Intoxicated by the spectacular success of the preceding weeks that had seen the retreat of the enemy army and the fall of Vienna, he had underestimated the fighting spirit of the Austrians. Wanting to act quickly, he had pressed forward too precipitately. The floating missiles had been the unexpected element that had shattered the impetuous advance of the French. Napoleon and his empire had almost been overthrown by some tree trunks, flaming barges and windmills. But the setback was only partial. With only twenty-five thousand combatants on the first day of battle and fifty-five thousand the next, the Emperor had miraculously succeeded in resisting a hundred thousand of the enemy, narrowly escaping total disaster. From then on Napoleon had only one idea in mind – to erase his defeat by pulverising the Austrians.

As soon as the news of the French retreat was known, Vienna rang with the peal of bells, sounding strange after the thunder of cannon fire, now finally silenced. Although the capital was still occupied by the French, it manifested its joy.

A grenadier lying near Margont declared: 'Obviously the bells are tolling for us!'

CHAPTER 5

MARGONT still felt tired in spite of a good night's sleep. His wound had stayed clean and the pain had lessened, becoming less bitingly acute and more of an itch. Jean-Quenin Brémond had prescribed rest, but of course, Margont had been up at dawn because he already had a thousand projects for the day.

The French army, massed on the Isle of Lobau, was licking its wounds. Margont rejoined his regiment and was happy to find that Lefine, Saber and Piquebois had escaped unharmed from the dreadful butchery to be known from now on as 'the Battle of Essling' or 'the Battle of Aspern'. He immediately began the search for the 8th Hussars, accompanied by Lefine.

'I don't understand what this is all about!' grumbled Lefine, his arms crossed like an obstinate child.

Fernand Lefine, although only twenty-five years old, was as devious as a bagful of monkeys. He was furious that Margont had interrupted him right in the middle of his horse-trading. He was illegally selling horses confiscated from Austrian dragoon prisoners to French troopers. The buyers paid a derisory price so they got a good deal, but it was less good for the seller because of all the intermediaries and accomplices taking cuts; but from little acorns great trees grow. Lefine was also cross that Margont had appropriated one of his beasts. If honest men started robbing the thieves, what would become of the world?

'I've already told you,' replied Margont.

In fact, Margont had not wanted to admit how attached he had become to the Austrian girl, whom he barely knew. So he had lied about his motivations, pretending that he had offered his help in order to gain access to her glamorous Viennese circle.

'The war is going to start again, Fernand,' he went on. 'Archduke Charles would have had to attack Lobau immediately after his partial success at Essling in order to defeat Napoleon. With our Emperor, if you don't crush him completely, and his entire army along with him, he will rise up again to annihilate you. In matters of war Napoleon does not accept happy mediums. But before the next confrontation, there will be numerous preparations. So we'll be trapped here for several weeks. Either we pass our time playing cards on this stupid island, or we are regularly invited to Vienna!'

Vienna, Vienna, Vienna! Margont could not stop thinking about that legendary city. Lefine shook his head. 'You're not giving me the full story, Captain. I know you. We're going to get involved in an escapade that doesn't directly concern us just because of your humanist ideals!'

Having said that, though, Lefine thought his friend might be right. The ruins of Aspern and Essling were still smoking, but already Napoleon had whipped his army into a frenzy of activity. They had started to build a bridge on stilts to provide a better link between Lobau and the west bank; they were setting up batteries everywhere, even on the tiny neighbouring islands; they were clearing the roads to make them passable; they were digging and nailing together bastions, depots for provisions and munitions, a forge, hospitals, barracks . . . The French army and its German allies were settling in. So obviously, if there was a way of going off to Vienna to have some fun, rather than labouring in the sun on this ant hill . . .

Margont, impatient as always, led Lefine rapidly into the midst of thousands of soldiers. Many were still asleep, exhausted by two days of combat. They were stretched out in the shade of the trees, their white breeches and dark blue coats almost entirely obscured by the high pale green grasses. The blows of felling axes cracked like feeble gunshot and the noise of saws filled the air like the buzzing of a swarm of bees building a new hive.

The 8th Regiment of Hussars were resting in the cool thickets, after their sustained attack on the Austrians. Margont spied three hussars passing a long-stemmed pipe amongst them.

'Could you tell me where I can find Lieutenant Relmyer?'

A quartermaster of cavalry caught hold of one of his plaits, twisting it round his finger. His green dolman was spattered with dried blood. 'What do you want to see our Lieutenant Relmyer for, Captain? If it's to tell him something, we can pass it on.'

'I must see him personally.'

'We'll make sure we tell him that.'

'Are you going to tell me where I can find Lieutenant Relmyer or not?' fumed Margont.

The quartermaster of cavalry puffed out his chest in the manner of a cock dealing with some lesser fowl come to squawk in his poultry yard. This infantry bird was lucky he had an officer's epaulette, otherwise he would have received a sharp peck.

'Captain, once when Lieutenant Relmyer was quartermaster, his lieutenant shouted at him for wearing non-regulation uniform. The exchange became heated. Relmyer insulted the lieutenant, who challenged him to a duel, or perhaps it was the other way round, and bam! The lieutenant was floored, and his shoulder run through. Now the poor bugger has a dead arm dangling and he serves in the equipment corps. He counts the wagons . . .'

The NCO spoke the last words sadly. For him it was a thousand times better to be a hussar – even a dead one – than a bureaucrat in the commissariat.

Margont looked surprised. 'Relmyer injured an officer? Surely he was arrested at least?'

'Captain Lidoine wanted to have him shot, but Major Batichut promoted him to lieutenant in place of the lieutenant Relmyer had floored. Now do you understand why we're not in a hurry to send you to see him? You never know, he might want to become a captain . . .'

Lefine recoiled instinctively. Better to stay well away from duellists. Duellists handed out death like others might hand out accolades.

The quartermaster shrugged and indicated the nearby willows. 'Don't say we didn't warn you . . . You can't miss him, he's practising with his sabre over there.'

Margont went off towards the thicket. Lefine hung back, gazing at the quartermaster's dolman. He was having a sort of vision. He saw the coagulated blood growing wet, liquefying. The stains glistened in the sun before beginning to run down, tracing wide vertical stripes on the jacket. The quartermaster took a puff of the pipe before frowning as he surveyed Lefine.

'Well, what are you waiting for? Mid-Lent? You won't get any tobacco, however long you hang about!'

Lefine moved off, telling himself that it must be the sun, the heat . . . The vision terrified him. This affair smelt of death. Wasn't there enough of that already with the war?

It was indeed impossible not to notice Relmyer. In shirt-sleeves and covered in sweat, he vigorously fought invisible assailants. He lunged, jabbed, parried, sidestepped in order better to attack, feinted . . . against a seemingly inexhaustible number of enemies. Or perhaps just one enemy that he was unable to vanquish. Margont was not a great swordsman – he had more or less mastered a few moves. Nevertheless he could tell that Relmyer was extremely gifted.

'It looks as if Relmyer has a few accounts to settle,' he murmured to Lefine.

'In that case, I wouldn't like to be in the shoes of whoever he wants to settle them with.'

'His adversary must be pretty dreadful to drive him to such rage.'

Relmyer turned in their direction, saluted them with his sabre and joined them, mopping his brow. His physique was impressive. What age was he? Twenty? His manner, assured without being arrogant, was that of an experienced man. On the other hand, his rosebud mouth, naïve expression and slightly infantile features were those of an adolescent. He therefore appeared both older and younger than he actually was.

'May I ask the reason for your visit, Captain?' His Austrian accent betrayed his origins.

'Lieutenant Relmyer? I'm Captain Margont and this is my

friend Sergeant Lefine. We have come to inform you that Mademoiselle Luise Mitterburg wishes to see you.'

Relmyer immediately barricaded himself inside his inner fortress, locking up his feelings so that they would not show. 'Yes, certainly, but later.'

'Mademoiselle Mitterburg and I met by chance. I helped her search for a certain Wilhelm . . .'

The name hit Relmyer like a blow impossible to parry. His face hardened, ageing him brutally, as if his age were more a matter of his emotions than his years. Suddenly the trilling of the birds seemed to irritate him and Margont thought that he was going to draw his sabre and slice through the poor robin sitting carolling on too low a branch.

'He's dead, I know. And disfigured! The two hussars I dispatched to find him described the state he was found in. I wanted to see to it myself but my captain forbade it. He finds me unruly. Unruly! I'm a cavalryman, not a horse!'

He tidied his brown curls and then managed to smile. 'You're a captain yourself: perhaps if you were to talk to him, he would let me go and investigate this business . . .'

Margont was infuriated. Like Luise Mitterburg, Relmyer had no compunction in soliciting his help. 'I know nothing about this affair, why would I go—'

Relmyer placed his hands on Margont's shoulders. 'Come, Monsieur! I can see you're a man of compassion! Won't you help an honest officer in distress?'

His tone might have sounded theatrical had there not been tears in his eyes. At that moment he could have been taken for a thirteen-year-old boy.

'Well, perhaps, it depends on . . .' stammered Margont, embarrassed.

Lefine suppressed the desire to hit his friend. If you always looked after other people, you ended up failing to look after yourself – a dangerous defect that he was at no risk of succumbing to.

'Mademoiselle Mitterburg is my sister, or as good as, and she's rich,' added Relmyer. 'She can lend you money, or give it to you . . . She'll do it without hesitating if I ask her to.'

Now Lefine was interested. If they were to be paid for doing a favour, that put everything in a different light.

'She'll get you invited to receptions,' continued Relmyer.

'I know, yes . . .' Margont cut in before Relmyer could also promise them the moon.

'But for pity's sake, for the love of Christ, you have to make my captain loosen my reins!'

'Tell me the whole story and I'll see if I can plead your cause with your superiors.'

They settled down in the shade of a large oak tree. While Relmyer finished unbuttoning his dolman, he contemplated his lieutenant's stripes. The silver chevrons contrasted elegantly with the dark green of the cloth. 'I'm not used to them yet,' he declared, smiling. 'I was only recently promoted, following a happy conjunction of circumstances.'

Relmyer leant back against the trunk but could not keep still, constantly trying to find a more comfortable position. 'I'm hunting a man. He's probably close by, perhaps in one of these forests . . .'

As he said that word, he made a sweeping gesture. There

were certainly forests round about. Their dark expanses dotted the countryside.

'I am Austrian by birth. I was abandoned at the age of one. I don't know why. Perhaps because my family could not afford to keep me. Or maybe my parents were killed in the war, or carried off by illness . . . or possibly I was the cruel result of the adulterous affair of one of my parents. I was placed in the Lesdorf Orphanage, north of Vienna. The children were well cared for there. It was the least that could be done, let me tell you, since several of the orphans had lost their parents in wars against the French, the Italians, the Turks or God knows who else. You were taught good manners, the Bible, patriotism . . .'

He laughed sarcastically – he was wearing a French uniform.

'Not to mention reading and mathematics, especially mathematics for the boys. You see, you have to be a good mathematician if you are going to become an effective gunner: measurement of angles, calculation of the curve of the shot . . .'

Lefine and Margont were perplexed.

'Gunner?' said Margont, astonished.

Relmyer smiled, a bitter, ironic smile. 'Of course! All these little boys orphaned by war were to be turned into soldiers. Wars are always hungry, so it is convenient that war nourishes war.'

He picked up a stone and threw it in an arc. 'Bang!' he joked when it landed. 'It doesn't work with everyone. Some marry and go into business or work the land of their new family, others move away, hoping to change their luck . . . but many do become soldiers. I met Luise in the orphanage.'

Margont thought he had remained impassive, but perhaps his

expression had changed because Lefine turned towards him as if he had given away his feelings. The sergeant's face registered enlightenment. He had just discovered the key to the mystery.

'She was abandoned when she was two years old. It's terrible! She was barely older than I was. We grew up together. When she was eight, a miracle occurred. The miracle that we all dreamt of. She was adopted. Her new mother was beautiful! Elegant, considerate, smiling . . . and her father, although less warm, was also happy, even if he didn't show it in public. The Mitterburgs are rich Viennese bourgeoisie. They came to Lesdorf because they couldn't have children of their own. They chose Luise after three visits. The day they took her away, we all clustered round the carriage, in case they wanted a second child . . . I'm sorry, I'm boring you with my reminiscences. Anyway, for a long time there were three of us: Luise, Franz and me. Since we didn't have any family, we made our own. Franz was our little brother, at least he was little in stature – he didn't know his date of birth. We spent all our time together. After she left, Luise often came to see us. Or she badgered her parents to let us come and visit her. Everything was shattered one day in April 1804. I was fifteen at the time.'

His body grew rigid. His recollections were extremely painful. 'Franz and I went for a walk in the forest. We were playing at . . . I don't know what at.'

He did remember, in fact, but since then, childish pastimes had exasperated him.

'We were playing hide-and-seek, not knowing that someone else was playing hide-and-seek with us. I don't know how long the man had been watching us. A few minutes? An hour?

Several days? Several weeks? We often went to the woods. Perhaps he had been spying on us for a long time, having worked out when we had free time. Or perhaps he came across us by accident. If you don't know the area around Vienna, you won't know that vast tracts have been cleared to make farmland. But several areas are still forested. It was springtime, the sun was shaded by leaves and the sunlight didn't travel far. If you left the beaten track, it was easy to get lost. I had just surprised Franz behind some shrubbery and I threw myself on him. We were playing at war.'

Relmyer shivered. 'I'm still playing at it today, in a way . . . The man appeared out of nowhere. He came from the forest, not along a path. I saw him briefly. He threatened us with a pistol and ordered us to turn round. I thought he was a robber, that he would let us go because we had nothing. But no. He forced us into the woods. We were walking in front of him and he was guiding us. He deliberately complicated the route. Finally we arrived at a ruined farm, very isolated. The road leading to it was completely obscured by branches and shrubs, the collapsed walls covered in ivy. He took us into one of the old buildings. There was a trap door, which led down into a cellar. After he had forced us into the cellar, he removed the ladder and left. He abandoned us there, imprisoned in that damned room like two birds in a cage!'

Margont felt the weight of oppression. Imprisonment, even imaginary imprisonment, was intolerable to him.

'Franz and I were left there for hours with nothing to eat or drink. Later I learnt that we had been missing for two days. We could barely see, the trap door was impossible to reach, and in any case the man had removed the lock. We shouted and banged on the walls but no one came to our rescue. Who would be out walking in that area? And anyway, the cellar was in a much better state than the external walls, and the ceiling had been carefully sealed. The man had fitted out the cellar so that no one would be able to hear us. By the second day, we were so weak that our captor would have been able to do whatever he liked to us without our being able to defend ourselves . . .'

Relmyer then related his escape and how Franz had disappeared by the time he got back. 'Franz's body was found the next day in another part of the forest, hidden under branches. He had been stabbed and also abused. Someone had mutilated his corpse in exactly the same way as Wilhelm's by carving a smile with a knife!'

Relmyer remained frozen, his face strained, as he recalled the horror of the body.

After a silence, Margont asked: 'How long did it take for you to find help and get back to the cellar, after your escape?'

'It's hard to say. I was so exhausted I wasn't exactly racing along, and of course I was lost in the forest. Eventually I stumbled on a path that led me out of the woods. I returned to Lesdorf and raised the alert. Unfortunately, I couldn't find the damned farm again. We had to wait for the police to arrive with several volunteers to organise a massive search and we finally found it. So I would say between seven and ten hours.'

Relmyer suddenly grew agitated. 'There should have been a hue and cry about the whole affair, but relatively little was said. Madame Blanken, who financed and managed the orphanage, did everything in her power to prevent people knowing about the crime. She wanted to maintain the reputation of her orphanage. Madame Blanken is part of the Viennese establishment and she has good contacts, so she had no difficulty in achieving her aim. The investigators were ordered to be very discreet and only two newspapers reported the crime. Madame Blanken did sincerely want the perpetrator caught, but I am convinced – and I always will be! – that her silence severely hindered the investigation. I, on the other hand, had different ideas: I wanted the affair to have as much publicity as possible. I hoped that would eventually flush out some witnesses. I also thought it was important to warn the Viennese! The killer might be preparing to strike again, everyone should stay alert until the killer had been arrested!'

The tension that Relmyer had felt at the time resurfaced as powerfully as before. 'My disagreement with Madame Blanken quickly became more and more virulent. Our points of view were completely incompatible. In the end she forbade me to mention Franz's death and every time I did in spite of her, she punished me! I was to "forget", leave the case to those who were competent to deal with it, and shut up! The man responsible was never identified. Gradually the police grew discouraged and abandoned their investigations despite my pleas and protests.'

'Why the bizarre desire to cover the affair up?' demanded Lefine.

'Because, in Austria, the establishment has an obsessive fear of scandal. Appearances are much more important than reality. The honourable reputation of an institution far outweighed the murder of an orphan. If the truth had leaked out, Lesdorf

Orphanage would have been harshly judged, and so would the police.'

'It's the same in France, and everywhere else,' said Margont.

'I couldn't stand the failure of the investigation and the indifference of most of the people involved. Besides, I was worried that the assassin would come after me; I had briefly seen his face. A few months later I fled. I had begun to detest Austria, so I left the country. I wanted to live off my own resources but, rapidly falling into poverty, I decided to enlist in your army. I chose the army because in times of war they take on practically anyone. I was guaranteed board and lodging. And I chose the French army because they were firing on the Austrians. But the real reason I became a soldier was to learn to fight. I acquired fighting skills; I am no longer defenceless.'

The three men found themselves staring at Relmyer's scabbard. They were all aware that it was a fearsome object guarding a blade that was the extension not only of a skilled hand but also of a determined will.

'I always knew that I would come back here to settle the affair. It's only that I have come a little earlier than expected. I would have preferred to wait three or four more years, to perfect my skills, to become a master of arms without peer.'

Relmyer's boundless vanity was childish. He passed from adulthood to adolescence to childhood in an instant, as if he were perpetually oscillating between these three stages of his life.

'However, my premature return is a good thing. Because the man is still here and he's killed again! Wilhelm was sixteen. Almost the same age as Franz and I when we were kidnapped!

We came from the same orphanage and, besides, I knew him: we used to play together sometimes. And most telling of all, there's that smile!'

'I wonder why the assassin mutilates his victims in that way?' asked Margont, baffled.

'I don't know, but I'll find out. I know that I can count on Luise, but that's not enough. I had put all my hopes on two of my hussars, Barel and Pagin. I sent them to look for Wilhelm but alas, Barel is lying somewhere between Essling and Aspern. As for Pagin, he's barely seventeen; he needs guidance. The other troopers in my squadron only care about themselves and the war, which, I do concede, is already a lot to think about. Are you willing to assist me?'

Margont appeared undecided and Lefine looked at him, willing him to refuse.

'I can help you out for the moment. We'll have to see for how long.'

Relmyer leapt to his feet, beaming. 'Thank you! Let's go and find my captain and get him to release me so that I can show you the spot where Wilhelm was killed. Pagin will come with us – he managed to find out quite a bit about the crime. Then I'll take you to where I was imprisoned. Perhaps you will notice something that escaped me.'

Margont was surprised by Relmyer's precise, coherent proposal. He must have thought endlessly about this investigation. Margont realised that, for reasons he did not fully understand, he had been drawn into a duel between two redoubtable adversaries, for the murderer, who had been able to strike a second time without being caught, was as formidable as Relmyer.

Overcome with joy, Relmyer embraced Margont, Lefine, then Margont again. 'Oh, Monsieur! I am so indebted to you! If ever anyone picks a fight with you, tell me and I swear I will have his guts for garters.'

Even his presents were stained with blood.

Instead of going to Relmyer's captain, Margont addressed himself directly to Major Batichut, whom he had heard much about from Piquebois. Batichut, a tough little hussar, did not even reply to Margont's salute.

'You're in the 18th of the Line? Do you know Second Lieutenant Piquebois?'

'Yes, of course. He's one of my best friends.'

Batichut's face lit up. Amazing! Here was one of Piquebois's friends! 'Why didn't you say so earlier? When you introduce yourself to the 8th Hussars and you know Piquebois, you should say, "I am a friend of Antoine Piquebois," not, "Captain Quentin Margont, 18th of the Line, Brigade such and such, Division so and so".'

Noticing Relmyer frowning, Margont explained to him that Piquebois was a former hussar of the 8th Regiment.

'No, Monsieur Plodding Infantryman,' corrected Batichut. 'Piquebois was not a hussar but *the* hussar! You would be lucky to find two as good as he in the élite platoon. An example to follow, Relmyer! At least to follow up until 1805, when, alas, he left the hussars after being seriously wounded, and went to become an infantryman. What a shame!'

It was not clear whether Batichut was bemoaning

Piquebois's injury, or his departure. Best not to ask.

'Please pass on greetings from Major Batichut! I met your friend at a duel when he was fighting some melancholy dolt from the mounted artillery—'

'With all due deference, Major, I'd rather not hear about it,' cut in Margont. 'I'm sure that Piquebois remembers you very well.'

Batichut was overcome with surprise and disappointment, like an attentive host whose guest turns up his nose at the main dish. Then he became angry when Margont made his request. 'You take Piquebois from us and now you want Relmyer! Would you also, by any chance, like my horse and my wife?'

Reflecting that it was not in the best taste to refer to his wife in this way, Batichut calmed down as suddenly as he had flared up. His outbursts were like storms in a teacup. Except on the battlefield . . .

'It shall not be said that I disappointed the friend of a hussar, even the foot soldier friend of a former hussar. Relmyer, you may go wherever you please, but if you miss a call to arms, you will be sanctioned.'

As the three men moved away, Batichut shouted, 'Captain Margont, ask Piquebois when he's coming back! Because he will come back one day, for sure, mark my words!'

CHAPTER 6

RELMYER was accompanied by three of his hussars. Pagin, who had scoured the countryside before finally finding Wilhelm's body, seemed to have forgotten the mutilated face. His blood, heated by the flame of youth, boiled in his veins and his ardour communicated itself to his mare, which was ready to set off at a gallop at the least provocation. Even the heat that streaked his face with sweat did not calm Pagin.

'How did you hear about the boy's disappearance?' queried Margont.

Relmyer pressed his lips together, annoyed with himself. 'I've been discreetly keeping a watch on the orphanage since we arrived in the Vienna area. It was easy for me to organise.'

Hussars were in fact always deployed across a wide area, and since they were observant and resourceful they acted as the eyes and ears of the army.

'I didn't know exactly what I was hoping for. I wanted to have news of the orphanage. Was it still there? Who worked there? I had a feeling of latent menace, but I've had that for years, ever since my kidnap. When I heard that one of the orphans had disappeared, that it was Wilhelm, I immediately thought, it's starting all over again. I didn't have any proof, of course, but it's what I firmly believed. I always thought that Franz's murderer would strike again. What was to stop him? I gave the order to search for Wilhelm, to interrogate people . . . I tried to persuade myself that he had only run away.'

'Why did he leave the orphanage?'

'He stole out on the night of his death. His friends don't know where he was headed, but he had taken all his meagre belongings so he had gone for good. It's an astonishing coincidence: as soon as I return, there's another murder.'

'I don't believe in coincidences,' declared Margont.

'Neither do I.'

'So what's the link between the two events?'

'I can't answer that question yet, although I keep asking it myself.'

'We will have to try to find the people who investigated Franz's death.'

Relmyer gritted his teeth to prevent himself from letting loose a stream of vituperation. The merest mention of the Viennese police made him want to hit something – the trees, the houses, the world. For a few seconds he was unable to reply. 'I'd already thought of that. As much as it pained me, I did make the effort to try to see those incompetent imbeciles, but I failed. One died last year of inflammation of the lungs. Two others joined the Viennese Volunteer force and were subsumed by Archduke Charles's army. The last one fled before the troops arrived. And to top it all off, when the police were evacuated from the capital they took most of their archives with them . . .'

Relmyer raised his chin and looked at Margont with sparkling eyes. He regularly forced himself to appear cheerful and sometimes even felt it. Changing the subject, he added: 'I like the way you put things. Very clear, very mathematical.'

'Really? "Mathematical"?' Margont had never heard the word used as a compliment.

'Do you like maths?' asked Relmyer.

'Not much.'

'That's a great shame! Maths is at the core of everything, it is the very essence of the world. It enables us to translate the complexity of what surrounds us into a simple, codified language.'

'The essence of the world?'

'The trajectory of a cannonball, the dome of a cathedral, the strength of a bridge, the speed of movement of an army, a series of attacks in a duel . . .'

'And that's what you think the world is? What about love, friendship, literature? Also just maths?'

'Not yet, but one day, certainly.'

Margont did not agree with this point of view and wanted to respond, but Lefine intervened with the consoling words: 'Not to worry, Captain, we won't be around to witness that sad state of affairs. The war will have killed us long before.'

The little group stopped on the banks of the Danube and the horses hastened to drink from the river. Behind them, the French troops and their allies were arriving at their quarters. Large shapeless masses, topped with a forest of muskets, moved slowly across the plains. The noise of their displacement, the muted hammering of thousands of steps and the clanking of arms and other equipment sounded almost ferocious. Messengers went to and fro at the gallop. The march of these titanic centipedes could be halted by three virtually illegible lines scribbled by an aide-de-camp trying desperately to take down orders rapped out by Napoleon. They would then be sent in a different direction.

'Look at all those islands,' commented Relmyer.

The majestic course of the Danube was indeed sprinkled with an astonishing number of small wooded marshy islands, covered with tall grasses . . . impossible to tell with the naked eye what their topography was like.

'Without even counting the part of the Danube that runs north from Vienna or south from Lobau, which is the largest island, you can see hundreds of them – they look like a labyrinth. The vagaries of the current either throw them up or obliterate them. I don't know why Wilhelm and the man we're hunting would have come here. But I know one thing: if you knew this area well, you could easily lose yourself in it, even if fifty soldiers were on your trail.'

'Which of these islands were they on?'

Relmyer's gaze sought Pagin, who was investigating the river, his horse submerged up to the chest. He was imagining himself parading in front of the Emperor, to announce that he, Pagin, of the 1st Squadron of the 8th Hussars, had discovered a ford across the river. No more pain-in-the-neck bridges collapsing! Unfortunately, others before him had searched and failed, and before long he would be swept away by the current, waving his arms in agitation. These days, it was always the Danube that had the last word. Relmyer signalled to him and Pagin came galloping back. The affair distressed him. He would dearly have loved to solve it for the two officers.

'It's impossible to tell, Lieutenant. I was able to interrogate only second-hand witnesses and they contradicted each other.

It was somewhere here, not far from Vienna, during the night of 19 May. The patrol was following the river when they heard a noise and saw two silhouettes on the one of the islets. They shouted out and then fired ... In the time it took them to commandeer a boat, the other fellow had disappeared.'

'Was the boy wet?'

'Soaking.'

Relmyer, pensive, stroked his horse's neck. 'They must have wanted to swim across. The bridges have been destroyed in several places by the retreating Austrians, and Archduke Charles has sabotaged most of the boats.'

Margont let his gaze slide over the surface of the water, seeking out the shimmers that caught the rays of the sun. 'The Danube's currents make it dangerous to cross. They must have gone over at night to avoid being seen by the sentries. And our man must have taken care to keep his pistol dry; he probably hid it under his hat. He would have been able to make use of the confused mass of islands to conceal their escape. Would you know how to do that?'

Relmyer shook his head. 'I don't think so.'

'So he knew the lie of the land even better than you. How did he meet Wilhelm? What did he do to persuade him to come as far as this? Where were they going? And for what? There are so many unanswered questions.'

Relmyer gave a bitter laugh, but it seemed to hide the salty taste of tears. 'So many unanswered questions? That's all I have, questions! Who is this man? Why does he mutilate his victims? How long will he go on killing? And how can we stop him?'

They frittered away several minutes trying to work out the exact spot where Wilhelm had been assassinated. They tried to find a boat first, but all the boats not already swiped by the Austrians had been requisitioned by the French. Pagin insisted on plunging into the water, bolt upright on his horse. The current bore him away and his horse began to turn its head from side to side, searching for firm ground. Finally the animal succeeded in reaching one of the little islands, but it was not the one Pagin had been aiming for. Despite his best efforts the hussar was only able to explore half a dozen islands.

Finally Margont exclaimed in exasperation, 'It's like looking for a needle in a haystack!'

'Even an entire regiment wouldn't be enough to find the island,' admitted Relmyer.

Pagin painfully made his way back to the riverbank, exhausted and trembling, and delivered his conclusion: 'This man knows the area like the back of his hand.'

Lefine clenched his teeth. 'We knew that already before wasting three hours here.'

Margont turned towards Relmyer. 'Why don't you show us the cellar you were locked up in?'

'I don't think we have time, it's already late . . .'

Late? It was midday! Relmyer wanted to return to the cellar, but at the same time he would have given anything never to have to set foot there again. 'All right. I'll take you,' he conceded with bad grace.

They followed the banks of the Danube back towards the north-west. Then they skirted round Vienna to the north.

Neither Lefine nor Margont had managed to visit that admirable city at the time of the 1805 campaign. All the riders except Relmyer looked towards it, avid to discover the least little detail about it even from afar. They lost time because there were troops in their path. The battalions had become muddled up trying to get round a mass of ammunition wagons. The light horse of the Imperial Guard, arriving in their turn, had decided to take the shortest route and simply galloped through the infantry. Bad idea. The resulting disorder rang with shouts, threats and injunctions. Behind this chaos could be seen the hand of Napoleon.

Lefine leant towards Margont. 'The Emperor is deploying his troops in the best way to confront the Austrian army, while still holding on firmly to Vienna. That will give pause to those who want to stir themselves to cause havoc behind us.'

Like every French soldier, Lefine still remembered the Viennese bells ringing out in celebration of the Austrian semi-victory at Essling.

Finally their way was clear and they were able to trot rapidly into the forest. It was denser and more massive than Margont could have imagined. Visibility dropped dramatically, as did the heat, which became more bearable. The hussars spread out one behind the other, a few paces apart. They held themselves at the ready, sabres or muskets in hand. Lefine and Margont were ill at ease. They passed a dead tree, suddenly revealing bushes, invisible the moment before. A group of shrubs trembled; was that just the wind? The tree trunks obscured their vision. If there were danger you would definitely not realise it until too late.

'How much further, Lieutenant?' asked Lefine.

Relmyer, lost in his memories, did not answer. Margont recalled an old history lesson. What was it now? Shortly after Jesus Christ, the Germanic Armin, chief of the Cherusci, annihilated three Roman legions that had imprudently taken a short cut through the Teutoburg forest. Margont moved up alongside Relmyer.

'I hope we're not going to linger here.'

'No.'

'Can you describe the man we're looking for?'

The irregular shadows of the foliage flickered slowly across Relmyer's tormented features.

'I'm tempted to say he was tall, but I was shorter at the time. His clothes were unremarkable, neither rich nor poor. His hair? Brown.'

'And his face?'

Relmyer grew agitated at that question. 'His face – I see it, but I can't describe it! It's like a splinter perfectly visible beneath the skin, but impossible to pull out. I only saw it briefly; then he made us turn our backs. It was so long ago . . . Everything is so vivid but at the same time blurry. He was thirty-five or a bit younger . . . with heavy eyebrows. No moustache or beard, blue eyes.'

'Would you recognise him?'

'Most probably. At least I think so . . .'

'And would he recognise you? Have you changed much?'

'Yes, I have changed! Today I know how to fight.'

Actually, the answer to Margont's question was obvious: Relmyer still looked very young.

'Let's put that to one side for the moment. What can you tell me about his hands?'

'His hands? He had two of them, each with five fingers. Flesh-coloured. Does that get you anywhere?'

'You must have seen his hands, at least the one brandishing the weapon. Was he right- or left-handed?'

'Right-handed, I'm sure about that.'

'He knew this forest well, according to what you've told me. Did he have the calloused hands of a woodcutter?'

Relmyer brightened. 'No, not at all! His hands were slender with clean nails.'

'Are you certain you're remembering correctly?'

'I'm not remembering, I'm seeing them.'

After a while, Relmyer stopped. 'It's somewhere near here that he surprised us. But I can't tell you exactly where.' He made an effort to overcome his apprehension. 'We have to go this way, now,' he added, forcing his way through a curtain of branches.

They abandoned the path they had followed up to that point. The interplay of greens and shadows became even more pronounced. The horses picked their way painfully through bushes and branches.

'We are a long way past Vienna now. You must have strayed far from your orphanage,' remarked Margont.

'At the time, I loved to ramble as far as possible. I had even thought of leaving, never to return. In the hope of abandoning my problems and grief at the orphanage. As if everything was their fault. But if I hadn't gone back of my own accord, I would have been dragged back by the police or the orphanage staff . . .'

They continued on their way in silence. Birds sang with full throat, not the least bit intimidated by the presence of the horsemen.

'Here we are,' declared Relmyer finally.

Margont and Lefine stared, unable to make out anything unusual. Tree trunks, foliage, shrubbery, bushes . . .

Relmyer leant over his horse, dumbfounded. Pagin joined him in three bounds of his horse, pistol at the ready. The area had been burnt. The bushes, ivy and tall grasses, which had previously carpeted the clearing, were all singed. The remains of the walls, eaten away by the depredations of time and bad weather, had collapsed. They lay there, a heap of blackened rubble. Relmyer leapt from his horse and hurried over to the cellar. The roof had given way. Relmyer froze at the sight of the spectacle, his boots in the cinders. His back shook, a pale indication of his inner turmoil.

'He came back and destroyed everything.'

Lefine and Margont dismounted in their turn and went over to him.

'That's just supposition,' objected Margont. 'Why would he do that? To—'

Relmyer rushed at Pagin, yelling, 'Damn your eyes! I ordered you to stay here lying in wait! I'm going to have you arrested!'

The young hussar paled, looking suddenly more dead than alive. 'I really wanted to, but it was impossible, Lieutenant . . . I couldn't do it on my own. Several Frenchmen have been assassinated by—'

Relmyer continued to fulminate, expecting the impossible. Margont intervened.

'If Pagin had stayed here, his incinerated corpse would have been laid out in the middle of these ruins. It would have needed fifty to stay and keep watch; one is useless. You don't have fifty troopers under your command. And even if you did, I doubt that your major would have let you do it.'

'I should have stayed myself then!' fumed Relmyer, going forward amongst the ruins.

'That would have made you a deserter. Your men would have been forced to reveal where you were and—'

The carbonised debris gave way under Relmyer's weight and he was suddenly buried up to his waist. He struggled to free himself, stirring up ash and staining his dolman and his dark green greatcoat with sooty marks. Then, realising how pitiful he looked, he pulled himself together and extricated himself. Margont crouched down beside him.

'Look at that beam beside you.'

The thick piece of wood, eaten away by the fire, had broken in two, but the extremities were still intact.

'The flames attacked it from underneath. The top is not burnt, and it's the same with the other beams. It's astonishing. It means that the fire that ravaged the cellar was started inside and not outside. Was there anything flammable in there?'

'No.'

'So branches were arranged inside first. You're right: this fire is linked to the cellar, and therefore to your affair. In fact there were two fires. The trap door is in a room where the walls act as a fire screen. The cellar was destroyed by the fire lit inside it, but I don't see how the burning twigs could escape from there, jumping over the walls and starting off new fires. So obviously there were two fires, one inside and one outside to destroy the surrounding area. If anyone had passed by, they would have thought that someone had abandoned a badly extinguished campfire. The fire outside was designed to hide the other fire, which itself hid any possible clues.'

'There were no clues. I had already examined everything from top to bottom.'

'When did you come?'

Relmyer, covered in soot and ashes, seemed to belong to the ruins rather than to the world of the living.

'Thirteenth of May. We were scouting out the area ahead of the arrival of the main body of the troops and I took advantage of that to come here.'

Why had the murderer returned to this spot? Who had burnt the area and why? Margont was drowning in conjecture.

Relmyer went over to the exit that he had escaped from formerly. The toy he had placed there had melted. All that remained of it was a little pool of solidified tin.

'That bird is singing offkey,' declared Lefine.

Margont was not listening to him. 'If the man we're after is responsible for this fire, he's particularly methodical. He's applied scorched-earth tactics to ensure that he's left as few clues as possible behind him. The only "evidence" is Franz, Wilhelm, the mutilations he inflicted on them . . . and you.'

Lefine froze, listening intently.

'There's another bird singing off key. Listen, will you?'

Margont made out a sort of far-off trilling, which seemed to be answered by another much closer one. It sounded like a bird, but which one exactly? Lefine threw himself onto his horse in panic.

'The Austrians!'

The whistling of a blackbird rang out, coming from yet a third direction. The French bounded into their saddles. A detonation sounded. A hussar's horse bolted, wheeling round on itself and whinnying. Pagin made to help it, but a bullet hit his own animal in the chest. The horse collapsed, its bit striking the stony ground harshly. Lefine fired his pistol into the thicket where the shot had come from. The leaves shook, perhaps because of the breeze, or possibly because a body had fallen behind them. Other trillings resounded, longer and much louder. Lefine rode his horse over to Pagin, who hopped on behind him. New explosions crackled. They were coming from all sides, mingling with the echoes of previous reports, so that the French felt as though they were being deluged with bullets.

'They're surrounding us!' cried Lefine, huddling down with Pagin gripping his waist.

They made for the forest, hammering their horses' flanks with their heels, though obstacles in their way slowed them down. Margont thought he saw someone and fired his pistol into a clump of ferns to his left. In response a shot cracked to his right and buried itself in the trunk of a pine tree, spraying his cheeks with fragments of bark. Although the horses were aided by the slight slope, Margont, too impatient, tried to make his mare go faster. The frightened, maddened horse entangled its legs in dead branches and to regain balance placed its shoe on a carpet of dried needles. The shoe slipped and the beast's head plunged downwards, almost causing Margont to lose his stirrups and tumble forwards. Three more gunshots rang out, but more for form's sake than to kill. The French were too far away to be hit.

Relmyer saluted Lefine as he would a colonel.

'If you hadn't picked up their damned signals, they would have caught us hook, line and sinker; none of us would have escaped. How would you like to join the hussars?'

'I've had my fill of that sort of thing today, Lieutenant.'

The horses continued down the slope at a hurried trot, constantly slowed down by the thickets and trees. Margont could make out the Austrians shouting something.

'Are they calling for reinforcements?'

Relmyer smiled. 'No, they're saying: Welcome to Austria.'

CHAPTER 7

LEFINE was furious. He was pacing back and forth under the roof of branches rigged up by Saber and Piquebois, near their tent.

'We were almost killed by the partisans!' It was the tenth time he had said that, as if he couldn't get over it. 'This inquiry – it's his battle, not ours!' he exclaimed for the nth time.

Margont was leaning against a tree trunk. This was the miracle of being an officer: the Isle of Lobau was being transformed at speed into a fortification but here he was enjoying free time! Lefine, meanwhile, was covered in sweat.

'What on earth did you want to get involved for? Is it because of that Austrian woman? That Luise Mitter-something . . . Why go hankering after a beautiful girl with problems when you could easily find two without? Oh, it's not only for her, is it? It's those magnificent revolutionary ideas of yours again, that drive you to take crazy risks!'

He took off his shirt to change it. His right shoulder bore the scar of a sabre blow, a souvenir of the Spanish campaign courtesy of an English light dragoon, and his stomach was scored with a gash from a bayonet attack badly parried. His collarbone had been shattered by a Prussian musket butt. The bone had knitted together strangely so that a bony ridge bulged under the skin as if trying to break free from his body. A pattern of burns carpeted his back, caused by fiery splinters from the explosion of a munitions box. The whole saga of the Empire could be read on the scarred skin of its soldiers.

'Being a Good Samaritan is not a quality, it's a defect.' He tugged on the new shirt so angrily he almost tore it.

Margont was cooling himself using a book as a fan. Assuredly, literature had many uses.

'It's not that. It's not just that.'

'Yes, it is, it's always that! "We have to take the principles of the Revolution to the peoples of other countries!" "Down with monarchy, long live Liberty!" You're always going on about it. You're a product of the Revolution, but it's not relevant any more. We were all so naïve! Yes, I believed in it all too: liberty and equality for all, peace, progress, a constitution guaranteeing the same rights for everyone . . . It's utopia, and you're still fighting for it! This army is full of soldiers who want to liberate the world. That suits the purposes of the Emperor who—'

Lefine stopped short mid-sentence, while Margont hastened to assure him that no one had heard. Criticising the Emperor was the quickest way of being taken for a subversive spy, a royalist, an agent of the Vendéens or a Jacobin plotter . . . For the past few years freedom of expression in France had become more and more restricted.

Lefine went on more quietly: 'The Emperor abuses the army! Why is half our army in Spain along with the Spanish, the Portuguese and the English, all butchering each other? We only had to set foot in Spain for us to be mired there up to our necks. When will there finally be peace? When we're all dead? And now there's you embarking on this search! All because it arouses your pity and you still believe you have to help those around you! After four or five more years' war, when everyone else will have been killed or will have abandoned all hope, you will be the last republican humanist.'

Lefine spoke those last words with derision. He burst out laughing and leant one hand against a tree trunk, sneering.

'The world has gone mad, but you are maddest of all!'

Margont was irritated. He was not easily offended, but even so . . . In fact, yes, he was easily offended, and now he was cross.

'I do as I please! Some people go and look after lepers or plague victims, others give all their money to the poor . . . I don't know, some people live just for themselves and others think a little about other people.'

'You're right, I agree. We just don't agree about where the happy medium is. Let's leave it to the Austrian police.'

'I've thought of that. But where are they, the Austrian police?'

A fair point. They were on the other side of the Danube, with Archduke Charles. Or in the woods, keeping a lookout for any French who dared to venture there . . .

'It's not as if the case will be solved if there's peace,' continued Margont heatedly. 'You heard Relmyer as well as I did! No one cares about the lives of a few adolescent orphans! Better to botch the inquiry so as not to cause waves because some people prefer it that way. Life is so much simpler when one closes one's eyes! And you, you ask me to do the same? Well, no, I'm not going to! Who stepped forward to help me when my family had me imprisoned against my will in the Abbey de Saint-Guilhem-le-Désert to force me to become a monk? I was six years old and I spent four years of my life there! Four years!'

Lefine was dismayed.

'You're comparing your story with Relmyer's? Oh, now that's dangerous! That's catastrophic!'

'Lots of people knew, but they said to themselves, "It's nothing to do with us." One day I appealed to the wine merchant who supplied the abbey. He told me, "I can't help you, kid, you're not my son." But the problem was, my father was dead. So who was I supposed to turn to, God? Anyway, it wasn't God who freed me, it was the Revolution.'

Margont stopped shouting but his tone brooked no negotiation. 'So I am going to involve myself in this matter; it will help me resolve some unfinished business, even if only indirectly. I'm convinced it will help me bury certain memories in drawers that I can finally close and forget.'

Now Margont smiled, laughed even. He felt better, having been able to formulate clearly what he felt in his deepest soul.

'You're not obliged to help me, Fernand. As you can see, I'm involved for very personal reasons.' He rose and tried to straighten his uniform. 'So, it's not because I'm a Good Samaritan,' he remarked. 'Can I count on you?'

'Of course. Because you're my best friend. I'm not as selfish as all that . . . unfortunately for me.'

Margont was openly delighted. His relationship with Lefine was complicated. Margont was too idealistic, too fond of dreaming and trying to make those dreams into reality. Lefine was the complete opposite. He was pragmatic, resourceful and his common sense rooted him firmly in the everyday. Margont needed Lefine; he helped him keep his feet on the ground. In exchange Margont provided the intoxicating excitement of his changing impulses and the grandeur of his Great Schemes. In short, together they found the balance between whimsy and reality, a balance that neither managed to achieve on his own. Several years of war had consolidated their friendship, especially since each had saved the other's life.

'So let's go and find Relmyer, and get him to take us to his former orphanage,' decreed Margont.

'But I still say it's dangerous to confuse this with your own personal history.'

CHAPTER 8

PART of the army was camped on the Isle of Lobau – IV Corps and also the reserve for General Lasalle's cavalry. As Relmyer served in the latter, he was just a short walk away from the 18th of the Line. But it was not actually possible to walk there because the artillery convoys blocked the way. Lobau and the surrounding islands bristled with cannon. There were cannon on the Isle of Masséna (each of the islands was nicknamed after a hero of the Empire, or an ally), on Saint-Hilaire, on Lannes, on Alexandre . . . six-pounders, twelve-pounders, even eighteen-pounders, and howitzers, not to mention the gigantic field guns seized in Vienna from the arsenals that the Austrians, in the haste of their retreat, had forgotten to sabotage. Altogether there were thirteen hundred mortar cannon acting as a deterrent to the Austrians. For them to attack would have been suicide. Napoleon was manoeuvring his resources to protect himself, but doing it in such a way that he would also succeed in foiling his enemies and regaining the initiative. For now Archduke Charles was obliged to wait for the French to mount an assault. He was, however, ready to receive them unflinchingly; he was well dug in around Aspern and Essling.

As usual Relmyer trained hard. But unusually, there were spectators watching him from a distance. One of these was Saber. Margont went over to him.

'What are you doing?'

In reply, Saber murmured admiringly, 'I'm learning. So young and already so gifted . . . He's like me.'

Margont, who was accustomed to his friend's overweening vanity, contented himself with watching Relmyer again. It was true that his attacks seemed to be devilishly precise. But were they extraordinarily so? Saber was also a very fine duellist and, until now, Margont would have assumed that he was better than Relmyer.

'Is he more gifted than you, Irénée?'

'He would lay me out stone dead in less than ten seconds. He's much better than me,' Saber conceded. 'Only in duelling, of course.'

Margont could not get over his surprise. Saber never complimented other people (except women, whom he flattered in the hope of seducing them, assuming them to be as avid as he was for a bit of love-making). Relmyer was truly a remarkable man – he seemed to make an impression on everyone.

The young hussar lunged, beat a retreat while parrying a storm of imaginary thrusts, suddenly attacked again, feinting, dodging . . . To Margont it all seemed like a Gregorian chant: very beautiful, but incomprehensible. Saber, on the other hand, had the necessary expertise to form a judgement and he was marvelling at what he saw, even going so far as to tap his thigh to prevent himself from applauding.

'He lives only for the art of the sword,' he said under his breath, 'without looking to left or right.'

That was totally untrue. Most people did not see past the image Relmyer projected. It was a brilliant image, so people looked no further. His violence covered up his suffering.

'He has natural talent and the compulsion to learn. He's nicknamed "The Wasp" . . . Bézut took him on as a pupil, but alas they fell out.'

Bézut? Probably another renowned master of military arms. Saber knew the most illustrious of them. He would have been their biographer had he not had it in mind to dedicate himself solely to his autobiography.

'I heard that from one of his cavalry regiment,' explained Saber.

That would definitely have been Pagin. Especially as he was one of the spectators.

'Why train so hard with a sabre when you can use a pistol?' Margont wondered aloud.

'When a pistol is empty, you're done for,' replied Saber. 'Pistols are also unreliable, imprecise and rarely fatal. In any case, I understand that Lukas Relmyer is also an extremely good shot.'

Relmyer caught sight of Margont and, interrupting his training, saluted him with his sword. Saber stood up straighter.

'I knew he had heard of me.'

Relmyer came over to Margont, sword still in hand. Did he never lay it aside? In spite of his intensive training, he still looked energetic, not showing the slightest sign of fatigue.

'Dear friend! Can I talk to you a moment in private?'

Saber stiffened, trying not to show his disappointment and jealousy. The other two men moved off together, leaving the admirers to rejoin their battalions.

'Before you say anything, I must warn you, you're in

danger,' declared Margont. 'If it is indeed the man we're looking for who set fire to the ruins of that farm, he is being exceptionally careful. If he knows that you went back there, he might well try to kill you. So you must always have an escort when you leave camp.'

Relmyer sheathed his sword, noisily clanging the hilt against the scabbard.

'I am my own escort.'

'I hope you'll take me seriously. Can we go and visit your old orphanage now?'

'Unfortunately I'm not welcome there. They were very angry with me for stirring up trouble before I left in 1804. It has to be said that, out of frustration, I did become aggressive. I actually struck the man in charge of the investigation. I was angry with everyone.'

His words plunged him into despair, and his hand came to rest on his sabre, his support.

'We're conducting an inquiry – that gives us rights,' decreed Margont.

Relmyer's eyelids drooped tiredly. 'Of course, but it's not as simple as that. Madame Blanken, narrow-minded, insensitive old witch, is still the director of Lesdorf Orphanage. As I've told you she has connections with the Viennese aristocracy. If you go ferreting around in her back yard, she won't be content with whacking you with her broom. Her outcry will bring down much more serious consequences on us.'

Relmyer went on in a tone that anger rendered as cutting as sword strokes, 'The Emperor wants Vienna to continue undisturbed, so anyone who causes trouble is heavily punished.

If a dozen countesses and wives of Austrian nobility complain about us, accusing us of sowing panic in an orphanage, we'll be summarily arrested. Believe me, La Blanken has a long arm and an effective fist.'

Margont backed down. Better to take time to inform yourself about a potential enemy before confronting them.

'In any case, without Madame Blanken's co-operation, our investigations will be fruitless,' Relmyer emphasised. 'That's why I propose that we take a different approach. I sent one of my hussars to Luise with a note, asking her to try to organise a meeting with Madame Blanken for us. She has answered saying that her parents are giving a ball. Napoleon is pressurising the Viennese to organise receptions. The Emperor wants to divert his officers and to show that he is so confident of victory that he regularly allows them to waste time in worldly discourse. He even invited actors from Paris to appear in the theatre of Château de Schönbrunn, where he has taken up residence. The Mitterburgs agreed because, like many Austrians, they are trying to have a foot in both camps. If Archduke Charles wins, they will be able to say they were forced to give the soirée, which is true. And if it's Napoleon who wins the war, the Mitterburgs' business will continue to flourish . . .'

Margont nodded.

'Franco-Austrian relations certainly seem to be complex, no one can make head nor tale of them! During the Revolution and the Consulate, Austria and France were enemies. Then after Austerlitz they were reconciled and French soldiers were told they must not criticise the Austrians because they were our friends. Today Austria is at war with us again. But no doubt, if

Napoleon triumphs, Austria will hasten to ally herself with him once more, to soften his anger and limit the extent of his sanctions!'

Relmyer appreciated the irony of these constant reversals of alliance.

'Many Austrians are patriots,' he declared, 'but there are others who run with the hare and hunt with the hounds. And those last are only following their emperor, Francis I, who turns his coat after each defeat.'

At that, he started to laugh at the insolence of his own behaviour.

'But let's get back to our investigation. Madame Blanken will be invited. She is always to be found at that type of reception. What's more, Luise tells me she's one of those whose allegiance goes both ways. During the ball we will be able to talk to her. Perhaps you will succeed in buttering her up and interrogating her? Are you still listening?'

'Absolutely,' replied Margont.

He was listening to Relmyer, but at the same time thinking about Luise. So he was going to see her again. Would she have the same effect on him as the first time he met her?

'The soirée is going to be on 31 May. We will just about have time to prepare our ceremonial uniforms. I would be delighted if Lefine could also come. Without him, we—' He did not finish the sentence. 'And the famous Piquebois!' he exclaimed. 'He's a former hussar, so I say he's one of us. Apart from those two, do you have any other friends?'

Margont looked over at the figure hanging about under a weeping willow.

'Lieutenant Saber, who's kicking his heels over there, and Medical Officer Brémond.'

'They will all be welcome! You'll see what Viennese balls are like. They're pure magic.'

CHAPTER 9

MARGONT went to the soirée accompanied by Lefine, Jean-Quenin Brémond and Relmyer. Saber and Piquebois were already there, having been released from duty earlier.

Their nocturnal journey across Vienna was slightly surreal. The darkness accentuated the majesty of the buildings and Margont thought he could make out the ghost of the Holy Roman Empire, which had been mortally wounded at Austerlitz but had lingered on until July 1806. Napoleon had finished it off by dismembering it, thus weakening Austria and creating the Confederation of the Rhine, a constellation of German states that orbited around France. Vienna was occidental clearly, yet the Orient also manifested itself without it being clear exactly how. The Turks had long since left Vienna, but the city still bore their trace, the imprint of their extraordinary culture. The long grandiose succession of façades was interrupted at regular intervals by enormous black holes. The streets and avenues bore the scars of the almost two thousand cannonballs and shells that had rained down on them during the night of 11 May. The capital had resisted as best it could with its fifteen thousand soldiers and some of its population. Napoleon was adept at showing magnanimity towards those who surrendered to him, but he was fearsome in the face of any glimpse of resistance. After the first deluge of missiles and their fiery aftermath had branded the night like red-hot iron, the Emperor had set himself to annihilate the city in thirty-six hours of widespread bombardment. Vienna had capitulated. Napoleon immediately had a proclamation read to his soldiers announcing that he was giving the 'good inhabitants' of Vienna his 'special protection'. The text further stipulated that 'wicked trouble-makers' would be subject to 'exemplary justice'.

Vienna was a strange mixture of past and present, West and East, monuments and ruins, grandeur and war damage – a melting pot propitious for every sort of concoction.

The Mitterburgs' house stood in a garden enclosed by an iron railing. The vast edifice, with its ochre façade, was reminiscent of a Venetian palace washed by a lagoon. Relmyer explained that the Mitterburgs had made their fortune in the coffee trade. The grandfather, now dead, was so fond of the beverage that he had made it his career. He had taken the trouble to learn Turkish so that he could negotiate his imports more easily, between the two Austro-Turkish wars. The drink became increasingly popular. Cafés sprang up across Europe and soldiers were annoyed when they were unable to get hold of it . . .

Lefine listened avidly. What a good strategy for getting rich! To guess today, before everyone else, what would become indispensable tomorrow. And he was indeed trying, trying to think of something . . .

They entrusted their horses to the servants, who hurried from carriage to carriage to greet the guests. A stiffly formal footman invited them to follow him. His tight white stockings made his legs appear spindly and his shoes grated on the inlaid parquet. They crossed a dark corridor bathed in the echo of music, laughter and conversation, and emerged into the light, noise and life of a large gallery.

A glittering crowd filled the long, wide room. Dresses with trains mingled with the sumptuous uniforms of Napoleon's Empire. Allegorical frescoes decorated the enormously high ceiling. The two long walls were adorned with large mirrors, amplifying the space and making the people appear more numerous. There were so many French windows in the wall overlooking the garden that the people appeared to move in a white luminous universe with gold panelling against a backdrop of green and darkness. Colossal crystal chandeliers, strewn with candles, hung low on astonishingly fine cords as if in reminder that even the largest and most brilliant worlds hung also by only a thread.

'Here's to coffee!' was Lefine's enthusiastic verdict.

To Margont, there was something strange about the dancing couples gaily bounding under a forest of raised arms, and the beautiful women installed in blue brocade armchairs decorated with gilt. Officers were everywhere: colonels, a few generals and some members of the general staff. Had Margont not seen the catastrophe of Essling, if he had just arrived in Vienna, he would have said to himself, 'What a party! What joy! Why are people saying the situation in Austria is so worrying? They must really have exaggerated the defeat at Essling.' Napoleon was a master of propaganda; he excelled at projecting the right image, at using the right symbols. The balls and plays that he propagated in Vienna were a demonstration to Europe that the setback at Essling was so insignificant that he was not even going to interrupt his worldly pleasures. So Prussia and England waited instead of involving themselves actively in the war, wary of an adversary who, even when hurt, continued to dance and smile. The joyous melodies of violins were as intimidating as cannon fire and bought Napoleon some time. It would not last and the Emperor knew it. Everything depended on the next battle.

Margont and Relmyer started to look for Luise while Lefine and Jean-Quenin Brémond went over to the buffet while studying the cartouches of mythogical scenes scattered over the walls.

Margont's glance wandered over the crowds in uniform. There were geographic engineers in their blue coats and bicornes, their eyes exhausted from drawing up maps of the exact topography of the interminable semi-islands littering the Danube; aides-de-camp serving one general and criticising all the others; Bavarians in light blue coats with breastplates in their regimental colours and tall black helmets bulging skywards; cuirassiers who had left their armour behind, and looked ill at ease, like crabs without their shells; hussars as colourfully attired as their reputation warranted; Polish Light Horse in blue and scarlet, who hated the Austrians almost as much as they hated Russians and Prussians, and who delighted in tormenting the Austrian nobles by 'accidentally' knocking into them; the élite police force in leather breeches and blue coats with red lapels, often in conflict with the French soldiers who rebelled against their authority; colonels with shakos topped with plumes or crests; bicorned generals whose importance could be measured by the sycophantic crowd that gravitated towards them ... And finally, at the summit of the pantheon of the imperial mythology, reigned the grenadiers of the Old Guard, giants made still taller by their enormous bearskins, which their terrorised enemies could spot from afar. These praetorians, who had never lost a battle and whose appearance signalled the death sentence for all those who stood in their way, were Napoleon's most trusted élite troops, which he called on only as a last resort. All the various soldiers chatted, drank, paid court, danced ... At the back of the gallery a monumental Dresden china clock dominated the scene, impossible to ignore. Its presence seemed to murmur, 'Hurry up, time is passing and life is short,' a message known and much repeated but none the less true. And especially true for these soldiers, who would perhaps all be dead in a month.

The Austrians were equally numerous: sympathisers of the French Empire, proponents of an Austrian revolution, or those simply wanting to mingle with important people.

Margont finally caught sight of Luise just finishing a conversation, but he was careful not to greet her or to point her out to Relmyer. She was sublime. Her white dress with puff sleeves was elegantly pleated in the manner of a toga, and seemed to diminish her pallor. She wore long gloves to the elbow. Her dancing slippers beat time, as much to the rhythm of her impatience as to the rhythm of the waltz. Round her waist she wore a red bow, where others had chosen golden or cream belts. The scarlet attracted attention and was emphasised by the flower pinned to her bosom. White and red, the colours of Austria, with the red on her heart. Luise was declaring her patriotic convictions. She must have been annoyed to see her parents welcoming the French into their home in this way. Her hairstyle had not changed and Margont was delighted because the new fashion for the Titus cut, very short and frizzy, left him cold. He did not understand why people longed to live in the manner of eight hundred years ago. And, happily, neither was she wearing one of those ridiculous crowns of wilting flowers straight out of an embroidered fantastical picture of the Muses. Luise had not spotted them yet; she was still looking about. How delicious it was to be able to observe a woman you were attracted to! Margont could have continued to watch her longer than was seemly. He wanted to savour the moment when she finally noticed him. He wanted to catch that instant of condensed time when the anxious quest ended and just before social niceties took over. That second of truth, when emotion and surprise make you briefly drop the mask that society obliges you to wear. Alas, Relmyer waved to Luise and when her expression changed to one of intense joy, Margont could not tell how much of that was for Relmyer and how much for him.

Margont and Relmyer skirted round the dance floor where couples, hands joined, arms raised, sketched complicated patterns in agreeable but artificial harmony. They passed in front of the orchestra, all powdered wigs, ochre livery, silk stockings and aggression muzzled by propriety; unleashed a storm of tut-tutting and fan-waving as they brushed past a group of young ladies in search of partners and reached Luise, who had walked over to meet them. She looked at Relmyer, her eyes shining with tears. Her distress, misinterpreted, earned him withering looks from scandalised ladies nearby.

'You've grown . . .' she stammered humbly.

Relmyer was equally moved. Thousands of phrases came to mind but they did not manage to say any of them. They were unable to express their evident joy, because their reunion emphasised the loss of Franz. Their couple was an amputated trio.

Margont did not exist for Luise at that moment and it pained him. Yet again, the past displaced the present and he did not belong to their past. Colour returned to Luise's cheeks and her voice grew firmer.

'I have so much to reproach you for, Lukas! You're lucky that I have forgiven you, you traitorous French hussar. You abandoned me, never wrote to me or sent me news, and you were too pig-headed, stupid and selfish even to let me know you'd returned to Vienna!'

She took his hand tenderly, to assure herself that this reunion she had so often dreamt of, although not in these circumstances, was in fact real. And also so as not to lose her brother again. Relmyer gently freed his fingers. Luise turned towards Margont. She looked radiant.

'You're very elegant in your enemy uniform. But I class you separately in a strange category of "enemy friends". I am delighted to see you, even though I would have preferred you in civilian clothes.'

'I would have preferred that too. Your colours are more reminiscent of a uniform than a ball gown.'

Relmyer turned his back on them.

'The old bat isn't here yet,' he murmured.

He was watching for her so avidly that he forgot about Luise and Margont. The latter hastened to take advantage of that.

'Luise – I can call you Luise? – there's something I've been dying to ask you. What did you mean exactly when you said that you had guessed that, in a way, I was an orphan?'

Luise had expected that question.

'Tell me about yourself and I'll answer you.'

Her tone was teasing but her expression serious. Margont entered into the spirit of the game.

'My father died when I was small. My mother couldn't support us any longer so sent me to live with one of my uncles. He took it into his head to make me a monk. A calamitous idea . . .'

Luise tried to imagine Margont as a monk. It was a disturbing image.

'He must have wanted to redeem his sins,' she hazarded.

'And I paid the price. I was shut up against my will in the Abbey of Saint-Guilhem-le-Désert, in the south-east of France. I wasn't allowed to see my family any more, nor to leave the abbey. I thought that I would never leave the place again. I felt utterly abandoned, like an orphan. I stayed there from the age of six until I was ten.'

Margont had presented his account in an orderly fashion. His summary resembled a report. But rage and sadness boiled within him, like pus in an abscess that would neither burst nor reabsorb itself, so could never heal.

'How did you escape? You must have driven those poor monks mad.'

'Actually that was one of my favourite tactics. However, it was the Revolution that liberated me – by suppressing by decree all religious communities.'

Luise shook her head. 'No, you liberated yourself. Someone can let you out of a prison, but your spirit can still remain a prisoner. I'm the same – I freed myself. It took me years and years . . . One day, at Lesdorf Orphanage, they taught us about earthquakes. I was terrified for weeks; I had nightmares. I kept thinking the earth was trembling. I imagined a country where the ground shook all the time, where houses collapsed and people walked about in streets devastated by every strong trembling . . . In fact it appears that these phenomena only last a few seconds. Humans can tremble for a lot longer than the earth can. Of course, my adoptive parents genuinely love me. But do you know why they chose me and not someone else? It's because I was good – very important, that – because I was in perfect health and I was a conscientious student. I read, wrote and sewed well and I had good manners. Sometimes when I get angry with them because we don't agree about something, I wonder if they'll send me back to Lesdorf for "breach of contract". Oh, I'm talking too much! It's your fault! And now you're going to think I'm ungrateful. But it's not true! I love my parents with all my heart. It's just that I'm frightened. Frightened of losing everything a second time, of living through another earthquake.'

She tried to shake off the sadness that had come over her and added cheerfully: 'Please excuse me. It's the gaiety here. Sometimes excessive jollity makes me melancholy; distress, on the other hand, has a galvanising effect. I often say that I'm like an inverse mirror that transforms black into white and vice versa. Which is lucky, since the world is much more often dark than light.'

Margont was gripped by a sort of euphoria, which annoyed him since he liked to believe that the mind controlled the body. He had just understood why the young Austrian girl held such fascination for him. They had both been abandoned. They had fought their suffering and had succeeded in dominating it using sheer force of will and their own philosophy of life. So Margont was a humanist because, in a way, he manifested towards other people the support and attention that he had found so cruelly lacking. Luise herself had constructed a nest, a cocoon, in which she lived happily with those she loved, and she had been ready to expend whatever energy was necessary in order to defend her little world, which Wilhelm and Relmyer also belonged to. And she had determinedly tried to keep them close to her. Margont and she shared the clear-sightedness of those who have been hurt by life, and the pugnacity of those who refuse to succumb a second time. They had suffered the same wounds and recovered by suturing the wounds in practically the same way. From their first meeting each seemed to have divined the other's scar, even before they had worked out what it was that attracted them to each other. Margont then realised that, contrary to what he would have expected, exposing the secret did not diminish in any way the feelings he had for Luise. Rather, the opposite was true. She seemed admirable to him, and he would have liked to forget everything else and lean towards her to kiss her. Luise blushed as if she read his thought, and she lowered her eyes. Margont in turn tried to guess what she was thinking. In vain. Relmyer spoke to them distractedly and Margont inwardly cursed him. Luise looked up at Margont again, her blue eyes sparkling.

'You're not as altruistic as I thought. You're helping us for several reasons and one of those is your past. I'm happy about that for you. In life, it's good to know how to be selfish.'

Had Lefine been there, he would have applauded. But he was systematically pillaging the buffet, swallowing quantities of canapés. Luise had arranged civilian clothes for him because his non-commissioned officer's uniform would not have got him past the footmen. He joined people's conversations, introducing himself as 'an aide to Commissioner of War Papetin'. He took great care to make his lies as clumsy as possible so that soon people were asking each other about him, discreetly, behind his back. They suspected him of being one of Napoleon's spies, the secret weapon of the Emperor, an ace up his sleeve. Perhaps he was that genius of manipulation, that master of astounding exploits, the extraordinary Schulmeister himself! People said – was it true, false or a bit of both? – that in October 1805 he had persuaded General Mack to believe that Napoleon and his Grande Armée were withdrawing in disarray to put down a widespread rebellion in the Vendée, supported by an English landing at Boulogne. Reassured, Mack had delayed in joining the rest of the Austrian troops. When he realised his error, he had been unable to prevent his division from being surrounded. His punishment: twenty-five thousand Austrians captured in the town of Ulm. Yes, this person was almost certainly Schulmeister since he looked nothing like any of the portraits that rumour painted of the celebrated spy. It was even said that Napoleon, who had regular meetings with Schulmeister, did not recognise him when he was in disguise. The Austrian aristocrats blanched when Lefine went up to them, causing him to bite his lips in order not to laugh.

Relmyer hopped nervously from foot to foot. He hated the celebratory atmosphere. Obviously the magic of Viennese balls, which he had spoken of, failed to stir him tonight.

'When on earth is she going to be here? The dirty scoundrel.'

He could not bear the wait. Margont realised that Relmyer was different from Luise and himself. Instead of relying on his strength of character, he fell back on his physical strength. He had trained ceaselessly, covering his body with a discreet but effective carapace of muscle and making his sabre into an extra limb. But at this moment physical strength was no help to him and impatience inflamed his anguish. He looked over at the punch the footmen in yellow livery were ladling out. After three or four glasses he would have felt so much better . . . but the large crystal goblets of orange or yellow liquid were like wells in which he could not risk drowning.

'I wonder if she's in that other room,' he said abruptly.

That sentence, peremptory and chilling, broke the rapport that had been established between Luise and Margont.

'But I don't see her,' he added.

Luise was entangled in a web of emotions. Anger, fear, impotence, despair, and disgust at her despair, all mixed together in a disturbing tangle. Paradoxically her face remained expressionless.

'You're never going to stop looking for the man, are you, Lukas?'

'No.'

Luise looked strained. 'So we'll be haunted by this affair for the rest of our lives! Suppose you never find him?'

Relmyer swung round, turning his back on them. His parting words were, 'Why don't you just enjoy yourselves! I'll come and tell you when Madame Blanken is here.'

Luise went over to the buffet. She asked for some cold water, then, annoyed by the mannered slowness of the serving boy, changed her mind and left the full glass on the sparklingly white tablecloth. She glared at Margont, pretending to be offended.

'Don't you know that it's not suitable for a young lady to be alone in the company of a man? If you don't ask me to dance immediately, people will talk.'

Margont longed to accept the invitation but he was intimidated by the grace of the couples whirling about on the floor.

'It doesn't matter if you don't know how to waltz,' Luise assured him. 'Let yourself be guided by me.'

That annoyed Margont. Ever since they had met, it had been like that.

Luise led him into the middle of the couples, to avoid being stared at. Margont rapidly felt befuddled by slight vertigo. He held Luise in his arms as everyone wheeled about them. The war was still so close. He had almost been killed at Essling and perhaps he would fall on the next battlefield. He could quite easily have only seven more days to live. He tried to forget about the investigation, the frenzy of past battles and the accumulating signs of the military cataclysm to come. The waltz with Luise represented a few stolen minutes away from the crazy chaos of the world. He accelerated the pace, staring at

Luise's cheerful face, allowing their motion to obliterate the rest of the universe. She smiled, showing glimpses of pearl-white teeth. The musicians also succumbed to the power of the music. The tempo took off, the conductor's gestures became expansive – now he seemed to follow his baton's lead. Then the music stopped abruptly. The silence was like a slap. Clapping crackled throughout the gallery. There was some quick toing and froing, and changing of partners, but Margont did not let go of Luise.

'Again!' he exclaimed quietly.

A new waltz started up. They twirled about in a haze of colour from the outfits and light from the candles, infinitely reflected by the mirrors and the gold panelling. The charm of the moment was enhanced by Luise's musky perfume. Margont imperceptibly tightened his grip on the young Austrian's waist. Time and thought seemed suspended and they were oblivious to the people round them. It was as if they were united in a capsule of emotion, which rolled endlessly in the light.

The orchestra broke off. Margont was looking forward to the next dance, but alas such persistence was unacceptable and Madame Mitterburg had her eye on her daughter. She dispatched the first fellow who came to hand to dislodge Margont. The man halted in front of Luise to request her pleasure, his shoulder nudging Margont's, indicating he was prepared to use force to eject the over-tenacious Frenchman. He was a lank, almost skeletal Austrian, the son of a good family who were friends of the Mitterburgs. He had served in the Viennese militia and had been careful to stay put when the French drew near to Vienna. Had he advanced, he would have been obliged to engage them in combat. Had he fallen back, he would have been obliged to join the Austrian army. So he had stayed where he was, allowing himself to be captured, whereupon Napoleon, wishing to propitiate the Viennese, had amnestied and freed all the militiamen on condition that they returned to their families.

Margont moved away.

He heard Luise say in astonishment to her new partner: 'Dear me, the Austrian army seems to have forgotten you in their retreat! Of course, when you depart in a hurry, you only take the essentials with you.'

Margont melted into the crowd, which was conversing in several languages. He spotted Luise and then lost her again, thanks to the movement of the dancing couples. The magic was broken, the music had become just music, and to add insult to injury the exertion had reawakened the pain in his side. That in turn brought back incoherent memories of the carnage at Essling. Instead of the harmonious melody of violins he now heard firing muskets and explosions, and instead of red dresses he saw blood.

Madame Mitterburg came to introduce herself. Her grey hair, lined face, the prominent veins in her hands and her husky voice all emphasised the great age difference between her and her daughter. Margont envied her for knowing so much about Luise.

'Luise has told me a great deal about you,' she stated.

Too much, in fact, she thought worriedly. She listened politely as Margont explained in German which regiment he served in.

But he hastened to assure her, 'I'm only a soldier because we are at war. As soon as it's all over . . .'

He stumbled over the end of the sentence. What did 'all'

signify? He no longer knew. Would the war be over one day? They had fought practically without a break since the Revolution, and even the brief periods of peace had tasted of gunpowder. It felt to him as if they had embarked on another hundred years' war.

'I mean, when there is finally peace, I will start a newspaper.'

The old lady listened politely, blinking from time to time. Because she said nothing it was difficult to tell what she was thinking. The word 'newspaper' always intoxicated Margont so he launched into a long explanation of his idea.

'Words are an antidote to the boredom of everyday life and help change the world. Newspapers and books stimulate the mind. It doesn't matter whether you agree with what you read or not, whether you laugh or cry, get angry or applaud. The only thing that matters is that we read something – anything at all! – that makes us react. And our reaction, our feelings, opinions and new ideas in turn make other things to discuss. They then feed the debate, they add to and propagate the range of the "chemical reaction".'

He was talking too fast, his German was deserting him and, realising this, he hurried to draw his speech to a close, convinced that his interlocutor was no longer listening.

'In short, I hope that my newspaper with its controversies and ideas will give the public something to read that will contribute to all the strands of thought that enliven and transform people's lives.'

Madame Mitterburg blinked again but said nothing. There was the sort of silence that makes you rapidly run through in your head the gamut of small talk that could restart the conversation, something unremarkable. The silence stretched out. Madame Mitterburg was still looking at Margont. He wondered if she was simply trying to fathom what it was about him that so appealed to her daughter.

'You must have a drink,' she declared finally. 'You've done so much dancing . . .'

She turned towards the buffet and asked for a drink. So much dancing? That was a bit of an exaggeration – he had danced two waltzes with Luise. He began to understand how far removed Austrian high society felt itself to be from the universe he operated in. In their world everything was regulated by a multitude of rules, codes, precepts and obligations. The slightest transgression set in train a flood of reactions designed to correct the misdemeanour. Madame Mitterburg was merely keeping Margont away from her daughter with this now rather ridiculous chat.

In the meantime, an Austrian nobleman had replaced the gangly creature, and others followed afterwards. So Luise danced but she did not derive any pleasure from it. Her waltzing was now just the conscientious application of the steps she had learnt in many hours of practice.

Margont thought of Relmyer. His criticisms of the investigation into Franz's death had ruffled society feathers. He had been told to keep quiet, but gagging him had only suppressed his words, not his feelings. This world defended its image and its privileges and considered scandal its worst enemy, the potential source of its destruction.

The waiter arrived with a crystal glass on a silver tray, and Margont had an impulse to send the whole lot flying.

Astonishingly, Madame Mitterburg seized the glass and said to him, 'Luise has had a great deal of grief in her life. Think about that.'

She put the glass in his hand, which she grasped tightly in both of hers. The crystal was freezing, her fingers burning.

'If you ever make her suffer, I swear that I will pay someone to kill you like a dog.'

With that, she left, abandoning Margont to his lemon punch.

Saber, who loved to gossip, joined him. With his head held high, accentuating his proud bearing, his glittering gaze and supercilious air, he looked like a brilliant general who had had to borrow a uniform from his batman, his own having been stained in heroic battle.

'Poor old Quentin, your beautiful Austrian has ditched you. Dance with someone else to make her jealous. It's even more effective if you dance with her best friend. The waltz sums it up: if you want to seduce an Austrian, you have to make them turn round in circles.'

Saber's words of wisdom ... Saber wanted Margont to introduce him to Relmyer but was too proud to ask. Margont decided to make him wait.

Jean-Quenin Brémond whirled past with a brunette in a white satin and silver lamé dress. She was gazing at him adoringly. Saber was rooted to the spot.

'Jean-Quenin's done well! All the girls love "Herr Doktor"! I'm happy for him.'

He had said this last in the tone of 'I hope he drops dead!' Even in matters of love, Saber went to war. His rivals were his enemies. He did not seduce, he executed manoeuvres. The heart of a beautiful girl was a bastion he set himself to assault, then abandon, broken under his heel. It was not the women who attracted him the most, nor the most seductive, that he paid court to, but the most unattainable. That way, he was able to boast about his 'victories'. And he was undeniably charming; alas, his Adonis-like beauty was like a spider's web.

'Antoine is not very lively this evening.'

It was true; Piquebois held himself aloof, leaning against a column, daydreaming. Distractedly he followed some of the couples with his eyes, but more because he was mesmerised by the movement than because he was interested in them.

The music stopped and Luise rushed over to Relmyer, who was becoming increasingly agitated. She dragged him off forcefully to dance a polka. Lefine, in his turn, went over to Margont, euphorically brandishing his glass.

'Schnapps – waltz, vodka – polka, punch – mazurka!' He emptied his glass with one gulp and concluded: 'Another pleasure snatched from the jaws of death.'

Luise smiled at Relmyer, exaggerating her joy to try to impart some to him. The polka, madly jolly, had the dancers leaping about. Officers and their beautiful partners jumped, turned and laughed. But Relmyer remained like an ice cube, detached from the warm ambience.

The polka came to an end and Relmyer immediately left the dance floor. Luise pretended to be out of breath to excuse herself from an officer of the artillery of the Imperial Horse Guard, in a dark blue pelisse edged with silver fur and dripping in gold braid. His voluminous rounded black fur bearskin transformed him into a colossus with an enormous head. He was extremely surprised as he watched the beautiful Austrian girl depart: the Imperial Guard was not in the habit of being defeated. Luise marched over to Margont.

Saber murmured hurriedly in his ear: 'She's coming! Talk to me, act as if you haven't noticed her and behave as if she's interrupting us.'

Act as if he had not noticed her? Margont had eyes for no one else. Luise spoke to him urgently.

'I'm entrusting Lukas to you. I want you to keep an eye on him. Promise me now.'

'In view of his duelling skill, it's more a question of asking him to protect me.'

'It's already done. Now it's your turn, promise!'

'I promise you.'

Luise held his eyes to seal the oath. Margont looked at her without letting his pleasure show. So she had made him promise to protect Relmyer! Saber was horrified.

'She's giving you orders! And you're going to obey? What will happen if women start to control everything?'

'The entire world is at war, so things can't get any worse than they already are,' retorted Luise.

Relmyer erupted into their midst, cutting off their squabbling like a ball running into a game of skittles.

'Madame Blanken is finally here, the *alte Funzel*, wicked, greedy old hag . . . Let's grab her straight away before she's embroiled in meaningless small talk with everyone.'

CHAPTER 10

MADAME Blanken was nothing like the portrait that Relmyer had painted of her. He had said she was unfeeling. Yet when she saw Luise she smiled affectionately. Her smile faded, though, the moment she laid eyes on Relmyer. Luise curtsied to her. Margont imagined a line of little girls, including Luise, curtsying in unison as Madame Blanken passed down a long corridor.

'Madame Blanken, please could you talk to Lukas for a few moments?' implored Luise.

The old woman turned towards Margont, who introduced himself.

'He's a friend,' explained Luise. 'He's helping us with our search . . . Lukas and Captain Margont would like to go to the orphanage to question Wilhelm's friends . . .'

Madame Blanken's face froze, giving her a steely look.

She said sternly, 'If they come anywhere near the orphanage I shall have them both arrested. And rest assured I will succeed in that. Very easily, in fact. General Lariboisière is staying with me . . .'

She pointedly ignored Relmyer. He clenched his teeth, as stiff as a blade. Luise tried to think of an answer, but there was none.

'Please let them. So that this saga can be settled as quickly as possible and so that we can finally be free of it! Allow Lukas to come, for pity's sake, so that he can find whatever is there to be found, and even if he finds nothing, he will finally be able to rid himself of this business!'

Madame Blanken took her hand. 'He's already been. Didn't he tell you?'

All three turned to look at Relmyer, who up until then had been ignored.

'Why did you not tell us that you've already been to Lesdorf?' fumed Margont.

'It wasn't important, and I didn't find anything. It was just before the Battle of Essling. Wilhelm had disappeared, I was very worried about him. May I remind you, Madame, that I barely had time to talk to two or three people before you threw me out.'

Madame Blanken went over to Relmyer.

'What cheek! How dare you complain about having been thrown out! After the scene you made? You forced your way into my orphanage, shoving the concierge and his son, you started shouting, demanding to see this or that person, you terrorised everyone by stomping furiously about the corridors . . . If you behave like a fox in a henhouse, you can hardly be surprised if the next thing that happens is that the farmer appears with a gun! We had to call the imperial police to get rid of you! It's lucky for you that Luise is so fond of you. It's only because of her that I turned a blind eye. That time! But if you come near Lesdorf again, you or your hussars, I won't be so lenient!'

'Why don't I come on my own?' proposed Margont.

'Same problem, same effect. You have to leave it to the

police. It's true that most of the police have fled Vienna, or have gone with the Austrian army. The few who remain already have enough to do keeping order, in accordance with your Napoleon's instructions. But, as soon as the war is over, life will return to normal and the investigation can start again. Until then, unfortunately we can only wait . . .'

Relmyer was incensed.

'Is that all? The man who murdered Franz has killed another orphan, and your idea is just to wait until the end of hostilities? As for the Austrian police, the most polite thing that can be said about them is that they are not known for their efficiency.'

Madame Blanken stared at him contemptuously.

'I suppose you have something better to suggest? You want to carry out your own investigation? You want to insult everyone and make a great hullabaloo! Where will that get you? Exactly nowhere! However, I do have something to show to you, and to Luise as well.'

She revealed a notebook that she was holding discreetly in her hand. Margont had noticed it a little earlier but had immediately forgotten about it. Now this little object had momentarily become the most important thing in the world.

'I thought that Luise would invite you this evening and that you would take advantage of it to try to speak to me,' she went on, still holding the notebook prisoner in her bony fingers. 'Despite our disagreement, I would like to prove that you are wrong about me. I have always done my utmost to protect the young people in my care. As the police failed in their inquiry, I carried out my own, in my own way. And I was meticulous; in fact I am still investigating. If you had not left, Lukas, I would have let you know my initial conclusions. As I would have let you know, Luise, had you not broken off contact with me because you held me responsible for Lukas leaving. I drew up a list of all missing orphans, not just from Lesdorf but also from neighbouring orphanages. Then I tried to find out what had happened to all those young people. I wanted to follow up each case to learn if any of the disappearances was in fact a kidnapping, or worse. I counted only forty between 1803 and 1809. I couldn't go back any earlier than 1803. After long investigation, either by me or financed by me, I was able to trace twenty-nine of them. I noted the names of those boys and girls, the dates of their disappearance, and when and where they finally reappeared, if they ever did.'

She held out the little book to Luise, who opened it, but Relmyer took it from her. The information was meticulously presented in neat scholarly handwriting. Madame Blanken was obviously happy to be able to prove her good faith. She smiled, confidently waiting for Luise and Relmyer to praise her efforts and apologise for having criticised her so often. But this was not at all what happened. Relmyer started as if struck by an invisible blow, and flared up.

'What is this nonsense? How can you write that Mark Hasach served in the army? You write that he disappeared in December 1804 and that he was killed on 2 December 1805 at the Battle of Austerlitz, which he took part in as a soldier in the Infanterieregiment 20 Wenzel Kaunitz. That's impossible! I knew him: he was also at Lesdorf,' he explained to Margont. 'His mouth was in a terrible state, full of broken teeth. Now having bad teeth is one of the few things that prevent you joining the army, because you have to be able to tear open the canisters with your teeth in order to pour the gunpowder into the chamber of your rifle. In any case, he hated soldiers because the war killed his parents.'

Madame Blanken frowned. 'I didn't know any of that. What exactly are you getting at?'

Relmyer leafed rapidly through the notebook, turning the pages so fast that some of them tore.

'And this one!' he exclaimed. 'Albert Lietz: disappeared in August 1805 and apparently died at the Battle of Austerlitz, in the Infanterieregiment 29 Lindenau. I also knew him. I promise you it is impossible that he would ever join the army! Albert was the biggest coward you've ever met. When he was fifteen, he was afraid of boys who were twelve and he let them bully him. Do you remember, Luise? He cried at the least little thing. He ran away from anything that came near him. It's unimaginable that he should become a soldier.'

'That's true,' confirmed Luise.

'A scaredy-cat in 1804 who transforms himself into a fighter in 1805? And here! Ernst Runkel. He disappeared in October 1805 and turns up dead at Austerlitz in the Infanterieregiment 23 Salsburg! Ernst, a soldier! All that bigot dreamt of was becoming a priest! He read the Bible all day long, he was in the choir, he bored us with his parables . . .'

'That's also true,' said Luise categorically.

'This information is all false!' concluded Relmyer. 'So where are all these boys really?'

Madame Blanken stiffened. The muscles in her neck contracted visibly beneath the skin.

'Lukas, you've taken leave of your senses! You're so traumatised by what you went through that you see kidnappings everywhere! All that does is convince me that I'm right: we have to leave this to the police. They have the necessary skill and they, unlike you, won't be blinded by emotion.'

'Right, so you're just going to abandon us all over again!' retorted Relmyer.

Margont intervened, fearing that Madame Blanken was on the point of hitting Relmyer, or vice versa – their views of the world and of how the investigation should be carried out were like chalk and cheese. 'Madame, where did you get your information?'

'From a friend, Oberstleutnant Mallis.'

'May we talk to him?'

'Why not? Just cross the Danube, ask for Infanterieregiment 59 Jordis and walk towards the enemy fire, you can't miss him.'

'Ah, I see . . . Well, could we keep the notebook?'

'I'll give it to Luise on condition that she gives it back to me in a few weeks. I don't want to lose it.'

'And how was Lieutenant Colonel Mallis able to put together the information?'

'At my request he consulted army records. The young people we take in have no family and no private means. When they run away to seek adventure, without any real plans, they quickly fall into poverty. So the army is often one of the only avenues open to them. Of the thirty boys I was able to trace, no less than ten had chosen the military. Eleven, in fact.'

'Didn't you say earlier that you were able to find only twenty-nine?' queried Margont.

'He's the thirtieth,' she replied, indicating Relmyer.

Relmyer was scarlet with rage. In a way, he was the living proof that there was no need to worry when a teenage boy disappeared; sooner or later, he would resurface. So his very presence gave the lie to his argument and this maddened him.

'Poor Mallis spent an enormous amount of time studying the lists of effective forces looking for all those names,' explained Madame Blanken. 'All those papers and . . .'

Relmyer stormed off and Luise followed him in silence. She was frightened without knowing exactly what it was she feared.

Margont thanked Madame Blanken before going over to join Relmyer. He was hunched over the notebook, drinking in the pages.

'Harald Tyler! He disappeared before me, in January 1803. He was found dead at Austerlitz, in the Infanterieregiment 9 Czartoryski! Another one! Austerlitz is being blamed for all these disappearances!' He skimmed the notebook faster and faster. 'According to this notebook, five of the missing boys whose names were in army records were killed at Austerlitz. The fifth was one Karl Fahne, of the Viennese Volunteer Chasseurs. Five deaths at Austerlitz? That's a lot.'

'But there were lots of Austrian casualties at Austerlitz,' said Luise.

'Even so, it's an astonishingly high count,' Margont put in. 'It's half of the boys who supposedly chose a military career. Yet at the Battle of Austerlitz, the Austrian army lost only about five per cent of its forces.'

Relmyer continued going through the names.

'And here! Ferdinand Rezinski! Disappeared in July 1803

and died at the Battle of Elchingen in October 1805. And this one, Georg Knesch, disappeared in January 1807 and died in training in May 1807, in the Infanterieregiment 49 Baron Kerpen. So actually of the ten boys who were said to become soldiers, seven are dead! Including Mark, Albert and Ernst! Now I would be prepared to swear on Christ that nothing would ever induce those three to choose to go into the army.'

'Then someone must have falsified the army's records,' concluded Margont. 'Perhaps some of these young men did actually die at Austerlitz. But it would be easy to add a name to a long list of deaths on the battlefield, to make a disappearance look like a casualty of war. And they were all, like Franz and Wilhelm, orphaned youngsters. I think we're talking about the same murderer. We're looking for someone who preys on boys, like a vulture: he thrives on dead bodies. It's thanks to the war that he has been able to find so many victims without people noticing. He must be delighted each time a new conflict breaks out; he must want there to be continual war. Perhaps he's one of those warmongers. I could well imagine that he might encourage war by rousing up bellicose minds, in order to satisfy his inclinations. He can then cover his tracks by burying the bodies in communal graves. Look, we won't even be able to tell the difference between the deaths he's responsible for and deaths incurred in the fighting.'

'Apart from Mark, Albert and Ernst,' insisted Relmyer.

'If you add Franz and Wilhelm, that's already five victims. More, in fact, because he must have struck in different orphanages to avoid drawing attention to what he was doing. One of the "Austerlitz deaths", this Karl Fahne, was from

Baumen Orphanage, and the boy who died in training and the one who died at Elchingen were from Granz orphanage.'

It was far worse than Margont had imagined. It was so appalling, he could barely take it in. He had been too confident when he had let himself become involved. Now he found himself on the edge of an abyss, and the view was giving him vertigo. He needed words, reason, logic. He would have to analyse the situation all over again, in the same way that Jean-Quenin Brémond, shaken by being unable to make a diagnosis, would perform an autopsy on the body of a patient with an unknown illness.

'Seven of the people in that notebook allegedly joined the army and died; of those seven, two disappeared in 1803, two in 1804, two in 1805 and one in 1807. But their names only appear in military records from 1805 onwards. So let's suppose that the man responsible becomes rattled by the investigation started when Franz's body is found in 1804. That's why he is so determined to falsify army records after the event. The murderer easily covers up his crimes. The only two times the bodies of his victims were found was when he was taken unawares. That happened with Franz, because once he knew that you had escaped, he could be sure that you would raise the alarm, and it happened with Wilhelm because he was spotted by a patrol. But I don't understand why he slashed them both. Did he do the same to the others? That smile betrays him and gives us an important clue. Yet the man tries very hard to leave as few clues as possible. One might think that he can't help himself mutilating the faces of the boys he murders, that it is beyond his control. When we understand why he does that, we will know a lot more about him.'

Relmyer stared obsessively at the notebook.

Margont continued, 'Several people tried to arrest Franz's executioner and to protect those who might be at risk, if he planned to kill again. But all these good intentions were thwarted by the murderer, and the police failed in their investigation. This lieutenant colonel, this Mallis, did he not think it odd to discover so many missing children killed at Austerlitz? He must have attributed it to chance, to ill luck. As for Madame Blanken, she has taken a good deal of trouble over her researches. She will certainly have concentrated her efforts on the ten orphans she could find no trace of, and since they are all alive and kicking, like you, she's been looking in the wrong direction. That means the assassin has succeeded in fooling everyone: the police, Mallis, Madame Blanken and the rest.'

'Not me!' objected Relmyer.

'Luise and you are the only ones who can prove he's changed the records. No one else knew the young men well enough to assert with confidence that they would never become soldiers. The victims are all from different regiments, otherwise the deaths might have been noticed. So he must have falsified central army records. Otherwise the murderer would have had to have an accomplice in each of the regiments and eventually someone would have talked. Now we have a trail to follow. We need to find out who fiddled the military registers. It's either the murderer himself or an accomplice.'

'An accomplice . . .' repeated Relmyer.

Until then he had thought of this struggle as a duel. That was the reason he had become first obsessed, then fascinated with that type of confrontation. Now there was a possibility that the struggle was even more complicated.

Luise could not hold back her tears. They rolled down her cheeks and splashed onto the décolletage of her dress.

'Now we know why he was so keen on orphans. Parents would never have fallen for it. They would have told that imbecile Mallis that the records were false! Then the *Oberstleutnant* would have demanded verification. As for Madame Blanken, she was doing all on her own work which should have been done by dozens of fathers, mothers, grand-parents, uncles and aunts! There would have been so many angry relatives stirring everything up and badgering the authorities that they would never have abandoned the search. Why are we always the ones to suffer? Isn't it enough that we have no family? Must we also put up with our solitariness attracting monsters like him?'

For the first time since they had found each other again, Relmyer expressed tenderness towards Luise. He took her in his arms, ignoring the outraged looks that people gave him. Margont envied him. He would have liked to be the one holding her. He felt that he had gone past the point of no return, that he had overstepped a limit without noticing. From now on, whatever happened, even if it took him one, two or even ten years, he would never give up on this case until it was resolved. In a way, he had become a second Relmyer.

Relmyer eventually released Luise, although she would have liked to prolong the moment.

'Wilhelm's murder and your return were no coincidence,' Margont added. 'The war brought you back here. And also led the assassin to believe that he could strike again with minimal risk. The dead on the battlefield are still being counted . . . If the man had not been surprised by a patrol, no doubt Wilhelm's name would have appeared on the long list of Austrian victims of Essling. The murderer takes advantage of combat. Most of the disappearances take place in periods of war, when the army is recruiting like mad and people vanishing is commonplace: men flee to avoid enlisting, or the opposite, they flee their families to join up . . . Kidnappings are lost in the mass of unexplained absences. As for the police, they are overworked and disorganised when the country is invaded. That makes it easier than usual for the assassin to cover his tracks: war has become his "hunting season". I tell you, he's a vulture! He is probably already tracking down a new victim . . .'

'Of course, he's going to kill again!' cried Relmyer.

Heads turned in their direction. The conductor of the orchestra glanced over at them and some musicians played wrong notes. He turned back and conducted more enthusiastically. The music grew noticeably louder. Relmyer went to stand in the middle of the dance floor, knocking into couples and being buffeted by them.

'It's no use playing *fortissimo*, they're all deaf!' he yelled at the top of his voice.

The orchestra ploughed on, but the dancers fled. Furious officers marched towards Relmyer, stunned guests looked at him in horror.

'Lukas Relmyer, the killjoy, wishes you an excellent evening!' he bellowed. 'Go on, dance, dance! One day you'll be forced to open your eyes and your ears!'

He strode over to a French window, flung it open and went out. He needed air. Margont followed. The couples reformed and took up their waltz again. The stone had sunk to the bottom of the pond and its ripples had already subsided.

Relmyer walked quickly, teeth clenched, his breathing ragged. Margont was hard on his heels.

'I understand why you're so angry, but the priority is to find the man and arrest him. Then you can go and settle your accounts with—'

'I can't stand their silence any more! It's ringing in my ears, it's deafening, it's killing me!'

Then something altogether amazing happened. Piquebois was leaning against a neighbouring building, looking up at the stars. When he heard Margont's voice he turned his head. Relmyer had never been introduced to Piquebois, yet the moment he saw Piquebois, he froze.

'Lieutenant Piquebois?' he asked.

'At your service, Lieutenant Relmyer, otherwise known as "The Wasp",' replied Piquebois, joyfully.

Piquebois's eyes were alight with excitement and a fanatical smile spread over his face. The two men had barely met, but already they had generated a spark of madness that engulfed them both.

'How about a friendly duel?' proposed Piquebois to Relmyer, who was already unsheathing his sabre, as if words were superfluous because their thoughts were in such perfect harmony.

Margont stiffened, pointing a threatening finger at the two officers.

'I order you not to! Lukas, put your sword away!'

Relmyer took off his pelisse. 'There's nobody but Margont here, so we only have one second.'

Piquebois threw his coat on the ground. 'Let's not waste time finding another one. Since Quentin is a friend of both of us, we can count him twice.'

Margont stepped between them, which could have been dangerous, had one of them taken exception to it.

'Lieutenant Piquebois, you will sheath your sabre immediately or I will have you arrested on the spot.' Already Margont was raising his arm to attract the attention of a sentry, who was paying more attention to mentally undressing the beautiful Austrian girls than to his watch. Piquebois was windmilling his arms to loosen up his wrists.

'Throwing us in prison will change nothing,' insisted Relmyer. 'We'll just persuade our gaolers to find us arms and then we'll entertain them with the spectacle.'

It was absurd, but true. Margont tried everything in his power to reason with them but the two lieutenants were no longer listening.

'In the 8th Hussars, everyone's always saying how unbeatable you are,' said Relmyer enviously.

Piquebois was exultant. 'They're exaggerating. And I've heard that you yourself are without peer. We absolutely have to fight.'

As they talked, they were sizing each other up, flexing their muscles and moving slowly and fluidly over to a lamp just behind the garden gate. They were engaged in a ritual of seduction and death, a dance that led gracefully to the tomb.

'Whoever touches, wins?' suggested Piquebois.

'Nothing better! Since it's purely intellectual, we should stop at first blood. In any case I don't want to slay you. The friends of my friends are my friends . . .'

'Of course you're not going to kill me, because once I'm finished with you, you'll need a stretcher.'

The sentry came to attention in front of Margont.

'Go and fetch a doctor. Ask for Medical Officer Brémond.'

'Ready?' demanded Piquebois.

'Always!'

Piquebois attacked with a sweeping stroke to his opponent's left side. The circular movement of one of his lunges could shatter an opponent's head like an eggshell. Relmyer dodged. Piquebois launched spiritedly into his favourite repertoire: attacks with arms not extended, beats, false attacks, feints, attempts to disarm, compound attacks, ripostes, parries, feint parries, aggressive sequences, unexpected retreats and many other moves as well, all punctuated by constant changes of rhythm. This staggering multiplicity of moves made him unreadable. Fighting Piquebois you never knew which foot you should be on. You were swamped by the calculated cacophony before submitting to the final blow, which was always completely baffling. His attacks were precise and difficult to parry, which is why Relmyer concentrated harder and harder on dodging nimbly or deflecting Piquebois's blade. Piquebois displayed a force that no one would ever have imagined from looking at him. When his sabre clashed noisily against Relmyer's, sparks flew and the Austrian grimaced in pain. The hussars were moving all the time to avoid being struck.

They both rapidly adjusted their techniques. Piquebois attacked less violently because Relmyer was not overwhelmed by his force, and instead became more precise. Relmyer stopped trying to tire Piquebois out, now that he had the measure of the Frenchman's endurance. The latter fought like a demon without either getting out of breath or tiring. Piquebois beat Relmyer back towards the corner between the concierge's lodge and the gate in the wall. With less room, Relmyer could not dodge as well. He tried to land a blow with the point of his sabre on Piquebois's face. He was aiming at the chin, but his offensive meant he had to reveal himself, and Piquebois parried and lunged in order to launch an immediate attack in the direction of Relmyer's flank. Relmyer, who had made his move to encourage this reaction from Piquebois, deflected his opponent's blade, whose trajectory he had anticipated, and his blade – just the point – went into his opponent's left shoulder. Piquebois blinked. A dark stain spread across his shirt. He looked at the wound with the same astonishment as if he were seeing a field of blue grass beneath a green sky. He collapsed and found himself sitting down with his legs apart and his sabre still in his hand.

Jean-Quenin Brémond hurried to his aid. The music from the ball in the background grew louder as the guests opened the windows to see what was happening. Piquebois ignored the medical officer.

'You're mad, Relmyer . . . Launching a false attack to make your opponent react is one thing. But launching a real attack for the same reason, knowing your opponent is of a very high standard . . . I almost killed you . . .'

Relmyer agreed. He was breathing quickly. He knew that he had diced with death.

'If I had feinted, you wouldn't have been taken in. I took a risk, yes. But it's you who's on the ground.'

Margont was choking with rage.

'Great, Antoine, bravo! Happy now?'

'Yes,' murmured Piquebois.

And the worst of it was, he really was happy.

CHAPTER 11

THE next day Margont and Lefine crossed the Graben, the avenue adored by the Viennese built on the filled-in trenches of medieval fortifications. Their eyes were red from lack of sleep, or perhaps they were splashed with Piquebois's blood. They stopped at the foot of the Pestsäule, the plague column, where they were to meet Relmyer.

'Can I ask a stupid question, Captain?'

Margont did not answer.

'Is Relmyer our friend or our future assassin?'

Margont's fury was evident from his clenched jaw, jerky gestures and pursed lips.

'That madman stabbed Piquebois!' he raged suddenly. 'As for Antoine, it serves him right if he didn't like being taught a lesson! He's as much to blame as Relmyer for what happened. Relmyer is like someone trying to climb out of an abyss. By helping him we increase his chances of success, but he might stumble and pull us into the void with him! We already have the Austrians to confront, and the partisans at our back, and somewhere out there there's a murderer who's as elusive as a ghost. And now to top it all off Relmyer has started wounding the people who're trying to help him!'

'His sabre is double-edged . . .'

'Did you see the duel?'

'No. I was too drunk to see anything except the buffet and the girls.'

'To think that Piquebois has floored I don't know how many opponents in his time. And against Relmyer, he didn't hold back, believe me!'

Lefine nodded. 'When Antoine draws his sword, he loses his head. It's as if his sabre starts to think for him.'

'Well, Relmyer dominated throughout the duel.'

Lefine drummed his fingers lightly on his palm in applause and this questionable joke irritated Margont even more.

'He'll live,' he went on, but Lefine paled, suddenly realising that his friend really could have died, that it wasn't just a macabre piece of foolishness resulting from his irrepressible personality. 'I went to see Jean-Quenin early this morning. He went on about a damaged scapulohumeral joint and severed tendons or something or other . . . Why can doctors never just give you a straight answer?'

'What else do you expect from people who study Latin?'

'Let's not exaggerate, only part of their books and anatomy treatises are in Latin. Although that's already too much for my taste. Anyway, I didn't understand what he said about the wound except that it's not fatal and Antoine will soon regain the use of his arm.'

'Great! More duels in prospect,' said Lefine with bitter sarcasm.

'That's out of the question!'

Relmyer had still not arrived. To take his mind off things Margont began to study the Pestsäule, several feet of High Baroque. In 1679 the plague had decimated Vienna; there had been a hundred thousand victims. When it was over Emperor Leopold I had had the column built to thank God for eradicating the epidemic. The Holy Trinity in gold metal sat atop a cascade of angels and humans. Leopold knelt praying, and beneath him a woman holding a cross symbolised Faith triumphing over the plague, embodied by an old woman naked on the ground, her skin loose and wrinkled. Margont thought of the column of the Grande Armée in Place Vendôme, which was not yet finished. How ironic in this time of war to have these two works celebrating the triumph of life (the Grande Armée column was made with the bronze of one thousand two hundred cannon captured at Austerlitz and in Vienna in 1805, because it was thought that the peace would endure).

Lefine let his gaze slide over the edifice, looking at each face in turn.

'After the great battle with the Austrians, they'll build a column like that,' he declared to Margont. 'But much, much higher and with even more people. It will be a huge pile of corpses that will touch the sky. At the top the Emperor will sit in splendour, pointing to Moscow or London, the site of the next column.'

Margont was getting more and more perplexed.

'Each war, instead of bringing peace, sets off new ones . . . We've gone astray somewhere and we'll never find our equilibrium again.'

Relmyer arrived. His rolling gait, his assurance and his dazzling uniform attracted glances from passing women and jealousy from husbands. His boots echoed on the paving stones just in case there were some who had not yet noticed him. He came to a halt in front of the two men and extended his hand. Margont shook it briefly and immediately launched into what he had to say.

'Do I really have to go on helping you? I don't want to find that by associating with you, I end up with your blade through my stomach.'

'That would never happen!' Relmyer spoke with the utmost sincerity. But was that sufficient guarantee? 'I swear that I would not have killed your friend,' he added.

He had that arrogance of masters of arms who believe they can wield their blade with the precision of a surgeon manipulating his scalpel. Margont spoke in clipped tones. 'If you take your sabre out again – even once! – on a whim, I will end our co-operation for ever. We'll investigate separately and too bad if that slows us down and plays into the hands of the man we're hunting.'

This threat plunged Relmyer into gloom.

Ashen-faced, he solemnly declared: 'I swear on my honour that I will never initiate any other duel until this business is resolved. However, I don't think you understand exactly what that fight represented for me. As soon as I hear people extolling the merits of a swordsman, I am riven with worry. I do my best not to think about it, to concentrate on my work, but I can't get it out of my mind and the fear grows. Only fighting a duel and winning brings me any relief. Well, relative relief, at least. I want to be sure – no, I need to be sure – that no one will ever be able to defeat me. I have to become invincible, more than invincible. I have to become untouchable!'

Relmyer looked strained. He had revealed the very core of his being: 'to become untouchable'.

'If you continue down that route,' Margont replied, 'perhaps you will be safe but you will also be alone, because everyone will be frightened of you. You will become untouchable in more ways than one.'

Relmyer did not respond. Margont was obviously still irritated.

'And another thing: do you expect me to believe that you want to deliver the murderer up to justice when you would happily run a stranger through? Do you take me for an idiot?'

'Of course not. I really do want to take him alive. Because it's not only him I want vengeance on, it's society's silence too. If I capture him there will be a trial, statements, witnesses, everything will be recorded. Finally people will take notice! We will finally be able to challenge that silence, justifiably . . .'

After a brief hesitation, he gestured towards the avenue. 'So are you coming with me?'

Margont acquiesced and fell into step beside him. They melted into the crowd of strollers, street-traders and prostitutes, 'the nymphs of Graben'.

'I've organised Pagin and Telet, another of my hussars, to find out about all the boys "killed in action",' Relmyer told him. 'They're going to go to all the orphanages, except Lesdorf, of course. I'm not going to get involved personally with that part of the investigation because I fear we will not get very far with it. The man we're hunting is too good at concealing his tracks. On the other hand, I can't stop thinking about the military records! We'll have to track them down so that we can find out who fills them in and therefore who could have allowed them to be altered.'

'Unfortunately I fear that we won't be able to,' declared Margont. 'Unless the Austrians have lost their minds. You would never let exact details of your troops fall into enemy hands: the size of your regiments, battalion by battalion, the identity of your officers and which regiments . . . Maybe the records have been removed by the Austrian army, or maybe we'll find what's left of them in a fireplace.'

Margont's arguments made absolute sense. But not to Relmyer. The young hussar swept them aside with an expansive gesture.

'At the moment that's all we have. I can only see one way of going about this. We'll have to go to the War Ministry and see if we can find, despite everything, a register or document that might help us.'

Lefine's eyes widened. He could imagine mounds of files, reports, letters . . . With the endless procession of wars, army numbers were growing all the time because of mass conscription and the integration of foreign contingents. Now France, Austria or Russia could easily boast hundreds of thousands of soldiers and militiamen. Bureaucracy had ballooned alongside this vertiginous growth in numbers. The bureaucrats maintained complete control and their innumerable verifications translated into millions of pieces of paper. The effectives had to be counted and recounted to establish how many active soldiers each battalion had, how many deserters there had been and what their names were, to check that each combatant did actually exist and that there were no 'phantom soldiers' whose pay could be appropriated by profiteers, to make sure the logistics (pay, provisions, uniforms, weapons and munitions, and billets) were correct . . . This last had to be especially closely monitored because there were so many crooked suppliers and corrupt officials swarming over everything.

Relmyer was annoyed at his companions' lack of enthusiasm.

'No one is forcing you! But we know how slow-moving and nit-picking bureaucracy is. What's more, the Austrian Empire is enormous: it includes Hungary, Bohemia, Moravia, Galicia, Slovenia, Croatia, Slavonia, Transylvania . . . Perhaps in the middle of all these papers there will be a copy of a report or the translation of a letter that has escaped the notice of the people charged with taking away or destroying all confidential documents. Don't forget the Austrian army did not reckon on being driven back by Napoleon. Vienna was evacuated in chaos and when everything is done in haste, people make mistakes.'

Margont looked sceptical. 'Well, such things do undoubtedly exist . . . But it would take months—'

'Well, I'll spend months,' persisted Relmyer. 'If necessary I'll find translators for Hungarian, Croatian, Czech, Slovenian, Polish, Romanian and the dozens of other languages and dialects spoken in this monstrous empire.'

Margont responded soberly to calm Relmyer down. 'The French have already searched the registers. Don't you think the Emperor has had the Austrian archives examined? Last night I asked one of my acquaintances—'

'One of *my* acquaintances!' corrected Lefine.

'Indeed, Fernand, and I thank you once again, even if I did

have to pay you both. According to this aide-de-camp to the general staff, no interesting documents relating to the Austrian army were found. So I propose another way of going about things, and if it fails, then, all right, we'll go and drown ourselves in the Viennese archives.'

'Another way of going about things?' repeated Relmyer, emphasising 'other'. He stood stock-still in the middle of the Stephansplatz. The Stephansdom, St Stephen's Cathedral, was endowed with a single spire because the silver and the energy needed for a second one had been used to shore up the fortifications before the first Turkish siege in 1529. Behind Relmyer this gothic steeple rose up, its disturbing patchwork of stone seeming to be the incarnation of the questions and worries of the young hussar.

'Let's speak to one of the people who fill in the records,' explained Margont. 'Indirectly, of course. We're going to have to convince someone sympathetic to the Austrian cause still living in Vienna to ask the partisans about it. Some partisans regularly cross the front line and could try to find the information we need. After all, we don't care about the actual registers, what we're interested in is the list of people who write them up. Now these bureaucrats must have followed the Austrian army in order to avoid being arrested and interrogated on the subject of enemy effectives. If these people understand why we are looking for this information, perhaps they will give it to us.'

Relmyer thought about this new approach, weighing up the pros and cons.

'It will take a long time, several days probably, but not as long as my approach, I concede. Unfortunately, it won't work.

We would have to find an Austrian sympathiser, persuade him of our sincerity, hope that he accepts and that he has enough credibility to be able to convince the combatants he has to ask. We'll never find such a man.'

Margont smiled.

'And what about Luise?'

CHAPTER 12

At first Relmyer had rejected Margont's suggestion in order to protect Luise, but then he decided to trust the Frenchman's instinct.

Margont and Lefine waited in the Mitterburgs' sitting room while Relmyer talked to Luise. A servant in bluish-black livery surveyed them suspiciously, which annoyed Lefine, who sank down on a sofa, crossed his legs and began to hum, '*Oh, it'll be all right, be all right, be all right. Hang the aristocrats from on high! Oh, it'll be all right, be all right, be all right. The aristocrats, we'll hang 'em all.*' The servant responded with an Austrian goose step. This archetypal scene made Margont despair. It summed up the paradox of the Empire. The French, hundreds of thousands of them, were starting wars to take the principles of the Revolution to the peoples of Europe, but instead of fanning the waves of republicanism, all it did was incite nationalism in its most aggressive manifestation. It had started with Prussia, then Spain, now the Tyrol and Austria . . . Where was it going wrong? Whose fault was it? How could it be put right before the Empire was crushed by a generalised European uprising against it?

Lefine noticed that the more at ease he appeared, the more irritated the servant became. He threw his head back and sighed nonchalantly.

'Why didn't Relmyer think of asking Luise?'

'I think he wanted to keep her as far away as possible from the investigation.'

'Possibly, but she's well and truly involved in it. Relmyer succeeded in dragging us into his struggle. Now, Luise is joining in as well. He's leading us one after the other to the edge of the abyss . . .'

Margont felt oppressed by the room although there was nothing exceptional about it, quite the opposite. A portrait of Mozart, comfortable armchairs with restrained floral embroidery, vases, a fireplace whose mantelpiece was covered with knick-knacks: statuettes, lacquer boxes, fans . . . Everything was in the classical style, even the antique paintings and the piano with a score open on it – *The Magic Flute*, naturally. The only original note was sounded by the collection of seven lead or tin soldiers displayed on a small round table. Two knights sculpted in exquisite detail dated from the eighteenth century. Their lead was worth its weight in gold. What was original was that all the figurines were representations from the Middle Ages. One of them was attacking with a lance, the other with a sword while sheltering behind a shield, a third brandished a mace . . . A handful of soldiers were launched into who knows what crusade. Margont realised that what irritated him about the room was its sterile conformism. Paintings of scenes from antiquity are in vogue? Quick! Over the sofa hang one depicting two columns and another of a temple at Delphi. Suddenly it is discovered that Mozart is a genius – what's more, an Austrian genius! True, he's dead and buried in a pauper's grave with three shovelfuls of quicklime, but let's not go on about the errors of the past. Instead, let's get hold of a copy of his portrait. That was all right. People led their lives in their own way, and so what if they decided to let others dictate their tastes? No, what bothered Margont was that it was this same attitude that encouraged the half-silence that cloaked Franz's death. The obsession to conform contributed to the rule of silence. Because if people submitted even in their own homes, it was unlikely that they would dare speak out and take a stand in public. Suddenly all these commonplace, predictable objects in the home of these well-off people appeared stifling and a little sinister.

Relmyer came in with Luise and the old woman who had been with her when she had been searching amongst the wounded men of Essling. The young Austrian contrasted sharply with the dowdy creature dressed in grey. Margont greeted Luise courteously under the inquisitive eye of her chaperone. Luise introduced her, speaking in French.

'Madame Hilde. I would have preferred a puppy, but instead I have this chaperone. Puppies yap, but they're affectionate and stop barking when you give them a sugar lump. Chaperones tittle-tattle, witter on and even bite sometimes. And you can't shut them in the salon when you want to go for a walk without them. Don't worry, Madame Hilde and my servant don't understand French.'

Madame Hilde intervened in an unexpectedly melodious voice: 'Mademoiselle Mitterburg, it would be more suitable if you spoke in German.'

'Yes, indeed. Alas, Captain Margont and his friend Lefine don't understand our language. It's very unfortunate.'

While Madame Hilde searched for a solution – should they

use Spanish? Or would she appear ridiculous? Would she be able to tell just by looking that no impropriety was being committed? – Luise declared: 'I agree to help you. But I can't guarantee that I'll get an answer. And even if I do it's not likely to be the whole answer. Hundreds of people are involved in the updating of the military registers so it's possible that some names are missed.'

'We'll use whatever they are prepared to give us.'

'And it will take days and days . . .'

'Is there anything we can do instead?'

Relmyer thought not. 'No, we have to search the Austrian archives from top to bottom! That's what we have to do! I'll begin immediately.'

Luise vainly tried to get him to sit down.

'But . . . you have to rest a little . . . this is wearing you out, Lukas. At least sit down for a few minutes . . . just to drink a cup of coffee or chocolate . . .'

Relmyer shook his head. Stubborn. Intractable. Margont felt obliged to go with him. His friend would not find it easy to get authorisation to consult the archives because of his Austrian origins. Relmyer was about to go out when he noticed the collection of figurines. He froze, stupefied. He looked over at Luise again and wanted to say something but the words wouldn't come, so he just touched her arm lightly under the scandalised gaze of Madame Hilde. Then the young hussar plunged outside onto the street as if he were diving into the sea.

Margont, although he himself walked fast, had trouble keeping up with him. Lefine followed at normal pace, far behind, shaking his head. Margont was annoyed at having had to leave

Luise, but he understood Relmyer's reaction. Relmyer was hurrying towards what he thought would be his salvation, much as he, Margont, had leapt at any possibility when he was trying to escape the Abbey of Saint-Guilhem-le-Désert. There was more at stake than arresting a killer and breaking the silence surrounding the affair. Relmyer also needed to liberate himself from the stranglehold of memories that kept coming back to haunt him, especially in periods of inactivity and in dreams. Yes, that was what this was – a war of liberation.

CHAPTER 13

THE Kriegsministerium displayed all the cold, oppressive grandeur of administrative buildings imbued with their own importance. The two sentries standing either side of the entrance presented arms to Margont and Relmyer. Their martial rigidity perfectly matched the façade.

Six other soldiers, grouped together in front of the marble columns, guarded the monumental vestibule. The duty officer had laid out his office so that he could keep an eye on the great staircase to his right and on the double doors opening on his left. Aided by two corporals acting as secretaries, he was applying himself to drawing up inventories; there was a strong odour, a mixture of wax, old papers, dust and leather. The officer had meticulously buttoned up his collar as protocol demanded, practically strangling himself to satisfy regulations. His red face, bloated by lack of circulation, turned towards one of the corporals.

'You've missed a line, Carrefond! A little mistake can lead to a great catastrophe! Another error and I'll transfer you to the *voltigeurs*.' He tore up the paper and flung it into the overflowing waste-paper basket.

Finally addressing the newcomers, he demanded: 'What do these officers want?'

Relmyer saluted him and explained what he was after, referring to but not explaining 'an extremely grave personal matter'.

The captain proved to be astonishingly friendly. He confirmed that they had not been able to seize the registers containing all the details of the Austrian army. He announced that, on principle, he was reluctant to let just anyone shuffle through what documents there were without official authorisation. Then he added that the French had taken over Vienna three weeks ago now. The archives that had remained in the capital had therefore already been partly examined. He made it clear that they were beginning to despair of finding anything at all of interest concerning the enemy army. So the Emperor preferred to rely only on his spies and on the reconnaissance carried out by them and their Russian, Polish and Bavarian allies . . . The duty officer concluded his discourse by saying that he did not agree to Relmyer ferreting about in the Kriegsministerium.

The refusal did not tally with the view expressed that the documents were effectively useless. Relmyer realised that there might be a way of changing his mind and laid out some twenty- and forty-franc pieces on the officer's desk. The gold coins shone in the sun like a constellation in an ebony sky. Lefine was astounded. What a madman, to carry around that amount of money just to bribe an official! Relmyer brandished a second handful that he began to spill noisily onto the desk coin by coin. The captain immediately picked each one up with the alacrity of a hen pecking grains. Now he was turning from red to purple. There in front of him was months' worth of a soldier's pay, a large chunk of Relmyer's life as a soldier.

'Come whenever you like,' said the officer obsequiously. 'I'll warn you if you ever have to hide yourself because of an unexpected inspection. The archives are stored on this floor and the one above. There are also several in the basement and in the attic, but they are the oldest ones.'

At that moment Relmyer felt a resurgence of hope, a resurgence that crumbled as soon as he had passed through the double doors.

The room, high-ceilinged and deep, was no more than a giant rubbish dump. Trampled papers and heaps of registers were strewn across the parquet. Interminable shelves blanketed the walls from floor to ceiling, some groaning with documents, others empty, having spewed their contents onto the floor. Lefine looked up, certain that the roof must be falling in. It appeared to him as if a deluge of shells had ruined everything in here, when Vienna had been bombarded. But no, the Austrians had pillaged their own archives and the French had exacerbated the disaster; it was chaos added to chaos.

Margont knelt down and picked up a ruined report written in a language he could not even identify.

'We don't know exactly what we're looking for, nor even if it's here, and everything is in such a muddle.'

Relmyer stood in front of one of the shelves and started to read the titles of the documents. Ten feet above his head, about halfway to the ceiling, a long wooden walkway was also weighed down with paper. Lefine joined Margont.

'Let's go. We'll come back and fetch him in ten years,' he proposed amiably.

In spite of everything Margont decided to help Relmyer. He tried to put some order into the madness, by proposing all sorts of ideas. He proposed using chalk to tick off the documents examined, paying more attention to the ravaged shelves and the torn reports as perhaps they had been sabotaged because they were the most important. He also proposed asking one of Relmyer's friends, who would understand what he was doing, to help. 'On condition that he doesn't run us through,' Lefine had murmured. And finally he proposed trying to find and question the men who had been through the papers before them . . .

However, little by little, Margont's determination wilted under the weight of the tons of written notes. He excused himself and left, accompanied by Lefine, abandoning Relmyer, perched on a ladder, a skiff adrift on an ocean of paper.

CHAPTER 14

TIME seemed to have frozen in an interlude before an inevitable acceleration would re-establish the normal course of things. The days slipped by, all spent in the same way: preparing for battle or relaxing. Nevertheless, a slight excitement gradually took hold of everyone. The whole of Europe was avidly watching this section of the Danube, this little blue ribbon that separated two armies drunk on their own invincibility.

Margont had been immobilised on the Isle of Lobau, fulfilling his military obligations. Today he was finally enjoying a day of liberty. At least he felt he was at liberty, a view that did not quite correspond to what the army felt. He was not supposed to move around without authorisation but he did it all the time. The French army had many soldiers who did not possess the proper disciplined spirit of the professional soldier. During an inspection, Margont had overheard a soldier addressing the Emperor informally. And, what's more, it was to complain about not having received the Légion d'honneur! Not only did Napoleon not bat an eyelid at this insolence, he effectively granted the decoration, having had the soldier's exploits confirmed.

A host of volunteers had enrolled to defend their country against invasion, to protect their newly acquired liberty or because they had been seduced by the glamour of victorious servicemen (and these volunteers received a rude shock when they discovered the true face of war). The conscripts, who were more numerous, had not asked to be soldiers. Having plunged their hands into a bag in front of their mayor and the police, they had drawn the short straw, the one that sent them to the front unless they had the money to pay for a replacement. All these people detested the over-rigid regulations, which they flouted whenever they could. Margont, who had volunteered in order to defend his revolutionary ideals, was in that category too. He often consigned his company to the care of Saber before disappearing. This time Saber was absent, so he left his men in the charge of Piquebois, who was gradually recovering from his wound. For some unknown reason, Saber was spending his time in a Viennese café, the Milano on Kohlmarkt, and only rarely came back, irritated and taciturn.

Margont and Lefine galloped off to Vienna. It was time to live again.

Vienna was crawling with soldiers looking for a good time. When Austrian women went shopping they returned home with their baskets full of eggs, vegetables and half a dozen declarations of eternal love; eternal, that is, until the end of the campaign. It was called going to market.

Margont and Lefine went to Luise's house where they were impatiently awaited. She flung herself on them while Margont still had one foot in his stirrup. She was overwrought and struggled to get the words out.

'Isn't Lukas with you?' she finally demanded, having barely responded to Margont's greeting.

‘We haven’t seen him for three days. He’s wearing himself out with his absurd searches. I think we will have to try to pull him out of the record office.’

Luise agreed. One servant took the reins of the horses while another one came over to join them. The Mitterburgs had left instructions that Luise was never to go out on her own.

While they were walking, Luise kept her fists clenched.

‘Why aren’t you looking after Lukas any more? This business is destroying him! Of course it’s not easy to do anything about it; he’s so stubborn! But you could . . . I don’t know . . .’

‘Let’s start by finding him.’

‘I’m doing everything to find the information he wants. Only, it’s so complicated . . . and, is it really what’s best for him? He’s already escaped from the man once. Trying to meet him again, he’s pushing his luck, playing with fire.’

Luise took Margont’s arm; he slowed down.

‘I lost my parents, then Franz. I don’t want anything to happen to Lukas. I couldn’t stand it.’

When they arrived at the Kriegsministerium the duty officer received them with the smile of a salesman welcoming his best clients.

They found the room in an even worse state of devastation than the last time. Relmyer just dropped the documents that were no use to him, drowning the disorder in his own chaos. Perched on his ladder, as though he had not come down from it since his last meeting with Margont, he let go of an enormous bundle that crashed onto a mound of papers with an explosive sound. Luise had to call him three times before he would consent to come and greet them. Although he had emptied an astonishing number of shelves he had undertaken only a tiny part of the Herculean task he had set himself. He looked dreadful. He regarded them with a deranged intensity through swollen, hollow eyes that were reddened as if rubbed by sandpaper. He had bad breath and appeared to be starving. His crumpled uniform stank of sweat, reflecting his inner turmoil.

'Have you come to help me?' he asked, with an exhausted smile.

Luise's demeanour changed completely. The minute before she had had tears in her eyes. She lifted her chin and spoke in clipped tones.

'We're taking you for a walk in Vienna. We'll also go to the gardens of the Château de Schönbrunn. They're so pretty . . . do you remember them? We used to go there . . .'

'Go for a walk?' repeated Relmyer.

He did not appear to understand. Anything not related to his obsession made no sense to him.

'Yes, go for a walk.'

'To Schönbrunn?'

Luise raised her voice. 'We're going for a stroll around Vienna and in Schönbrunn! Do you think I'm going to let you kill yourself with these papers? I demand that you leave here!'

Her voice reverberated, bouncing off the walls of the Kriegsministerium as it did off Relmyer's closed mind.

Without really agreeing the young hussar let himself be

dragged off. Luise decided that first of all her brother must eat. Margont proposed that they go to Café Milano so that they could see Saber.

CHAPTER 15

THE Milano's sign was an enormous copper coffee pot held by a little black boy. Margont took an instant dislike to the crowded noisy café and wondered how Saber could possibly spend entire days here. Lefine, who was having all the same thoughts, indicated the billiard table as a possible reason, but Margont was not totally convinced. Saber was installed in a corner of the room. As was his way, he had taken the place over. His table was buried under maps, books, gazettes, and letters. His very bearing, sitting with an air of complete confidence and concentration, gave the impression that he was at home, and that he had graciously agreed to have his office turned into a café. He was in discussion with two other lieutenants. None of the numerous customers who were having to stand dared to ask for one of the empty chairs, which were piled with a jumble of letters.

Margont joined them and introductions were made. One of the lieutenants, Valle, bestowed an exquisite smile on Luise, who signalled her lack of interest by turning to order coffee and bread before 'forgetting' to listen to the slew of compliments that the officer was giving her. She liked to keep her distance. Saber, who was cold towards Relmyer, annoyed with him for having wounded Piquebois, brusquely made space on the empty chairs by throwing their contents onto the ground and reorganising his documents.

Like Margont, Saber loved both coffee and the effect it had on him. He drank it with exaggerated, mannered gestures. A waiter brought a tray with myriad cups, an immense coffee pot, a pitcher of milk and another of cream. Vienna was a paradise for lovers of coffee. Saber turned his into honey with dollops of sugar. Luise filled Relmyer's up with cream, not because that was the way he liked it, but to give him some nourishment. Margont liked his pure, strong and bitter. As for Lefine, he chose to 'sweeten it' with schnapps, having swiped a bottle off the counter. Luise only started her drink when Relmyer had already drunk two cups. Margont had to press the servant accompanying Luise to dare to accept a cup. The man was astonished to be treated as an equal, and this little incident was to sow the seeds of republican ideas in his deepest thoughts.

The very fact of being served coffee, of doctoring it according to one's taste, was a delicious pleasure and one that was enhanced by the company of friends. It was a very agreeable moment ... Margont temporarily forgot the war. Unfortunately Saber hastened to remind him of it.

'This is Europe.'

Lefine stared, realising that Saber was indicating the maps. Maps! All the general staff were looking for those. They changed hands for extraordinary prices, as though they were valuable pictures! Or gold! And there they were, right in front of his eyes!

'These are the Austrians,' announced Saber, knocking over the sugar bowl.

The Austrian troops had possession of part of the world – a little mound of sugar represented Archduke Charles's army.

Saber also placed sugar in the Tyrol, in Italy and in Poland. Then he used breadcrumbs for the French forces and their allies.

'Now the Russians: sugar or crumbs?' he joked.

He opted for crumbs, even though the Russians were not proving reliable allies. In 1805, they had fought with the Austrians against the French. Four years later, new political alliances had redrawn the map, but Tsar Alexander I played a double game. As for the stubborn Russian soldiers and generals, they were loath to support the French and the Polish (especially the Polish, whom they hated). So, when Archduke Ferdinand's forty thousand troops invaded the Grand Duchy of Varsovia, a state that was allied to France and defended by only six thousand Poles, Gallitzin's Russian army, which was supposed to help the Poles, did not exactly hasten. And as the Russian army was already very slow when it was trying to go quickly, to say that they were slow in this instance was to understate things; it would be more accurate to say they were fossilised. As a result, Napoleon ran the risk of having to deploy thousands of soldiers just to shore up the Grand Duchy of Varsovia and to protect himself to the north.

But, Saber exulted: 'Poniatowski, the general in charge of the Polish, had them well and truly. When he understood that he would not be able to resist the Austrians head on, he decided to bite them in the tail.'

As he said this, Saber placed the Polish crumbs in Galicia, to the south of the Austrians. He placed the bread as reinforcements, because that Austrian province had previously been Polish and welcomed Poniatowski as liberator. Archduke

Ferdinand's sugar troops retired precipitately into Austria so as not to find themselves dangerously isolated. Not only did this manoeuvre not succeed in weakening Napoleon, but it was actually detrimental to the Austrians, preventing Ferdinand's troops from joining those of Archduke Charles, which had to continue to fend off the impetuous Poles.

'That Poniatowski, what a genius!'

Saber beamed. Now he was Poniatowski. He wanted to manoeuvre the Polish troops, to continue the fight. Why had they stopped when they were doing so well? Saber had taken part in numerous battles, he had found himself soaked in blood – his own and that of his friends shattered by round shot – yet he persisted in considering war like a game of high-level chess. His dreams of grandeur were impregnated with blood. For a long time Margont had been annoyed with him, considering him to be insensitive. But today, he was less certain. Saber was protecting himself by burying his head in the sand. The day he opened his eyes, he would be overwhelmed and destroyed.

'The Tyrol! Rise in rebellion, General of Tyrol!' exclaimed Saber.

Thousands of mountain folk, furious that treaties between the powers had placed them under the control of Bavaria, had taken up arms. Their leader, Andreas Hofer, an innkeeper, had had some success in leading ambushes, attacking isolated posts, storming Innsbruck and even harassing the left flank of the army in Italy under Prince Eugène, Napoleon's stepson. In the German states Major von Schill and the Duke of Brunswick were also agitating. The Austrians prayed for a generalised uprising but they still feared Napoleon's might too much. Saber seized his cup and noisily crushed the Tyrolean sugar.

'Insurrection repressed.'

In Luise's opinion Saber was undoubtedly a bloodthirsty madman. She had also heard that the Tyrolean rebellion had not yet been beaten. The 'sugar' had certainly been dealt a severe blow, but that blow had only succeeded in fragmenting it and its 'grains' continued to pose problems for the French. Saber continued his demonstration – French officers and some Austrians had joined them, forming an attentive audience, and now he was talking more to them than to his friends. Saber was admirably well informed. Normally officers of his rank only knew about the state of their own company and any other titbits they overheard over supper. But Saber was convinced that he would be promoted to marshal one day and he behaved as if he already was one. His map began to make sense to Margont.

The Austrian plan was clever. It combined great sweeping manoeuvres to attack the French and their allies everywhere, at the same time. In the north, in Poland, and in the south, in Italy, with forty thousand men under the orders of Archduke John; in the centre with Archduke Charles and round the edges using the partisans. This strategy forced Napoleon to disperse his force and gave notice that the Austrians were determined to open the conflict out. This was not a Franco-Austrian war, but a European war, with France and its Italian and German allies on one side, and on the other Austria and all its allies: England, Prussia, certain German states . . . And what about Russia? Austria wanted to spearhead a vast coalition.

However, as is often the case in situations like this, the

potential allies were hesitating. England had promised to dispatch an army to Holland, but constantly delayed doing so. On the other hand, in Spain and Portugal, the Spanish resistance and Anglo-Portuguese troops continued to recruit numerous French soldiers. When Napoleon recalled his contingents stationed in Spain to strengthen his position against the Austrians, he weakened his position against the English. He counterbalanced this by winning a victory against the Spanish, but he learnt immediately afterwards that an insurrection had erupted in Austurias and he feared that the Royal Navy was behind it. Each conflict now took on monumental proportions because everything was linked. If Austria fought Napoleon again, Prussia would join in, guerrilla warfare would ravage Spain once again, and the English would this time send an army to Holland. Russia would probably join Austria. One error, one defeat, a single false step and the Empire could collapse completely, neighbour by neighbour, country after country. Margont lived in an extraordinarily precarious world. If the Empire collapsed would the ideals of the Revolution founder with it?

Saber's finger tapped northern Italy and moved south-east to the gigantic Austrian Empire in Hungary.

'The Italian army has pushed back Archduke John's Austrians. The Emperor is scoring points in all the secondary theatres of operations and he is calling for reinforcements to prevent Archduke Charles from joining up with his own reinforcements. The more Napoleon destabilises his adversaries, the more the rebels' ardour will cool.'

The principal armies resembled two queens face to face in

the middle of the chessboard, both immobilised, while elsewhere the pieces were ceaselessly manoeuvring and annihilating each other. At the end of all these moves, one of the two queens would feel sufficiently protected by its pawns to take action.

'He should be made a general!' decreed an enthusiastic captain.

'Well, not really . . .' murmured Saber with false modesty.

Luise came closer to the table, the prelude to a brutal storm.

'There's no blood in your game. I'll add some.'

As she spoke she tipped the coffee pot over the map. The puddle of coffee spread in a lake, soaking up the crumbs of bread and dissolving the sugar. Saber was too polite to reproach her; he merely withdrew his documents precipitately. Relmyer burst out laughing like a child, which made Luise relax. Saber, furious, was preparing to leave when suddenly he froze.

'He's here . . .' he murmured.

His anger had evaporated. Margont wondered who could have produced such a miracle. Normally his friend would not forgive such a humiliation; he endlessly rehashed past slights that everyone else had forgotten. Margont looked round at the customers. It couldn't be Napoleon – the walls and ceiling would have been reverberating to the cries of 'Long live the Emperor!'

'Maestro Beethoven is here,' repeated Saber.

Margont leant towards Luise. 'Who's Beethoven?'

She shrugged. 'A composer. He was very successful in the past and his sonatas have earned him some followers. But he hasn't managed to win the heart of the public and his detractors are legion. He's no Mozart—'

Saber reacted violently. 'It's Mozart who's no Beethoven and not the other way round!'

He made more sense when he was talking about the war.

'So who is he, this Beethoven?' Margont asked impatiently.

Luise pointed out a strange-looking man of about forty. Red hair was escaping here and there from a badly brushed grey wig. Thin and husk-like, he resembled a solitary insect forced by hunger to go out foraging. Absorbed in his thoughts, he lived entirely in another world exclusively woven from music.

'He hasn't had the best of luck,' added Luise. 'They were on the point of showing *Fidelio* here, in Vienna. That was at the beginning of May. But when people learnt that your army was on the way, no one wanted to go to the opera any more. The notices are still up on the walls . . . Add to that the fifty million contribution demanded by Napoleon to punish Vienna, which led to a host of exceptional taxes, and the high cost of living thanks to the presence of your soldiers who devour everything . . . Beethoven can't have an easy life, that's for sure. In times of war, in order to survive, most musicians are forced to eat their scores.'

No one was paying any attention to this regular customer. Beethoven did not have to place an order; since he was a habitué, the waiter knew to bring him coffee and cream. Saber was visibly excited.

'Have you never heard his Third Symphony? It's fantastic. He dedicated it to Napoleon!'

At these words, Luise stifled a laugh but said no more. She wore the joyous impatient expression of someone who knew what little catastrophe was about to take place and was keen not to ruin it. Saber would not stop talking about the maestro's melodies. For his part, Margont, who was incapable of reading a score, understood little of what was going on. Saber had chosen to quench his absolute thirst with the great wins and the disasters of military life, but it seemed his thirst also extended to music. Without wars, would he start to churn out musical scores? Saber grew breathless.

'It's the fifth time I've seen him. He always just slips in.'

'Have you spoken to him?'

Saber groaned. 'No . . .'

Margont had seen his friend's bravery at first hand on the battlefield and here was Saber speechless in front of a man he admired.

'Herr Beethoven, I am Lieutenant Irénée Saber. Allow me to say that I find your work absolutely sublime.'

Beethoven did not react. He drank his coffee, still wrapped up in his thoughts. His face and his gestures betrayed tension. His dreams were filled with rage.

'Herr Beethoven?'

A customer came to Saber's aid.

'He's almost deaf,' he said in hesitant French, covering his ears with his hands to make himself clear.

'How can a musician be deaf?'

'Why not? He could hear before.'

'Yet he's still composing . . .'

'He hears in his head.'

The Austrian tapped his temple as he said that. He burst into the raucous laughter of a pipe-smoker.

'No one takes him seriously,' he added.

'Don't say that. He's a genius, you . . . hypocrite!' retorted Saber vehemently.

The customer beat a retreat, glass in hand, disappearing into the crowd. Saber smiled again and leant towards Beethoven's ear, raising his voice.

'Herr Beethoven? I'm Lieutenant Saber. I wanted to tell you—'

The maestro swung round suddenly to face him. His face was covered in scars, the result of smallpox, and his glasses magnified his eyes.

'Don't talk to me! Damn you French!'

His cheeks had become purple, emphasising the whiteness of his voluminous, old-fashioned cravat.

'What's become of your revolution? You launch your wonderful republican ideas on the world and then you found an empire! Napoleon has betrayed us all!'

'I want to talk to you about your music . . .'

'Let go!'

But Saber had not touched him. Beethoven hurried to the door, knocking into customers.

The owner leant over his counter to shout: 'Herr Beethoven! You haven't paid! It's not free here for musicians and poets.'

'I'll pay for him,' declared Saber, throwing a handful of kreutzers at the owner.

Disconcerted, he rejoined his friends. When she did not like someone, Luise could be scathing. She looked at him contemptuously.

'If I may correct you, Beethoven did not dedicate his Third

Symphony to Napoleon, but to the revolutionary, Bonaparte. At the time he used to harangue the nobles in the public gardens to tell them that all men are equal, that monarchy was a thing of the past . . . As Beethoven is an extraordinarily touchy man, persuaded that all the world is out to get him, he's always involved in confrontations. He fell dramatically from favour when your Bonaparte became Emperor. He destroyed the title page of his Third Symphony, which is now called the Heroic Symphony, and it is dedicated to one of his patrons, the Prince Lobkowitz. Oh, yes, it's such a shame that Beethoven ruined your sugary war game.'

CHAPTER 16

IT was hard to persuade Relmyer to come to Schönbrunn. The Hofburg Palace was the official home of the Court, but it was decaying and rather impractical because of its dispersed buildings. Emperor Francis I preferred the Château de Schönbrunn. So did Napoleon, and he had installed his headquarters there. To show the Viennese that the little setback at Essling had in no way dented his determination, he regularly reviewed his troops at Schönbrunn, that symbol of Austrian power. Today, as frequently happened, an assorted crowd of people hurried into the gardens to watch the spectacle.

An immense park had been decked out in the French style with flowerbeds, shaped hedges, lines of trees . . . Symmetry was the golden rule. A fountain of Neptune, statues and fake Roman ruins paid homage to the fashion for antiquities. Right at the end, on a little hill, a pavilion with columns presided in splendour, an invitation to gaze at the view. This park was not of its time. Schönbrunn was like a little version of Versailles. The ochre façade suggested appeasement. It was governed by subtle mathematical and architectural rules. The result, harmonious, elegant and aesthetic, was a pleasure to behold. In front of the château, several regiments waited. Their white gaiters, breeches and tunics shone in the sun, contrasting with the dark blue of their coats. As the Emperor was not yet there, there was complete stillness.

Lefine was overcome with a fit of the giggles.

'You would think that time had stopped down there.'

The crowd pressed against the sentries charged with keeping it at a distance. Soldiers mingled with the Austrians, some curious and some sympathetic to the republican or imperial cause. Several women had secured places at the front to charm Napoleon. Were they being seductive? Defiant? Greedy? Did they harbour ambitions? Was it love or fascination? Some were so exquisitely beautiful that the Emperor could not fail to notice them if he were to pass close by.

Margont noticed that Relmyer had a sort of tick. His eyes were moving all the time. They ricocheted from face to face, rarely lingering, never finding repose. He had acted the same way in the streets, but here the mass of people accentuated his behaviour, making it more obvious. He's looking for him, thought Margont. If Relmyer suddenly saw him here – or thought he saw him, because his memory of his gaoler had altered over the years – how would he react?

A clamour arose. There were shouts, and cries of 'Long live the Emperor!' A black berlin arrived, escorted by the chasseurs of the Imperial Guard in their green uniforms, their red pelisses thrown over their shoulders, their sabres unsheathed. There followed an interminable, sumptuous procession of officers of the general staff, the gold embroidery on their blue coats sparkling. The cavalry were distinguished by the originality of their uniform. One of them, a dragoon, wore a dark blue coat and a crested copper helmet in the style of Minerva, decorated with a black plume and banded with sealskin; another, the Mameluke Roustan, wore babouches, red baggy trousers, a short blue jacket and a white turban (his ostentatious presence was a reminder that Napoleon, when he was still Bonaparte, had conquered Egypt, albeit briefly). This river of prancing colour and the frenetic excitement of the public contrasted with the immobile, impassive infantry of the line. The crowd tried to draw nearer, but could not get past the sentries barring its way.

Lefine sounded a sour note: 'That's right, long live the Emperor! We won't be saying that when we receive our pay late.'

Napoleon stepped out of the berlin. Emaciated at the time of the Consulate, he had now become stout. His neck was so short that his round head seemed to perch directly on his torso. In spite of the heat he wore a long grey greatcoat and his black bicorn. He was strikingly short, but radiated energy and an intimidating authority. This contradiction was unsettling. Many Viennese hated him. They had come to gaze at 'the monster'. Many times they had imagined how they would sneer at the Emperor, taunting him as a dwarf, a bloody tyrant, a jumped-up nobody, an ogre . . . but now they were struck dumb. They had counted on seeing 'the vanquished man of Essling' and instead they were faced with a leader bubbling over with self-assurance. It had been said that during the battle everything had gone wrong for him. Yet the Emperor smiled, joking with an aide-de-camp. He was behaving like . . . like a conqueror! In reality Napoleon was projecting an image and he imbued it with astonishing realism.

A general shouted an order and the soldiers briskly presented arms. Moving stiffly, Napoleon began to walk along the line, his hands behind his back, accompanied by two officers of his general staff and two colonels. Sometimes he would pause in front of an infantryman long enough to pose a question, or to repeat one of his sayings, which the army took up in an endless echo: 'Soldiers, I am pleased with you' (the evening after Austerlitz), 'War between Europeans is civil war', 'Action and speed!', 'That can't be allowed: that's not French!' . . . Margont could not understand how Napoleon could appear so serene while his world was at risk of collapsing any day now. Such self-control inspired confidence.

Now I'm falling under his spell, he reproached himself.

Napoleon speeded up, hurrying, hurrying. The crowd groaned, put out. Was he leaving? So soon? Was he not going to approach before he left? The Emperor questioned two other colonels, turned about and hurried off towards his escort. Some soldiers shouted again, 'Long live the Emperor,' while the beautiful girls made eyes at the sentries to try to get them to bow. An imperceptible eddy ran through the crowd in response to Napoleon's slightest gesture. Margont watched the little grey figure go back up the white and blue line of soldiers.

Suddenly two boys escaped from the throng, pursued by a corporal. Other sentries came from behind to bar their route. The two young men had underestimated the speed of reaction of the infantrymen and were taken unawares. They took stones from their pockets and hurled them in the Emperor's direction, yelling, 'Long live Austria!' Their stones landed in the flower-beds as Napoleon, who had noticed the incident, disappeared into his berlin. A grenadier grabbed the outstretched arm of one of the boys and yanked it upwards, forcing the boy to let his missile go, like a giant disarming a midget.

'Little beasts! I'll tan your hide!'

There were protests from the public. How old were these two daring lads? Fourteen? The commander in charge of the cordon let them go, saying, 'We only hunt the big game.'

'We'll get them when they're big then,' retorted the grenadier bitterly. 'And then it won't be the belt, it'll be the firing squad.'

Margont caught Relmyer by the arm. He was unaware that he was pinching him.

'That's how our man operates! That's how he was able to drag Wilhelm with him. Wilhelm wanted to join the Austrian army and his murderer led him to believe that he was going to help him cross the border and then to enlist.'

The crowd broke up around them but Margont was not paying attention to that.

'It's impossible to cross a river while threatening someone with a pistol. And you can't pass through enemy lines with someone who wants to be noticed and is trying to escape from you. That doesn't make sense. If the murderer had regularly run risks like that he would have been caught long ago. He must have discovered that Wilhelm was hostile to the French.'

'But how?' Relmyer immediately asked.

'He must sometimes go to the area around Vienna. He has already done that at least once, when he was taken by surprise with Wilhelm on the road back.'

These words reinforced Relmyer's feeling of an invisible threat that he had had now for so many years. A latent, formless, malleable danger, a sort of thickness in the air, which was both variable and oppressive.

'He looks for boys who are critical of the French,' went on Margont. 'He could very well be here now, in the crowd, and have noticed the demonstration made by those two young boys. See how easy it would be. And it would be easy for him to elicit confidences, since he is Austrian. He's worked on his technique. Now instead of forcing, he convinces. He doesn't threaten any more, he seduces. That way he can easily lead his victim where he wants him; the victim willingly co-operates. He has adapted to circumstances and uses them to his own advantage. He chooses someone in French territory and takes them over to the Austrian side before taking advantage of them. He does admittedly run risks crossing lines, but with his exceptional knowledge of the woods and marshes of the area, the risks are limited. Moreover, riding between the two zones confuses things and helps him cover his tracks. Anyone who disappears in the French zone will only be looked for in that zone. Our man therefore puts his victims out of reach of anyone who might help them.'

Spelling out his deductions, Margont was cocooned in a universe of concepts, theories and speculation, spun out of ideas. This protected him, keeping at bay emotions, which Relmyer, on the other hand, felt the full brunt of. Wild-eyed and sweating, he appeared ready to succumb to rage, or exhaustion, or perhaps illness . . .

'Wherever he goes,' he said, 'he will never be out of my reach.'

'Now he's choosing people whose name their nearest and dearest would not be surprised to find on a list of men killed in action. He's covering his tracks even better than previously.'

Margont looked again at the long line of regiments a general was addressing. The scene was exactly the same as earlier but, to him, it now meant something different. Now it seemed menacing. It was no longer reassuring; on the contrary, it had become the involuntary ally of peril. The soldiers broke rank, as the grains of a wall of sand rapidly disperse.

'The more troops arrive, the closer we are to the moment of battle. We can almost say with certainty that the man we're seeking will try to get hold of another boy before the next confrontation. Whatever the outcome, the war will move on far from here, either following the retreating army, or it will be suspended. So the murderer has an incentive to act quickly.'

Relmyer's torment was without end. 'Perhaps it's already too late.'

'I don't think so. It would be very risky to kidnap another young man from Lesdorf. Two disappearances so close together would attract attention.'

'Several of my hussars are keeping a watch on the orphanages in the area and will spot him if he approaches.'

'No, he'll go looking elsewhere. But he will still need several days to pick out a potential victim and to gain his confidence. However, time is against us.'

CHAPTER 17

THE days passed; military routine was established. It was almost possible to forget that shortly people would die in their thousands . . . Lefine was leaning against a chestnut tree, contemplating the branch of the Danube that separated the Isle of Lobau from the Austrians. He liked having a few moments to himself in a calm spot, far from Margont, whose constant activity tended to wear his friends out. Sure enough, here he was on his way over. Lefine cursed himself for not having taken himself further away from the regiment. He could tell what Margont was about to say.

'Let me guess: your investigation is not progressing any more; you're going round in circles. The Emperor is everywhere at once, the army is struggling to accomplish a thousand tasks, the Austrians are entrenched beyond Aspern and Essling . . . Why are we bothering? Look on the other side of the Danube: it's exactly the same over there. Why don't we just stop now; there would be half the world for Napoleon and the other half for the Austrians? We would leave them Russia, India, China, Japan and all that they can find beyond, if there is anything beyond . . .' Lefine spread his arms wide to illustrate the proof of his idea. 'The world is a big pear: we'll halve it equally.'

'Instead of talking nonsense, you could think about our investigation. You're the one who always has ideas . . .'

'Oh, I have thought about it, would you believe! I've even thought of a suspect.'

'You have? Who would that be?'

'Relmyer. If he's the murderer, it explains everything. It would have been easy for him to lead Franz to that old deserted farm because they were friends. There he killed Franz for some reason or other: vengeance, jealousy, unnatural desire, or bloodlust. Then he invented the story of the "evil stranger" to cover his tracks. That's why the man we're hunting leaves as few traces as a ghost – because he is in fact a ghost who exists only in your head.'

Margont realised that Lefine did not really believe any of that. Nevertheless the latter expounded the theory as if he did believe it because he knew that it vexed his friend. Subjected to Margont's authority, from time to time he enjoyed reversing the roles.

As Margont turned pale, Lefine went on with increased assurance, 'No sooner does Relmyer return than a new crime is committed. That's no coincidence. Relmyer wanted to do to Wilhelm – whom he knew! – what he had done to Franz. But he was surprised by a patrol he managed to escape from because he had lived in the region. As for those orphans killed at Austerlitz, they were actually killed at Austerlitz. We both fought in that battle, didn't we? Have you forgotten all those dead and wounded littering the ground? You're in love with Luise and you're confusing your childhood story with hers and Relmyer's. So Relmyer is able to manipulate you. You're looking everywhere for a murderer who's right under your nose and who must be laughing up his sleeve. Sometimes he who shouts loudest has the most to hide.'

Margont was so shaken he had to lean against a tree.

'How you can imagine something so horrifying?'

'I'm not imagining anything. I'm opening my eyes and observing humanity. Whilst you're torturing yourself with your hypotheses, I have done my researches to try to verify mine. Relmyer did not murder Wilhelm: he was with his hussars when the sentries spotted the two figures on the little island. Besides, if Relmyer had killed Franz he wouldn't have taken us to see the farmhouse – he would have kept us well away.'

Margont looked taken aback. 'You really believed that Relmyer could have . . .'

'Of course.'

Lefine was capable of evoking the worst abominations with fatalistic resignation while Margont persisted in ignoring that facet of the world.

'Why didn't you mention it?'

'Because you wouldn't have listened to me. So I had nothing to suggest. But I did eliminate a potential suspect.'

Although he did not agree with Lefine, Margont recognised that he was right about one thing: Margont did identify with Luise and Relmyer's personal histories. The memory of his years shut up in the Abbey of Saint-Guilhem-le-Désert was still vividly painful. He had suffered not just from the loss of liberty but also from the pressure to become a monk, that is to say, to become someone he was not. At the time, his family had thought that what they felt counted, and not what Margont wanted. It was one of the main reasons that he had later become a fervent follower of the republican cause. Because the

Revolution considerably reinforced the rights of the individual. To be able to be true to himself was, in the final analysis, all that he wanted. Was that not all that Luise and Relmyer were after too? But in order to do that, they had first to track down this man.

In his mind his childhood memories constituted a sort of monster. A monster taking up too much space in his consciousness, bloated from having gorged itself on dark emotions, on rage, sadness, abandon, hate and dismay. Margont knew that he would never succeed in striking it down definitively. But he wanted to subdue it, to bridle it and tie it up somewhere, as if it were a frisky horse that, once tied up in its paddock, could not harm anyone. You could not change your past, but you could change the way you thought about it. Should Margont succeed in helping Luise and Relmyer overcome their pasts, he would fortify himself and consign his own beast to a corner of his mind. At least, that was what he hoped. That was also the reason that victims helped other victims.

Lefine was right on two points, in fact. Margont was in love with Luise. However, something was preventing him from drawing close to her, from trying to seduce her: it was their respective pasts and Relmyer's. Standing between Margont and Luise there were three monsters that he was wrestling with.

Lefine went over to the riverbank, intrigued.

'What on earth is that fish?'

Across the water glided a boat equipped with three light cannon and propelled by twenty rowers.

'The Emperor has decided to have a flotilla patrol the river and harass the enemy observation posts,' replied Margont. 'He's also using small boats to intercept anything that could damage the bridges. And he's manned I don't know how many islands with soldiers and batteries, even those up beside Vienna. So now no one will be able to tell where his army will pop from for the big battle. He's having reinforcements rushed in from all over the Empire, he's undertaking reviews . . . In short he's being incredibly active while the Austrians are just waiting.'

'They're not just waiting, they're digging in,' corrected Lefine, a proponent of defensive war methods, since war was less bloody for defenders than assailants.

'Prince Eugène's Italian army is going to confront the Austrians under Archduke John again. If Eugène wins, he will come to back us up and Napoleon will probably launch his offensive. The situation is endlessly evolving, time is pressing and we, we are stuck here, slouching in the sun, without any ideas! It's already 8 June!'

'Why don't you go and search the archives with Relmyer then?'

'That would achieve nothing! In any case, I can't read German very well, so to try to decipher illegible writing when I don't know what I'm looking for . . .'

Four hussars appeared from behind some trees – an adjutant of the 9th, two troopers from the élite company of the 7th and a young sabreur of the 5th. The variety of their uniforms made an iridescence of colour animating the gliding motion of their horses. They were like exotic birds, combining the colourful plumage of robins with the ferocity of birds of prey.

The men approached Margont. The sun played on their gold braid.

'Would you by any chance be Captain Margont?' enquired the adjutant with extreme courtesy, too much courtesy.

His rosy lips and his moustache with the curled tips might have made him look rather ridiculous, but any hint of a smile, and you would find yourself challenged to a duel.

'I am. And whom do I have the honour of addressing?'

'Adjutant Grendet. And this is Warrant Officer Cauchoit, Trumpeter Sibot and Hussar Lasse.'

The face of the warrant officer was extremely scarred. The surface of his skin was like a fencing manual. Sabre fencing, of course; for him that was all that counted. He owned two sabres, one very curved, like a Mameluke's weapon, and the other almost straight. He looked disdainfully at Margont's sword. The adjutant went on in the same unctuous, honeyed tone.

'We have been looking for Lieutenant Relmyer, of the 8th Hussars, for several days. They call him the Wasp sometimes, or the little lieutenant because of his youth and childish countenance. But of course you know exactly to whom I'm referring . . . Very unfortunately he is never to be found with his regiment. However, I am told that you know him. Can you tell me where we would be able to find him?'

Margont was an excellent liar. He could thank Lefine for advice on the best techniques.

'I've known Relmyer for only a few days and I don't know where he could have gone. May I ask why you are looking for him?'

'It's very annoying,' lamented the adjutant. 'We would be so happy if we could speak to him.'

At these words the trumpeter burst out laughing.

'Speak to him about . . .?' persisted Margont.

'Well, you see, Captain, Relmyer wounded Lieutenant Piquebois. Yet Lieutenant Piquebois is a very fine swordsman. So we would like to know if Relmyer would agree to show us his technique.'

Margont was outraged. 'You want to challenge Relmyer to four duels?'

The adjutant shrugged to indicate his disappointment. It did not surprise him that Margont did not understand. He had always considered that foot soldiers and cavalry belonged to different worlds.

'We don't fight duels, Monsieur Infantry Officer; we make art! Very well, we'll be on our way. Tell your friend Relmyer that we're looking for him. He will easily find us in our respective regiments. Explain that I would be very much obliged if he would respect the order of hierarchy in his encounters with us. The highest in rank first, of course.'

The warrant officer was last to leave. Just before he did so he threw out: 'Please say hello to Antoine Piquebois for me.'

His finger traced the length of one of his scars, running diagonally through the chequered pattern of the welts. Margont suddenly remembered him. In 1804, Piquebois, then a hussar, had floored him with a sabre stroke. Officially it had been recorded as a training accident . . .

After the hussars had gone, Lefine announced: 'I'm going to try not to get too close to Relmyer. That way I won't be too grief-stricken when they bury him in two or three weeks' time . . . because even if he succeeds in knocking off those four strapping fellows, there will be more, and still more. For Antoine, all that calmed down after he was wounded at Austerlitz, because he changed completely after that. He's no longer a swashbuckler ready to fight at the slightest challenge. Except when he sees Relmyer! But Relmyer, he does everything to attract the calamity that is duellists!'

'He doesn't mean to. He has only one idea in his head: to find the man he's looking for. Look how little he takes Luise's feelings into account, even though he regards her as his sister. And that fortune that he spent to be able to examine the archives at the Kriegsministerium. Imagine what else he could have done with all that money? No, he attracts death without even being aware of it.'

Lefine was appalled at this.

'The problem is that death is blind,' he declared. 'It's stalking Relmyer but it could just as easily get us by mistake!'

'Relmyer is tied to his past. He won't really start to live until he has broken the ties.'

'There are other ways of freeing yourself from a rope than tugging to make the bulldog attached to it come and bite you.'

'He only knows how to do it his way.'

'Listen, about that dog . . .'

Pagin galloped over to them. As he felt he was not getting there fast enough – the world turned too slowly for his liking – he was gesticulating. That would have saved time had anyone understood what his waving arm signified. He brought his sweating horse abruptly to a halt, causing it to whinny.

'Captain, Sergeant: Lieutenant Relmyer wants you to know that he's found what he's looking for in the registers. He's going to try to find the person concerned. If you want to go with him, you will have to follow me immediately.'

CHAPTER 18

RELMYER was everywhere all at once. He had gathered a dozen hussars from his squadron and he walked from one to the other, checking their arms and giving orders. An Austrian peasant, unwillingly forced to be their guide, sat stiffly on a mount controlled by a non-commissioned officer. Relmyer, already overwrought, grew even more excited when he saw Margont. The latter had seen similar expressions in hospitals when a victim realised that the bullet inside them was about to be extracted. In certain cases, the relief caused rapture.

'Here you are at last!' cried Relmyer to Margont and Lefine, shaking them by the hand. 'We have a lead! We have a lead!'

He held out a letter written in German. It was dated 3 May, just before the French had occupied Vienna. Relmyer did not have the patience to wait for Margont to decipher it.

'It's the copy for archiving of a letter written by a certain Limbsen to a secretary at the Ministry of War called Homkler. Look here, and there!'

His excitement was making him confused.

'This Limbsen explains that he has been put in charge of an internal inquiry concerning the military registers. One of the men responsible for keeping the documents in good order had noticed the anomalies in the lists of effectives of the Infanterieregimenter 20 and 23! Those were the regiments that Mark and Ernst were supposed to have served in!'

Becoming more and more agitated, he raised his voice. 'Limbsen verified the relevant registers. He suspects a certain Johann Grich of being responsible for the errors. In this letter, according to procedure, Limbsen asks Secretary Homkler – Grich's superior – for authorisation to question him. We don't know if Limbsen ever did so. I would imagine not. The Austrians have had other things on their minds since our troops arrived in Vienna.'

'Why does he suspect Grich?'

'That's not made clear in the letter.'

Margont was finding it hard to believe in this miracle.

'Where did you find this document?'

'In the chaos of the archives. I told you we had to look there! Now, we've wasted enough time, let's go! Let's pay Johann Grich a visit. According to the letter, he lives in Mazenau, a hamlet a few leagues north of Vienna.'

Lefine was suspicious.

'Lieutenant, why all the hussars and a guide?'

Relmyer spoke calmly, as if he had inadvertently forgotten a minor detail. 'I found out a bit about Mazenau: it's in a forest.' In the face of Lefine's fury, he immediately added: 'It's on the French side. If Grich had lived on the other bank, everything would have been more . . .'

Lefine shook his head at this. 'Because you would have gone there anyway?'

Pagin brought his horse closer to nudge the flank of Lefine's mount.

'Infantrymen only know how to advance in line, in their thousands, elbow to elbow, once the artillery have carefully prepared the terrain. Let's proceed as normal: let the hussars do the work and then join us in a week when it's all over. We'll tell you—'

Lefine was not amused.

'Insolent at seventeen, dead at twenty.'

Relmyer was worried. His eyes searched Margont's.

'You are coming with us, aren't you? Having you there is very important to me.'

'I'm coming. I've promised Luise I'll look after you, and I have decided to help with this affair until it's resolved.'

Lefine grunted his agreement. Relmyer bounded into his saddle with the dexterity of the hussar. Margont held out his arm to calm his impetuosity.

'Allow me to warn you that you are in great danger: four hussars are searching for you to fight duels with you.'

'Only four?' joked Pagin.

Relmyer greeted the news with equanimity. He was used to it, and in any case, he had somewhere to go and the rest of the world was irrelevant to him at the moment.

'Is it because of my duel with your friend Piquebois? Unfortunately it's just like that.'

'Just like that?' choked Margont. 'Everywhere, all around you, people are pointing sabres in your direction and . . .'

He could not even finish his sentence, he was so put out by Relmyer's calm.

Lefine leant towards him. 'Methinks we have been taken for idiots.'

Three of the four hussars in question had just appeared behind them, sneering. The hussar from the 5th Regiment rode out in front. The two élite troopers were behind on either side, ready to encircle Relmyer should he try to escape. Adjutant Grendet was nowhere to be seen. Perhaps he was lying in wait nearby or perhaps he was looking for Relmyer elsewhere. Lefine felt like a hare that, believing he has escaped a hunter, now sees the snout of the hunter's dog ferreting around its form.

'They followed us and we didn't notice anything! But I'm usually so careful!'

'What is this nonsense?' fumed Relmyer.

'You'll leave one for me, won't you, Lieutenant?' asked Pagin, his hand on the hilt of his sword.

Lefine was already moving away.

'Hussars are as twisted as their sabres!'

'Remember your promise,' Margont said fiercely to Relmyer.

Relmyer was very diplomatic. He explained his proposed expedition without going into detail about the reasons for it and insisted that it could not be delayed. He won himself a reprieve but the three hussars insisted on coming with them, which Relmyer agreed to. The hussars were convinced that Relmyer was trying to escape them and did not intend to let him out of their sight. Relmyer, smiling again, set off, indicating with a sweeping gesture that everyone should follow. Three duels were hanging over him, but he paid them as little heed as if they were three specks of dust on his pelisse.

CHAPTER 19

THE little troop made its way north. They skirted Vienna before plunging into the forest. Margont lost all sense of direction and had no idea where they were. He had deployed some of his men as vanguard and some on the flanks. He scanned the area, his gaze seeming to slide through the foliage. The green and scarlet troopers were redolent of drops of bloody sap scattered over the vast vegetation. The trees, giants weighed down with leaves, seemed to crush them in their vertiginous grasp. They formed a sort of palace of alarming proportions. Had it not been for the war Margont would have liked to lose himself here.

The three duellists followed Relmyer. The two élite troopers never spoke to the hussar of the 5th Regiment. They only knew each other because of the magnetic draw of Relmyer's blade to theirs. Yet Margont told himself that he was hardly less idiotic than they were. Had he not become involved in this business for complex motives, which he couldn't share with anyone else? Twenty men found themselves united here but for very differing reasons. None of them belonged to the same world.

'Is it much further, Lieutenant?' asked Lefine.

Relmyer asked the guide in German. The guide's back sagged as if the officer's questions were blows.

'No, a little more than two leagues, Monsieur,' he replied fearfully.

Margont spoke quietly. 'Is it really impossible to avoid those duels?'

'Clearly I won't be able to escape them. As soon as we've finished questioning this Grich, I will have to fight them.'

'What?'

Relmyer spread his hands slightly. 'They will never leave me alone unless I agree to fight them. We will fight at Mazenau, which will suit everyone. We won't lose any time and they will get what they want in a quiet spot. On the Isle of Lobau, we risk being disturbed by a superior officer opposed to duels, or by the imperial police with their excessive zeal. I remember the promise I made you but this is not a situation of my making.'

In spite of the shade, Margont was sweating as if he was under a midday sun.

'Three duels . . . The first will perhaps be one. But if you're wounded the second will be a murder, an execution!'

'Not at all. If I'm hurt we'll examine the wound together. If it's decided that the wound is superficial, my adversary will be declared winner and I will go on with the next duel.'

Margont interrupted with a gesture. He could no longer bear these rules and the logic that conferred an illusion of rationality on the madness.

However, Relmyer, caught up in his explanation, continued: 'Of course, a serious injury would mean the end of fighting, but there would be a problem if the wound was disputed. If a unanimous view cannot be amicably reached, we will have to ask the opinion of a doctor whose word will be final. Exhaustion postpones the duel by one day, a serious injury postpones it to the day following complete recovery.'

'But why? Why take still more risks?'

'You're asking that question because you don't understand the life of a renowned duellist. Of course he attracts other duellists avid to fight him. He's famous and everywhere he is feared in the same measure as he is admired and envied. He makes money giving lessons and winning duels that are wagers he gambles on. He progresses rapidly up the ranks. Without my sabre I would not be a lieutenant. Lieutenant at twenty years old! Certain women – superb ones, I can tell you – are ready to do anything to have a well-known swashbuckler hold them in his arms.'

'And all that's worth risking death for?'

'It's worth risking death ten times over. If any one of these sabre-fighters succeeds in piercing my chest, that life will be his. Take Pagin, for example. A few months ago he was afraid of everything and everyone. His apprenticeship with the sabre has transformed him. Look at his assurance today, his *joie de vivre* . . . that's why he's always dashing about the place: he is catching up the years that he lost in inertia, held back by his fears.'

Margont chased away the flies buzzing round his horse's head, endlessly irritating it.

'You are just like him. Pagin is "fortifying himself with iron" to confront a nameless danger that torments him. You're acting the same way. Except that you have a clearer idea of the threat you're confronting.'

'Yes and no. Only in part. I was damaged by what happened to me. My sword is my crutch: take it away from me and I'll collapse. I am grateful to it for helping me to walk again but at the same time it reminds me of the past and it attracts duellists.'

Margont looked at him with a mixture of compassion and fear: in his eyes, Relmyer was suffering from a malady that was little by little increasing its stranglehold on him.

'You started to train with the sabre to learn to defend yourself. But arms are like wine – in the end they take you over. Lukas, you have become the scabbard of your blade.'

'As long as this investigation remains unresolved, I will not be able to give it up. Afterwards, I will try . . .'

Warrant Officer Cauchoit rode closer.

'You're making it too complicated. Better to have ten days of glory than ten thousand of mediocrity.'

'What a magnificent epitaph,' replied Margont. Then, turning to Relmyer, he added: 'Let's suppose that you win these three duels: how many duellists will be attracted by that triple . . . success?'

'All of them of course! My duel with Piquebois is not the only reason for this situation. My reputation carries weight. It's not very easy to—'

To chase away the flies Relmyer's horse had just lifted its head when part of it burst open under the impact of a shot. Margont, his face splattered with blood, saw the horse collapse on its side as Relmyer was thrown to the ground, a leg and a stirrup in the air, his hands pulling on the now useless reins. This first bullet was immediately followed by a concert of detonations. A hussar in the vanguard, mown down, fell backwards, while the mount of his companion collapsed along with his trooper. Clouds of white smoke appeared everywhere: in the thickets, behind the trees . . . A grey silhouette took aim at Margont but Lefine immediately fired his pistol, catching the figure in the thigh.

'It's the militia! Death to the Landwehr!' cried Cauchoit.

Sabre in hand, and dragging his trumpeter friend and some hussars in his wake, he charged straight at a mass of infantrymen that had formed in front of them. These Austrians were not professional soldiers. They had thought that the surprise and success of their first volley would send the French into disarray. The thirty amongst them who had just made themselves defenceless in order to adjust their sights were struck head on by the troopers. The warrant officer moved as if in a trance. His sabre attacked furiously, wounding, killing, killing, wounding ... The trumpeter aimed his blows exclusively at faces and throats, leaving nothing behind him but dead and disfigured bodies, dehumanised corpses. The troop of militia disappeared beyond a clearing; the carnage had sewn confusion amongst the Austrians. Although they were still more numerous, and for the most part sheltered behind trees, many of them fled, vanishing through the vegetation. Others continued to riddle the French with gunfire. The poor guide they had pressed into service was taken for a traitor and received two balls in the back. The hussars plunged at a trot into the wood, laughing in the face of their fear. They passed no one without mowing him down with their pistols or laying him out with their sabres. Relmyer, already on his feet, having freed himself, but covered in his horse's blood, feverishly scanned the thickets. He paid no attention to his men or to the battle that raged around him. He pointed in the direction of the shot that had killed his horse.

'It's him! He killed Franz! Him!'

Such a coincidence was impossible. Had Relmyer been driven mad? Or had they been betrayed? In the woods, the officer Relmyer was pointing to detached himself from the combatants to take flight. The Austrian wore a grey coat with red cuffs and lapels. The elegance of his uniform contrasted with the coarse coats of certain of the militia. Light brown hair could be seen under his black bicorn, braided with gold. Margont briefly caught a glimpse of the man's face. He seemed to be in his forties. Relmyer had launched into the woods in pursuit, his pistol in one hand, his trusty sabre in the other. All about him there was carnage. The hussars, although very much inferior in number, definitely had the upper hand over their adversaries. They attacked and charged at anything that moved. Their horses plunged into groups of militia, knocking into bodies, and the troopers wielded their sabres as though they were mowing the grass. Margont found himself facing a wave of Austrians in disarray. How many were there? Dozens? He thought he was going to be slashed to pieces but his very presence exacerbated the panic of the fleeing Austrians. But the tide of humanity ricocheted around him and the militia scattered in other directions. Margont wanted to pursue them, but hands were raised all around him. He had just taken fifteen prisoners. A hussar burst out of a thicket brandishing his sabre. It was the trumpeter from the élite company. He whirled like the wind into the midst of what he took to be a pocket of resistance and launched an attack towards the face of the horseman he took to be the leader of the rabble. Margont scarcely had time to duck down by his horse's neck. The point of the sabre pierced his shako. He wanted to cry out to set the trumpeter straight, but he was long gone, chasing other moving figures. Had he really been mistaken in all the confusion? Margont seized one of his two horse pistols and had to fight against the urge to shoot at the horse of the madman. Pagin arrived in the meantime, his sword bloody, his face scratched by branches. He looked in astonishment at Margont and the captives.

'Victory!' he bellowed, standing up in his stirrups, his sabre pointing towards the sky.

His shout made the fifteen Austrians flinch.

Relmyer returned at the run. 'He's escaping! Pagin, your horse!'

The hussar did not dare protest and got down from his mount. Margont tried to say something, but Relmyer bounced into the saddle and set off, spurring the horse until it bled. Margont followed, abandoning Pagin, who, disdainful of the prisoners, looked for someone to fight. The two horsemen overtook Warrant Officer Cauchoit, who was a terrifying sight. He was covered in blood and had eviscerated everyone who opposed him. He was a veritable angel of death.

Margont found himself in an artificial clearing. Some Austrian horses were stamping and restless, tied to branches. At the other end of the expanse of felled trees, figures were fleeing on horseback.

'He's not far ahead of us!' cried Relmyer.

Margont and Relmyer's horses dashed along, devouring the distance. They were far superior to the old nags the Austrian army furnished the militia with. Little by little the fleeing man became easier to make out. The officer with the bicorn pointed his weapon in their direction.

'That's him!' shrieked Relmyer.

'Duck!' warned Margont.

A detonation sounded but the ball missed its target. The fugitive changed tactics, tugged on his reins and disappeared into the forest. Relmyer was quivering.

'He's heading north-east. He wants to get over to the Austrian side but the Danube is blocking his way.'

The two pursuers were engulfed in their turn in the woods. The figure of the Austrian appeared and disappeared intermittently. Margont used shot after shot from his horse pistol, trying to hit the Austrian's mount, but in vain.

'We're miles away from our army!'

'Where did he go?' agonised Relmyer.

The man seemed to have been swallowed by the vegetation. Margont slowed his horse and saw him cut off down a path.

'That way.'

The fugitive had taken a badly maintained path. Margont had just made out his grey uniform through the jumble of thicket. Relmyer, who had almost got lost, had been overtaken by his friend and was hitting the flank of his mare with the flat of his sabre. His horse took off like a whirlwind at twice the speed of Margont's mount, forcing him off the path. Margont steadied himself and settled back into his galloping rhythm. He felt fear swelling in him. He was now convinced that nothing about the fugitive had anything to do with chance. He and Relmyer saw only a random labyrinth of vegetation whilst their adversary moved as easily as if he were strolling about the streets of his hometown. Margont no longer felt like a hunter tracking a wolf; he felt like a pike throwing itself onto a fish-hook.

He shouted to Relmyer: 'He knows this forest: it's he who's masterminding this chase, not us!'

Relmyer was not listening to him. He was noticing something else. The militiaman's horse was not up to the tactics of its rider, and was starting to show signs of fatigue. His own, on the other hand, neck stretched out and nostrils quivering, was eroding the distance that separated them. Margont was struggling not to be left behind; he was not experienced in chasing people on horseback. The branches whipped his face, confusing him, while the bushes murdered his legs and the flanks of his horse. Relmyer, paying no heed to these inconveniences, brandished his sabre, promise of devastating retribution.

The terrain was now gently sloping, which meant the horses speeded up. The fugitive manoeuvred his horse between obstacles. He suddenly cut off to the right, abandoning the path to head into an entanglement of little bushes. The vegetation swallowed him up. It was an astonishing choice of route: on the path beyond there were fewer obstructions and so it was much faster. Relmyer continued on straight. Margont chose to follow the tracks of the runaway to close the trap. In spite of his advantages, the man was slowing down. Relmyer left the path in his turn and gained on him. He came level with him fifteen paces to his left. He was going to overtake him and cut off his route when the militiaman and his horse seemed to subside, as though the ground had given way beneath them. The slope he had been descending had suddenly become much steeper. Relmyer was now looking down on the fugitive, who descended still further. Relmyer's horse reared. His frightened whinnying terrified the young hussar. Relmyer, clutching his reins, guessed rather than saw the danger. His mind could not interpret the chaos of images it was receiving: sky, trees, a rocky outcrop . . . Relmyer lost his balance and crashed into the stony ground. That was what saved his life. When the legs of his horse landed, one of them encountered the void. The beast toppled head first and crashed to the ground fifteen feet below. It rolled over, kicking up dead pine needles, and finished up against a tree trunk, its broken neck forming a right angle.

Margont's attention had been deflected. When he looked again at the man he was pursuing, he barely had time to duck. The man had stopped and, turned towards Margont, was aiming his pistol at him. He had chosen his moment to perfection, proof that everything had gone as he had planned. Margont tugged frantically on his reins. The ball struck his horse in the neck and it went sprawling on its side. Shaken by his fall, Margont was drowning in pain. He freed his sword and tried to get up, but collapsed, caught by one of his stirrups. His mount, in agony, vainly tried to get to its feet, trapping Margont on the ground, his right foot crushed by the struggling animal. He tried to free himself while brandishing his sword. He was not going to be taken like this! He thrashed about like a wild thing. The militiaman looked at him, hesitating. Had he had another pistol he could have finished off the wriggling worm. He had taken hold of his sabre, but worried that the captain might wound him with his sword.

The Austrian decided not to linger. There might be others following him as well. The man spurred on his horse. A stone ricocheted off a tree trunk nearby. Standing on top of the rocky outcrop, Relmyer was throwing stones at him, hoping to knock him out. Stones! Pathetic . . . Margont finally freed himself but a red-hot pain invaded his side. His wound had opened up.

CHAPTER 20

MARGONT was resting stretched out on some straw, his side in flames. Lefine came to sit down beside him. Margont watched him woozily. In preparation for being sewn up again he had been made to drink brandy and a concoction of laudanum, opium, cinnamon, cloves, wine and saffron. He was in a field hospital set up in a large farm in the village of Ebersdorf. All the wounded from Essling finished up here, either to recuperate or to die. The walls and the beams were impregnated with the odour of gangrene and blood. Even months later, the place would smell of death, haunted by those who had perished there.

Margont tapped his friend's knee.

'Thank you! Without you I'd still be there waiting for help.'

'That would have been what you deserved! You galloped off like furies; several times I nearly lost you. Happily your route was not difficult to follow with all those broken branches and trampled bushes.'

'We really almost got him.'

'No, he almost got you! Groups of militia were circling the front line from north to south. They were crossing the Danube in boats or by ford or by the bridges that are still standing, to come and support the partisans who were already at our backs. Everyone knew that, but no! Relmyer and you, you're always deaf to such things. A fine result, in truth!'

Seeing Margont's grimaces of pain, Lefine took pity on him and held out his water bottle.

'A drop of wine from the Wachau?'

Margont drank almost half of it.

'That Austrian officer is definitely the murderer we've been looking for, Fernand. Not only did Relmyer recognise him, but also he deliberately fired at Relmyer before dashing off without giving any thought to the battle. He only mingled with the soldiers for one purpose: to kill Relmyer. And he would be dead had his horse not raised its head at that moment.'

'The Wasp was saved by flies . . . Yes, you're right. But I don't quite understand what was going on . . .'

'Neither do I. Let's sum up what we know and try to see more clearly. First of all, I don't think our man is a professional soldier. A professional fighter would have tried to finish me off. He was not sure of succeeding even though I was injured on the ground and caught up in my stirrup. By the same token, when he did fire at me I was only a few feet away from him. He could have aimed at me but he preferred to make sure of his shot by wiping out my horse. He's good with a rifle but not so good with a pistol.'

'But over half the soldiers in the militia are originally from the regular army. They come directly from the army or, more often, they are veterans or have been invalided out.'

'He's too young to be a veteran, called back to service. As for being an invalid, right at this moment that applies to me more than to him . . .'

'Maybe he is a professional soldier but a non-combatant. An officer in charge of supplies, or a penpusher . . .'

Margont was feeling more and more groggy. The pain, like his thoughts, was becoming less sharp, more diffuse. Sometimes the pain would come rushing back, making him clench his teeth and clarifying his reasoning, setting off glimmers of clear-sightedness in a fog of blurred thoughts.

'No. If he had served in the regular army, he would have followed it at the end of 1805, when it was marching against us. But he was definitely in Vienna then because Albert Lietz and Ernst Runkel disappeared at that time, one of them in August, and the other in October. That means that there are several arguments pointing in one direction: our man is a civilian who enrolled in the militia. But he is an officer, either a lieutenant or a captain.'

'Monarchies are keen on preserving the social hierarchy. Other officers of the Landwehr and the Volunteer force come from Viennese high society; they're aristocrats, rich bourgeois, high-ranking functionaries . . .'

'We're progressing! When one is lucky enough to be one of these "important people", one can easily be tracked down. Perhaps our man is keen on hunting. That would explain his aptitude with a rifle and why he knows the forests round about here so perfectly. Did you interrogate the prisoners?'

'They are as mute as carp. We captured fifty of them. Soldiers of the Landwehr of Lower Austria, and Viennese Volunteers.'

Margont shifted all the time, trying to find a less painful position.

'We have to find out as much as possible about these two types of troops. Our man wore a particular uniform.'

'I noticed that. Infantrymen are issued only with ill-cut grey overcoats with red facings they have to sew on themselves. Some of them don't even have those and have to use their own coats. That devil of a man you chased after had a magnificent grey regulation coat with impeccable scarlet facings. But that would be the case for most officers of the Landwehr and the Volunteer regiments.'

Margont could not hide his disappointment.

'So his uniform tells us nothing about him. Which units did we confront?'

'At least two companies, one was the 3rd Battalion of the Landwehr of Lower Austria, and the other was the 2nd Battalion of the Viennese Volunteer force.'

'So our man is an officer in one of those two battalions?' Margont pulled himself up immediately. 'Unless he was wearing a fake uniform – although that doesn't seem possible because how would he have justified that to his superiors? – or he was accompanying the battalions but didn't serve in either of them. He's so tricky that you would expect him to have covered his tracks yet again. He knows the woods so well that he could have convinced the two companies to take him along as a guide to help them organise the ambush.'

'While you're waiting for an orderly to be free to stitch you up, I will go and find out what I can. According to the last estimates, Austria has lined up more than a hundred thousand militia. And to that they have added the Volunteer regiments. So their lieutenants and captains can be counted in their thousands . . . The man we're looking for lives in Vienna or nearby. The militias are organised by region. A priori, he must therefore serve in the Viennese Landwehr, in the Landwehr of Lower Austria or in the Viennese Volunteer regiment. Let's begin by finding out about the two battalions that attacked us. That will already be a start.'

Margont racked his brain for an idea, for a new approach.

'If we succeed in convincing one of the prisoners to give us the names of the officers of the two battalions . . .'.

'I don't think they'll even know them. The Landwehr was hurriedly thrown together in June 1808. A hundred thousand militiamen had to be organised in under a year. As for the Viennese Volunteers, that's an old formation that has disappeared and been resurrected regularly since 1797. It's made up of civilian volunteers who were exempt from serving in the Landwehr. The Viennese Volunteer force hastily re-formed on 1 March while we were marching on Vienna. Most have been soldiers for only three months and they are even more confused about this war than anyone else. Did you notice, several of them didn't even open fire during the attack, because certain regiments of Austrian hussars also wear green pelisses. They took Relmyer's hussars for Austrians and they shouted at them to stop fighting; it was a misunderstanding!'

Margont sat up and was overcome by a wave of pain, which jerked him sharply out of his alcoholic haze.

'So how is it possible? We are relentlessly looking for someone and they turn up in front of us, as if by magic! Where is Relmyer? I want to talk to him – oh, yes! I would be grateful if you would bring him here.'

*

Relmyer had been wearing himself out trying to extract information from the prisoners, but in vain. When he came to see Margont with Lefine, his face cleared.

'You seem to have recovered already.'

'Lukas, you must take us for imbeciles!' retorted Margont. 'It's absolutely unthinkable that this was a coincidence! Someone betrayed us by telling our man the route that we were going to take.'

Relmyer blinked at this reception.

'If it wasn't a coincidence, well . . . there must have been a leak . . . Perhaps one of my hussars mentioned it to someone . . .'

'He's lying to us,' Lefine told Margont.

Margont suddenly made the link between two apparently unrelated events and everything became clear. He pointed furiously at Relmyer.

'It's you who betrayed us. This expedition came about in exactly the same way as your duel with Piquebois. Antoine is fiercesome with a sabre, so you knowingly launched a risky attack. Thinking you had made an error, he dodged and launched his own attack. Antoine could not pass up such an opportunity to triumph! His attack obliged him to expose himself in his turn and your riposte hit him. Your first attack, which put you in danger, was solely intended to incite your opponent to act. So, you launch your second attack and the biter is bit; your opponent collapses, skewered. You arranged it so that the man we're tracking learnt that you were going to lead an expedition into hostile territory. That journey through the forest was your "first attack". It led your adversary to show himself in order to try to kill you, which permitted you to counterattack.'

'It's true,' admitted Relmyer. 'I have been preparing the plan for several weeks, even before I met you. It's what I call "the tactic of the false weakness". It worked! We've seen him again, I sparred with him!'

Margont flushed with anger. 'It was a suicidal tactic! We all nearly didn't make it!'

'I thought, I hoped, that he would try something, but how could I have guessed that he served in the militia and that he would throw himself on us with a crowd of soldiers?'

'Is that all that you have to say to justify that carnage?'

'No, that's not all I have to say in my defence!' stormed Relmyer. 'Certainly there could have been many deaths and it would have been my fault, but I could very well have been the first victim! I was the bait. I thought my hussars and you would be the hook, not a second worm. I gave myself a one in two chance of surviving his shot and that was the reason that I needed you! Had I been killed I would have died knowing that I was bequeathing the investigation to Pagin and to you two.'

Lefine was appalled. 'This man is insane!'

Relmyer persisted, supporting his discourse with great sweeping gestures, which were not normal for him.

'It has nothing to do with madness, it's mathematics! If your opponent is an exceptional horseman, attack him while he's having lunch at an inn! Everyone has a weak spot and that's where you have to strike him! The man I'm looking for is a remarkable defensive tactician. He hides his traces, never draws attention to himself . . . So I harassed him, irritated him with my provocations, more and more. Until his exasperation obliged him to seek a direct confrontation. I acted like a beater who makes so much noise to frighten the prey that he eventually leaves his hiding place. I forced him to attack and reveal himself, which was so different from his normal way of proceeding that he showed himself much less effective than usual. That's why the ambush was a big setback for him: badly prepared, badly organised and badly executed. On the other hand, as soon as our man returned to his favourite tactic – hiding in the forest, avoiding head-on confrontation, using treachery – he regained the upper hand. If you abandon me, I won't hold it against you, of course. Pagin and I will in the end flush this wolf out of the forest!'

'How did the man find out that you were looking for him? How did he know where to find us when?'

'I told you: I've been preparing my trap for a long time. I have been endlessly planting clues wherever I've been so that he understood that I had returned and was searching for him. I put little tin soldiers along approximately the path where he kidnapped me, in the ruined farm and around my old orphanage. Children's toys in the places that linked us: the message was clear. And then there was the ruckus I made at Lesdorf Orphanage, the official and unofficial complaints by Madame Blanken, the scene with the police and magistrates when I tracked them down in Vienna to complain about their incompetence . . . Everyone was talking about my return.'

Margont pressed his injured side so that the sharpened pain would chase away the effects of the alcohol again. Lefine, understanding what Margont was doing, shook his head, alarmed. Margont did not take his eyes off Relmyer.

'When I went with you to explore that ruined farm, it had been burnt down. Apart from the fact that he wanted to burn any possible evidence, it was his response to your provocations. He was letting you know that he had received your message loud and clear, that it was in your interest to abandon your search and that, if you continued, you would end up like Franz and Wilhelm! He was trying to scare you.'

'At first, I was shocked,' conceded Relmyer. 'But then I was happy! My plan was working, the man was starting to panic.'

'The scene you made at the ball was all part of your plan!'

'Absolutely. And I also left a tin soldier on poor Wilhelm's freshly dug grave.'

Relmyer's assured façade was crumbling. Another facet of his personality started to show through the tatters.

'What choice did I have? To sit on the terrace of a *Kaffeehaus* on the Graben, sampling the coffees all day and hoping to see him pass by? No, I had to force him into an error, and to do that I had to lower my guard. Yes, I almost got myself killed, but see how we have progressed, thanks to my plan. Now we know that he serves in the militia and that he's an officer! I'm going to find out all about the Landwehr and the Viennese Volunteer regiments! And all that in addition to the clues we might find in the registers . . .'

'Ah yes, the registers, let's talk about those properly! What exactly was that report that threw us into the lion's mouth. Is it a fake?'

'Of course it's a fake! I suspected as much. It was too good to be true. Vienna is crawling with spies and Austrian sympathisers, and we know our man sometimes crosses over to our side of the line. He must have asked one of his acquaintances to find out about me. He learnt that I was spending my days in the Kriegsministerium. It was even easier to discover since I was doing everything possible to make it known. Obviously he must have understood that I was on the trail of the registers. All he had to do was make up that false letter . . . I can only dare to hope that he wrote it himself: but all the same he wouldn't make us a present of his handwriting.'

'How did he get it into the Kriegsministerium?'

Relmyer lowered his gaze. 'I didn't find it there, in fact. A Viennese man sold it to me. He claimed to work for the army and to have stolen a heap of documents just before Vienna fell to the French. He said he wanted to make money selling them to the French. According to him, he was keeping a watch on everyone who went into the Kriegsministerium, trying to find out what they wanted and seeing if that corresponded with what he possessed: maps, reports, files on officers, inventories, the layouts of fortified buildings . . . I offered him a tidy sum in exchange for a dozen letters relating to the Austrian army. Only the one I showed you had any bearing on our case. The Viennese man must have been hand in glove with our murderer. Unfortunately the murderer used an intermediary. I know that because while I was launching my expedition, two of my hussars, who were discreetly following the Viennese fellow, grabbed him to interrogate him. He described the individual who had contacted him and paid him to make sure I received the false letters. The description did not tally at all with the man we're looking for. Alas, it has not been possible to identify him.

I turned in the charlatan to the general staff. If he really does possess confidential documents, our marshals will be very interested by what they find at his house.'

Relmyer did not care about the war. His remark was merely an attempt to placate Margont and Lefine, but it failed dismally.

'It was a dirty trap!' responded Margont. 'You knew it: that's why you pretended that you found the document yourself. It looks as if our adversary did not even bother to finesse this story of the trade in stolen documents. I believe that he suspected that you had guessed that it was just a trap! It's as though together you had agreed a sort of rendezvous! The two of you, you agreed to play the game! And you, Lukas, you even limited the size of your escort so as not to dissuade him from attacking.'

Relmyer rapidly assessed these words.

'I don't know if he knew that I was a willing victim of his trap. But your friend Piquebois had definitely spotted that my first attack was intended to incite him to act. He believed that his assault would prevail anyway.'

Lefine concluded, exasperated: 'And here you are, all in disarray except for our enemy. Lieutenant Relmyer, you have manipulated us since the beginning because you knew that we would oppose your tactic of the earthworm on the fish-hook!'

Relmyer could not justify himself any further. He turned away from them.

'I am truly sorry. But I would do it all again if I had the chance. I will leave you. I'm going to Mazenau, even though I'm sure that Johann Grich is an invention of our murderer. But you never know. In any case, this business is nearly over one way or the other.'

Saying this, he left. Outside three duels were waiting for him, three possible deaths.

CHAPTER 21

THE two élite hussars were waiting in the sun. NCO Cauchoit had unsheathed his sabre and was amusing himself using it to reflect light into the faces of the passing soldiers. Oh, if only he could annoy one of them into challenging him! But no. They hurried past, pursued by the light, or they let their retinas burn gently, pretending not to notice anything. Cauchoit was having fun when Relmyer came out of the hospital.

'I'm not waiting any longer, Officer!'

'Where has your companion gone?' queried Relmyer in surprise.

The NCO glowed, like his blade.

'I laid that pretentious hussar of the 5th out cold while we were waiting for you. You must have seen his stretcher-bearers as you came out. Let's fight here! What better place for a duel than a hospital?'

He was almost in ecstasy. Like a lover on the point of climaxing with his sabre.

'Victory at first blood?' he proposed.

Relmyer nodded. Yet he had heard that Cauchoit was a sudden death expert. Of the nine 'first blood' duels that he was known for, seven had ended abruptly with the death of his opponent (and this figure assumed that the hussar of the 5th Regiment was going to survive). He was nicknamed 'the widow-maker' . . . Cauchoit had the falsely innocent cruelty of a little boy who finds it funny to throw the cat in the fire.

He took off his pelisse and his dolman and held them out to his friend, the trumpeter, who willingly played the role of coat-stand. Every gifted duellist seemed to have a beatific disciple, a Pagin. Relmyer put his belongings in a wagon stained with dried blood. The sharp sunshine made the white of their shirts dazzling. Cauchoit talked all the time he was warming up, trying to unsettle Relmyer. He mentioned his past successes, hinted that Relmyer was a coward . . . For him the duel had already started: his comments were his first strokes.

Relmyer was not listening to him. He found himself in an internal turmoil with which he was all too familiar. His past resurfaced and invaded him, like black water flooding brutally inside him. A man stood opposite and wished him harm. The features of Franz's executioner imposed themselves on Cauchoit's face. This confusion of identities, of time, of histories and general contexts generated a hellish chaos in Relmyer's mind. He was terrified of seeing the man triumph anew and walk away to commit other crimes; the idea obsessed him. He had reached the point where he was no longer paying any attention to what was happening around him, to the extent that he felt he was in a sort of corridor, his only exit blocked by an enemy. Relmyer felt the irrepressible conviction grow in him that he must vanquish this man so that he could escape this tunnel, rejoin the world and resume normal life. It was as if his opponent were the stone in the cellar, which he had to make fall in order to free himself.

Relmyer had to control this whirlwind of emotions and to do this he had his blade, which hid an entire universe. The teaching he had followed, the training sessions, his reflections on the meaning of violence, the ability of mathematics to express the most apparently confusing phenomena in the simplest terms: all these interacted to channel the forces jostling within him. Anger, sadness, rancour, rage, anguish, hate, dismay, painful memories and unresolved grief: he managed once again to make all these currents converge towards one aim. To annihilate his opponent. Cauchoit temporarily became the focus of all his suffering.

Cauchoit strutted gracefully, the beautiful embodiment of death.

'I find there is something of the chicken about you,' he taunted Relmyer. 'The way you ran away after we were attacked by the grey mice of the Landwehr reminds me of the stampede in the poultry yard when a fox appears. I would wager that your blood has the ruby colour of pigeon blood!'

Relmyer saluted him with his sabre. Cauchoit responded in the same way, then immediately lunged, trying to stab Relmyer in the side, clashed with Relmyer's weapon and withdrew for fear of a counterattack. A simple test that he judged conclusive. Then he charged at Relmyer. In response to this head-on tactic, Relmyer produced a complex compound attack. He pretended to parry a lunge to the throat but at the last minute dodged and feinted towards Cauchoit's chest to threaten his left shoulder. Cauchoit, caught short, beat a retreat.

Relmyer immediately unleashed a frenetic succession of assaults: attacks, composite attacks, false attacks, attacks to the left side, whipped strokes, feints, jabs, false parries, beats, ripostes, parries, unexpected sequences . . . He aimed for one side, then the other, the waist, the head, the throat, the side again, the thigh, the right wrist, the left hand . . . Relmyer seemed to be able to do whatever he wanted. During his duel with Piquebois, he had studied his tactics. He had, as it were, ingested them and now reproduced them in his own way. Cauchoit, disconcerted, uselessly parried a false attack to the abdomen and received a circular blow full on the temple, which landed him in the dust.

He got up immediately, put his hand to his head and looked at his bloody palm.

'It's nothing! What a relief! I thought for a moment I was bleeding.'

Fury made his cut inaccurate. Relmyer dodged and plunged his sabre into Cauchoit's thigh, pitching him for a second time to the ground.

'You can see it better now, Monsieur?'

The trumpeter Sibot looked at his friend writhing in pain but the sight made no sense to him. He persisted in thinking that even though he could see Cauchoit on the ground, in reality it was Relmyer who had been defeated. He took several seconds to take in the true situation. And then hesitation gave way to raw violence. Sibot thrust the point of his sword in the direction of Relmyer's face, bounding forward like a cat. Had he hit his target, the first blood would have been Relmyer's, flowing from his burst eye, and at the same time from his brain. But Relmyer had been sharpening his reflexes for a long time and he was able to parry the blow even when his adversary's blade had already almost completely obscured his vision. He counterattacked immediately, thrusting his sabre into the musician's shoulder. The bone cracked, blood spurted, the man collapsed and Relmyer found himself motionless, bespattered and dazed, alarmed by his uncontrollable capacity to trigger violence all around him.

Stretcher-bearers hastily gathered up the two élite troopers.

Margont noticed the agitated throng pass in front of him and disappear into the little room where he himself had been sewn up. The floor was roughly flagged. After a few operations and one or two amputations, the accumulated blood was sluiced away with large bucketfuls of water.

Margont and Lefine were silent a moment, amazed at what had happened.

'When Relmyer is not chasing after death, it's death that comes to him,' concluded Lefine, finally.

Shortly afterwards the figure of Antoine Piquebois appeared framed in the entrance. Four hussars of the 8th Regiment accompanied him. They were friends from his old regiment with only one desire: to convince him to become a hussar again. To them, their friend's invalidity was because he was not thinking straight, not for any physical reason. They surrounded Margont and Lefine.

'Don't tell me that you all want to fight a duel with Relmyer!' said Margont, irritated.

'Not at all. We're not at his level, alas,' Piquebois reassured him. 'Dear friend, I've heard all about your chase and your wound . . . You know how I love horses. No beast understands man better! Between man and horse a harmony can be established that . . .'

Words failed him. There was a gap in his discourse right there where he would have liked to express the heart of it. A tic played at his lips.

'All right, if no one understood what I was trying to say, let him learn to ride a horse. But there is one particular case – just one! – where an event transcends our love of horses.'

'One particular case, just one!' echoed the hussars.

'It's when the first horse is killed under you in combat! In God's name, that's a baptism! It's like the first girl one beds!'

Piquebois and his companions produced goblets they had been hiding behind their backs. A warrant officer held one out to Margont.

Piquebois, joyously excited, shouted: 'In honour of the first horse killed under my friend Captain Margont!'

Everyone emptied their goblets, the warrant officer clinking for two people since Margont refused his glass.

'You're all stupid!' exclaimed Margont. 'I was almost killed, I . . . Oh, get out! Go on!'

Piquebois and his companions went on their way, laughing. They were young and there was a war on: life was sweet. That was the way they saw the world . . . In spite of the shooting pains travelling through his battered body, Margont turned to Lefine.

'Why am I surrounded by idiots?'

'It's because you attract them, damn it!'

'Listen to me: Jean-Quenin thinks I will be able to leave hospital the day after tomorrow, so I'll leave this evening. That will be good enough; he is always too cautious. Go and see our major and tell him from me to make sure Antoine doesn't leave our regiment; he can tell him that he's putting him on guard or that there's going to be an inspection of the company, or anything at all that will keep him there . . . Because otherwise the malady of our friend Antoine, the "hussar manqué", will recur and we will have two Relmyers for the price of one. Can you also find me a new horse and keep me informed about the prisoners? If one of them finally decides to talk . . .'

Lefine sniggered. 'Isn't it enough for you, all that's already happened?'

'No!' persisted Margont. 'It would take a great deal more than that to make me give up.'

'For heaven's sake! At the rate things are going, you'll soon have your "great deal more"!'

But Margont was no longer listening. Luise had just arrived in the company of a hussar that Relmyer had sent to inform her what had happened. She was in tears and the man had to point out Margont before she spotted him. She crossed the room, lifting her pale blue dress slightly, but the bloodstains had still accumulated at the bottom and were gradually creeping up the azure material. She stopped in front of him.

'Is it serious?'

'No, it's nothing.'

'Why did you let yourself get wounded?'

She leant over him. Margont thought she was going to kiss him, but she slapped him hard.

'Idiot!'

She immediately left as the wounded soldiers guffawed. Lefine shrugged his shoulders philosophically.

'There are some days when everything goes badly and others when things go even worse . . .'

CHAPTER 22

By 11 June Margont had recovered. Lefine was regularly absent pursuing his research, and Relmyer was still spending all his time ferreting through the archives of the Kriegsministerium. They were all to meet up in a café on the Graben to take stock.

Margont, the first to arrive, already had three empty cups in front of him when Lefine joined him, accompanied by Relmyer, whom he had gone to uproot from his world of papers. Pagin was not far behind, of course; he followed Relmyer like a shadow. Relmyer was his mentor, the ideal older brother he had never had.

They all ordered coffee while they waited for Luise, who was also to join them. The ambience was noisy and smoky. The *Kaffeehaus* was always full. Soldiers gathered there in spite of the high prices. Prostitutes sat on their laps and hung round their necks wearing daringly low-cut dresses, which they lifted to show off their legs. They roared with laughter when the men fought over them. Some drunken infantrymen came in, loudly calling for wine, and went angrily off again when they discovered there was none left. The owner and his sons hardly knew which way to turn.

'Before we begin, I'd like to give you something,' Relmyer announced.

Give them something? Lefine looked expectant. He still

remembered the cascade of gold that had fallen from Relmyer's hand onto the desk of the clerk at the Ministry of War. Relmyer lined up three tin soldiers on the table. The figurines, horsemen painted in three colours, seemed to challenge the coffee cups.

'To me they are much, much more than toys. They represent our "soldiers' oath". After the inquiry into Franz's death was abandoned, Luise, some friends from Lesdorf and I swore never to renounce the hunt for Franz's assassin. I organised the ceremony – a secret meeting in the dead of night, in one of our bedrooms. To seal our pact I had the idea of using tin soldiers. Seven of us swore the oath.'

'Where are the five others?' asked Lefine.

Relmyer's voice became halting and bitter.

'I lost track of two of them. One of the others serves as an NCO in the Austrian army. The two remaining ones are here in Vienna. I went to find them. They told me they considered that the saga no longer concerns them. One of them even said that our "soldiers' oath" was the fantasy of a handful of angry boys. He added, "Today we are adults." Well? What do you think? Am I just a child who hasn't managed to grow up?'

His explanation lent new meaning to the figurines.

'That's why I chose the tin soldiers to signal my presence – so that our man would notice me. They are testimony to my determination never to give up.'

Pagin picked one up and brandished it in front of his face. Margont took one as well. The object was heavy, and weighed down by the oath associated with it. Lefine took the last one, although to him it was all a kind of game rather than a real pledge.

'I bought them for you,' continued Relmyer. 'I wanted to retrieve the ones from my former friends but they had lost them or thrown them away. Only Luise kept hers, in her drawing room.'

'She even added some of her own, perhaps to compensate for those she felt had disappeared with the other conspirators,' hazarded Margont.

'To think that as soon as I came back I went to find them and not Luise! Now that that has been sorted out, let's see where we are. Luise is late, but I can't wait any more.'

Margont related his discussion with Lefine in the hospital. Relmyer said that so far he had not obtained any results, either at the Kriegsministerium or following his interrogation of the man who had stolen the archive material. Although military documents had been found at his house and the general staff were studying those, large sums of money earned from his illicit trade had also been found. As for Johann Grich of Mazenau, he most certainly did not exist, nor had Pagin been able to find out anything about the disappearance of the young boys supposedly killed in battle.

'I have news!' Lefine announced proudly. 'Our man serves in the Viennese Volunteer regiment. One of the prisoners finally talked! He revealed that it was an officer of the Viennese Volunteers who planned that attack. But he does not know his name or his battalion.'

'What do you mean, someone talked?' Relmyer was annoyed. 'I ask every day and I'm always told there's no news!'

'That's because the men who interrogate the prisoners will

never reveal what they learn to you,' replied Lefine. 'They suspect you of being a traitor. You are of Austrian origin, and it's you who led that expedition that was almost annihilated. If Major Batichut and your colonel had not sprung to your defence, in this current climate, you would have been interrogated yourself by the officers charged with the struggle against the partisans.'

Once more, Relmyer felt betrayed. There were so few people ready to help him that they could all be gathered together round a café table, a derisory fragment of the world.

'If our man really serves in the Viennese Volunteers and not in the Landwehr,' continued Lefine, 'that gives us several clues about him. The Landwehr is a militia created by Archduke Charles when the Austrian army, like so many others, began to be puffed with pride. Service in the Landwehr is obligatory between eighteen and forty-five, with a great many exceptions stipulated in the regulations: invalids, students, people indispensable to the smooth functioning of society – teachers, different kinds of merchants, policemen, administrative employees, doctors . . . The principle of volunteer regiments is to incorporate at the last moment the largest possible number of those exempt from service in the Landwehr.'

Margont rejoiced. 'Conclusion: there is every chance that our man has a job that exempts him from serving in the militia. But whatever he does is not enough to excuse him from the Volunteers. He's an officer and we know that he is probably not a military man by training. So why does he have such a high rank? Because he's a personality: a big landowner, a noble, a high-ranking administrative official . . .'

Margont's face lit up as he spoke. He was pursuing this inquiry with tenacity, refusing to become discouraged, and he was jubilant at every step forward.

'Perhaps he works at the Ministry of War? That way he would personally have access to the military registers. If not, if he is a high-ranking administrator he will have contacts: his position must have helped him ensure that someone manipulated the lists of regimental losses. Fernand, we must find out the exact causes for exemption from service in the Landwehr.'

'Alas, that's impossible. The Austrians have not left us such a document.'

'How many Viennese Volunteer regiments are there?'

'There are six battalions of six to nine hundred men. The sixth, so nine hundred soldiers, participated in the defence of Vienna and was finished off when the city fell, so forget them. In the three thousand five hundred Volunteers that remain, there must be a good one hundred subaltern officers.

'Why did he volunteer?' wondered Margont aloud.

'To defend his country . . .' Relmyer suggested.

'No, he doesn't care about his country. Look at the considerable efforts he's taken to commit his crimes. He devotes a large part of his time to preparing his kidnappings and afterwards, covering his tracks. I think his crimes are the only thing that really interests him in life.'

'So, it's to be able to attract his prey better to where he wants them. Like he tried to do with Wilhelm.'

'No. There's no need to be a soldier in order to pretend to be one. In my opinion, he was forced into the Volunteers. Or he joined up loudly declaring his "patriotism", or he would have had to seek new employment. So I think he's an important functionary.'

'That's speculation,' objected Relmyer.

'True. But we can state with certainty that he was not very patriotic during the ambush. He abandoned his men just after firing on you. Seeing the officer who had organised the ambush flee contributed to triggering the collapse of the Austrians. His action was solely personal, he couldn't give a fig about that battle.'

And neither could you, Lukas, Margont added to himself.

Everyone had delivered the information they had gathered and conversation petered out. Their investigation was stalling again and still Luise had not arrived. The war had, though. Everywhere soldiers were strolling: Bavarians who felt more affinity with the French than the Prussians, whose desire to take over the whole Germanic world was growing; Saxon infantrymen who joked with the French dragoons who had sabred them a few years earlier at the Battle of Iéna; officers striding with determination, avid to bound to the top of the hierarchy; artillerymen who talked too loudly because their cannon had gradually rendered them deaf . . . Margont could not believe how much the army had changed since 1805. Between 1805 and 1809 was but a short time, yet 1805 seemed to belong to a whole different era. At the time of Austerlitz, the French army had been made up of volunteer troops and hardened combatants. Now the allies – Italians, Saxons, Württembergers, Hessians, Bavarians, Polish . . . constituted an increasingly important part. And they had often previously been enemies. As for the number of French conscripts, they had become dangerously elevated in number. These soldiers, inexperienced and more or less motivated, replaced the veterans killed on the battlefield or mobilised for guerrilla warfare in Spain. The Empire depended on its army. Now Margont detected little fissures . . . and this re-awakened his fear of dying. That fear inhabited every soldier. You grew accustomed to it as best you could, but regularly, without warning, it overcame you. Margont reacted. He needed more life, immediately, even here!

'*Herr Ober!* Coffee, cream and patisseries!' he ordered.

'And some schnapps!' added Lefine.

The waiter brought them everything straight away, smiling to himself as he imagined the look on their faces when he presented them with the bill . . .

Luise finally arrived, accompanied by the two hussars whom Relmyer had ordered to protect Luise in this city full of soldiers. She did not reply to their greetings and put a piece of paper on the table in the middle of the cups and the crumbs.

'Here are the names of several people who maintain the register of effective Austrian soldiers. There are thirty-two of them.'

CHAPTER 23

THE days slipped by. Summer had succeeded spring, and the heat was becoming unbearable. The military climate, like a crystal goblet placed in the middle of the oven of these days of heat wave, was approaching the point at which it would explode into a titanic battle. Now Napoleon was spending his days reviewing his troops. By the same token he frequently inspected the bridges, worried that the Austrians might use their tactic of broken bridges that had been so successful at Essling. The bridges, impressive pieces of workmanship, were now all over the place, as though it had been necessary to build them ceaselessly in order to forget the constant collapse of the first ones. They linked the west bank of the Danube to the Isle of Lobau and to the neighbouring islands, and the islands to each other, weaving a sort of spider's web. Lampposts had even been installed on certain of the bridges, which were protected with landing stages on stilts upriver, fortifications loaded with cannon, troops, a flotilla of ten gunners and myriad little boats.

During this period Margont, Lefine, Relmyer, Pagin and Luise tried to find out a little more about the thirty-two suspects by questioning the reluctant Viennese prisoners. They hit so many obstacles that they gradually became discouraged. Relmyer was convinced that the assassin had tampered with the registers himself. So many names had been added that an accomplice would in the end have guessed what was going on, and who would agree to be associated with such ignominy? As a result, against Margont's advice, he began to strike off the names of those who manifestly could not be the murderer. He treated them like suspects who had been cleared; he saw everything in black and white, with no grey areas. What's more, if his hypothesis was not correct, there was a risk that their inquiry would fail, and Relmyer simply could not contemplate such a thing. He therefore persisted in hoping that one of the biographies and one of the descriptions tallied with what they knew about the assassin. And there was another problem. Their list of suspects was necessarily incomplete. Relmyer, knowing that, became more and more tense. The passage of time obsessed him, and at night he was on the verge of exasperation. According to him, no one was making progress fast enough. They met regularly in a café to review the situation, but even the café ambience no longer relieved their tension.

On 14 June, in Raab, Prince Eugène, won a great victory against Archduke John's forces and his Hungarian reinforcements. On 24 June, he defeated the Austrians again, supported this time by the Croatians. So Prince Eugène found himself free to join Napoleon. A short time later, the first elements of his army could be seen arriving. Day after day Eugène's divisions appeared. Each one was like a weight adding to Napoleon's side of the scales, tipping the balance more and more in his favour.

On 30 June, everyone was once again seated round a table in a Viennese café. Luise revealed what she had learnt about the various names on the list, but whatever she was able to tell them, it was never enough to satisfy Relmyer.

'In short, this Monsieur Liedel is married, has two children, brown hair and he lives in the Naglergasse,' he said, starting to lose his temper. 'Perfect. And so? We can't go and see him because he serves in the Viennese Volunteer force and is stationed on the other side of the Danube. He might be our man but equally he might not. That's the twelfth like that. They all work in the same ministry, they're all in the same boat, and in any case no one wants to talk to us about them because we serve in the French army!'

'Let's search their homes for a portrait,' proposed Lefine.

'I'm not sure . . .' demurred Relmyer doubtfully.

Having your portrait painted was a costly habit of the aristocracy or the bourgeoisie: not everyone did it. There was also another, much more intractable problem.

'If we act like that, I doubt we'll even get as far as the fifth house,' warned Margont. 'The inhabitants will complain about us, we'll be taken for looters, and shot. Perhaps with a little luck we'll only spend a few days in prison and we'll be released the day before the great battle . . .'

'I'd do it!' Pagin defied him.

Relmyer thanked the young hussar with a tap on the shoulder.

'Quentin is right. The confrontation is imminent, so the Emperor is being more respectful than ever to the Viennese.'

'We'll have to meet one of these men,' repeated Margont for the nth time.

'After all, they haven't all joined the army or fled the capital,' said Luise. 'We must surely be able to lay our hands on one of them.'

Margont scanned the list. Relmyer had covered it with his minute, angry handwriting, adding information and ink stains.

'Stop rereading the list endlessly!' he exploded.

Margont's forefinger indicated a name: Konrad Sowsky.

'That one is crossed off!' Relmyer declared angrily. 'We're not progressing fast enough: must you keep going back over the same things?' As Margont's forefinger was still indicating the man, he added: 'That's not our man, Sowsky is obese.'

'Yes, I know that's the reason you've struck him off,' replied Margont. 'But how obese is he?'

Relmyer stared at him as though he were mad. Luise intervened.

'He must weigh much more than a hundred kilos. I was able to talk to his wife and to certain of his neighbours who described him to me. They told me that Sowsky moves with extreme difficulty and that he gets breathless very easily.'

'Therefore it's impossible that he's our man,' Relmyer repeated.

'Just as it's impossible that he serves in the Viennese Volunteer force and that he is with the Austrian army, contrary to what his wife claimed to you, Luise. No Volunteer battalion would accept an invalid into its ranks. He must have stayed in Vienna!'

CHAPTER 24

THE house was small, squashed between two much larger buildings; an insignificant dwelling in a modest district. While Relmyer repeatedly hammered on the door, Margont turned to Lefine and Pagin.

'Fernand, go and take a casual look round. You, Pagin, make sure none of the neighbours leave, otherwise one of them might attract the attention of the gendarmes. But no brutality!'

Finally the door was opened by an Austrian woman with black hair streaked with grey pulled back in a chignon. She stood in the doorway, barring entry.

Luise spoke to her softly: 'Do you remember me, Frau Sowsky? Luise Mitterburg. I came the day before yesterday to ask you about your husband.'

'He's not here, I told you.'

'I can vouch for these two officers.'

'He's here and we're coming in,' cut in Relmyer in an uncompromising tone. 'We would like to talk to him.'

Madame Sowsky gave in, seeing that it was useless to annoy the hussar any further by defending the lost cause of her lie . . . Her husband was easy to find. He was sitting in the gloom in his bedroom, the coolest place in the house. As Margont's eye fell on him, he felt immense pity. His wife was over forty years old, but how old was he? It was impossible to tell. His excessive fat stretched his skin, filling out the grooves of his wrinkles. His protuberant stomach was literally crushing him in his armchair, and his legs, swollen and reddened with oedema, were putting him on the rack. He must have weighed a hundred and eighty kilos.

'He's ill, like his father before him,' sobbed his wife. 'Shame on you! May God strike you down!'

'We won't stay long,' Margont told her tactfully.

Relmyer stared at the suffering man. His own pain was just as intense, even if it was much less visible. It was a little like looking in a mirror – the body in front of him was a reflection of his spirit. This bitter thought increased his aggression.

'Herr Sowsky, I want to speak to you about the army registers,' he announced menacingly in German.

The man smiled. 'Your accent is impeccable. You're Austrian?'

These few words were enough to exhaust him. His obesity was slowly strangling him, compressing his lungs. Relmyer was going to continue when Sowsky waved a languid hand.

'It's no use! I am a patriot, Monsieur, and you are a traitor. Torture me, kill me if you like – that will hardly be an effort for you as I'm already dead – but I will never talk.'

His face was becoming purple, the price of having spoken so many words. But Sowsky had something more to say. He raised his arm: 'Long live Austria!'

His wife, in spite of her anguish, looked at them defiantly.

'Do you know why he works at the Kriegsministerium? It's because his health prevented him from becoming a soldier. You can cut me up in front of his eyes, he won't say anything and I, I will shout at him to remain silent.'

Margont was disorientated by the turn of the conversation.

'No one is going to torture anyone. The military registers have been falsified. Names have been added to the list of losses but the people added, young boys, have never served in the regiments in question. I'm talking about the Infanterie-regimenter 9, 20, 23, 29 and 49, and the Viennese Volunteer Chasseurs. We only want to know the name of the employee responsible for that.'

Sowsky said nothing, but his face, now attentive rather than stubborn, gave him away. The manipulation had been discovered and Sowsky knew about it. The seconds ticked slowly by, like the passing of time before a rolling coin falls on its side. The coin landed on the wrong side.

'I won't tell you anything. The affair was discovered weeks ago . . .'

He had to pause to catch his breath. So the document that Relmyer had searched so hard for in the Kreigsministerium did exist. However, Relmyer would never succeed in finding it. On the other hand, he was in the presence of someone who had read the letter or whatever it was that had been spoken of.

'An inquiry has been started,' went on Sowsky with difficulty. 'It was interrupted by the war but, after the retreat of your army, the investigation will be taken up again.'

'I'm sure there's a suspect! What's his name?' shouted Relmyer.

'I've forgotten.'

Obviously he was lying.

Relmyer tried to control himself. How far would he go in order to oblige the man to speak? To resolve his quest was he going to become a disgusting executioner like the murderer he was tracking?

Margont spoke in measured tones. There was already enough tension in the room without adding to it.

'Did you ask why these falsifications took place? Do you know what happened to the young men concerned?'

Sowsky did not answer. Yes, he had asked himself that question several times. Like all honest functionaries, cheating appalled him.

'They were assassinated,' continued Margont.

Relmyer did not move. Sowsky's eyes turned away. He had not imagined anything so atrocious. He had thought that the young men were rogues trying to escape justice by passing themselves off as war deaths.

Relmyer went over to him and murmured: 'My name is Lukas Relmyer. Relmyer: that name was almost added to those other "errors".'

Margont held out the list of suspects. 'Please tell us who he is.'

Sowsky hesitated for a long time. Finally he spoke.

'He's not on your list. Because he was fired the very day it was discovered that he was behind the manipulations whose significance we did not know. He claimed he was innocent. After the end of the war, he will be summoned before a military tribunal. His name is Hermann Teyhern.'

'What does he look like?' Relmyer pressed him.

'I never met him. I have only worked on the army registers for a short while.'

'Is he in the Viennese Volunteer regiment?'

'All that I heard about him is that he lives in the village of Leiten.'

Relmyer thanked him and left precipitately. Now that they had the wolf's den, the hunt could begin.

CHAPTER 25

RELMYER hastily assembled a new detachment of hussars, but this time they skirted round the forest.

The village of Leiten was on the top of a hill and slid towards a valley carpeted with fields. Teyhern's house was set apart, isolated by a large wood. Relmyer and his men encircled it.

The vast stone building dominated a courtyard enclosed by a wall. All the shutters were closed, giving the place the appearance of a fortress. Relmyer took hold of the axe fixed to the saddle of his mount. He was going to smash in a window near the door, but Margont advised him to choose one at the back. Relmyer obeyed and attacked the shutters with force, creating a noisy shower of splintered wood.

When he went into the house, he was struck by a sharp anguish. The gloom reminded him of the forest in which he had almost been killed. He crossed the room in a flash, bumping into armchairs, not taking the time to accustom his eyes to the darkness, and opened one of the other windows. He could not repress a cry. In the salon thus revealed hung the portrait of the man for whom he had been searching for so long. The painting, which was small, decorated one of the walls, in the midst of some landscapes.

The picture brought back the memory of his kidnapping. He allowed himself to believe that the man was standing in front of him. An abyss opened up inside him, but Relmyer refused to look away. It was another ordeal that he inflicted on himself, yet more training to reassure himself that he was ready. He walked up to the portrait, and stared at those motionless blue eyes, holding the gaze that seemed so lifelike.

The soldiers went through the house and its surroundings from top to bottom. But they found nothing. The absence of feminine clothes indicated that Teyhern was a bachelor. He owned two rifles displayed on a rack. The rooms were tastefully furnished: pictures, French furniture, marquetry chests, Turkish carpets, porcelain or crystal vases . . . Relmyer went four times to the cellar, obsessed with the idea that a young boy was dying there, in a recess that they had not noticed. He tapped the walls to see if they concealed a hiding place, looked for a trap door leading to a second cellar, opened a barrel that contained only wine . . .

Then he returned to the salon, on the way moodily knocking into Pagin, who had not seen him. He let himself drop into a Louis XV armchair, just opposite the portrait, his legs stretched straight out in front of him.

'I'm going to wait for him here,' he announced. 'For five more years, if necessary.'

Margont was keen to think through all the hypotheses and rank them, as an entomologist would classify insects into species and subspecies.

'This could be the man's house, but it might not be. If—'

Relmyer, leaning his elbows on the arms of the chair, gesticulated. 'We've got his portrait and the business with the registers! A portrait is personal; you don't go giving them to your friends!'

'Well, quite. I've also verified that there's no indication of any break-in other than ours. So the assassin did not come in here secretly and put that picture on the wall.'

Relmyer looked at him in fury. They were almost there! Why bother with all this speculation? Margont lifted the portrait and the other pictures, trying to see whether the parts of the wall underneath, protected from the light and dust, corresponded exactly to the outlines of the pictures. This examination was inconclusive and only succeeded in enraging Relmyer further. The artist had not signed the painting. It must have been done by a little-known artist who would be impossible to find.

Margont proposed something else: 'I'm going to show this portrait to the neighbours to confirm that it really is Teyhern.'

'No!' said Relmyer. 'I'm going to wait here to ambush him. If we question the neighbours, we'll be noticed. Someone will warn him that the French are after him and know where he lives. It's imperative that Teyhern does not know that we have identified him.'

Lefine was of the same opinion.

He added: 'In any case, we have already seen with Sowsky and his wife how difficult it is for us to learn anything at all from the Austrians. The villagers will say that they don't know Teyhern, whether it's him or not . . .'

For the first time for five years, Relmyer felt a real sense of tranquillity take hold of him.

'I'm in his lair! He will come back here, perhaps before the great battle, perhaps afterwards. And if he dies in combat, I will hunt out his body, even if I have to dig up a hundred thousand Austrians in public graves!'

'Wait here?' ventured Pagin. 'But, Lieutenant, you can't abandon your regiment. You'll be accused of desertion . . .'

'Exactly. That's why I'm going to stay on my own.'

Pagin was on the verge of tears. His role model was collapsing in front of his eyes! Relmyer was a lieutenant at twenty, and already famous thanks to his prowess with a sabre. General Lasalle, that mythical hero, had come to seek him out to cross blades with him in friendly fashion. Lasalle had applauded when Relmyer had hit him – without hurting him – for the third consecutive time. His colonel, Laborde, expected him to be promoted to the rank of captain of the élite force at the end of the campaign. And Relmyer was abandoning everything! For something that happened so long ago! Pagin could not understand it at all. He wanted to run at the portrait, to brandish it and smash it on the floor. In a sudden flash of intuition he realised that Relmyer was sitting rigidly to prevent himself from dashing at the portrait.

So he exclaimed: 'I'll stay with you, Lieutenant! I'll kill him! I won't miss, I swear it. By Christ, I'll skewer him and disembowel his body just to be sure!'

Relmyer shook his head, imperturbable.

'You can't sacrifice everything!' Margont told him, annoyed. 'What's more, if you're taken, you'll be shot. After all's said and done, the man we're looking for will well and truly have assassinated you, but indirectly!'

Relmyer smiled, deaf to all other logic than his own, and swiftly held out his hand.

'Thank you, Quentin! Without you I would never have identified him. There are no words for me to express my gratitude.'

Relmyer shook his hand, pressing too hard.

'Good luck, Lukas,' said Margont.

'Luck does not exist. There are only consequences.'

'We will go back and tell Luise the situation. Would you like us to give her a message?'

'Tell her that she is my adored sister and that I entrust her to you, should events prevent me from seeing her again one day.'

Everyone resolved to depart, abandoning Relmyer, his eyes riveted to the face of his enemy, installed like a king in his throne.

CHAPTER 26

On 1 July, Napoleon set up his new headquarters on the Isle of Lobau, by this time generally known as Napoleon Isle. The general staff installed themselves there with great pomp. The Imperial Guard, ten thousand seven hundred strong, was set up around the Emperor's tent. General Oudinot's II Army Corps accompanied the Emperor. IV Corps received the order to leave Lobau to join the other corps, which were massing near the village of Ebersdorf. Only VIII Corps commanded by General Vandamme would not participate in the battle. The Emperor had decided to leave it behind in Vienna, in order to prevent any attempt at an uprising. The actions of the Austrian partisans had proved successful, mobilising at the back several thousand French and Westphalian soldiers.

Napoleon was living up to his reputation as a great tactician. He had a bridge built, named Baillot bridge, linking the Isle of Lobau with the east bank. That bridge was situated to the north of the island and was facing in the direction of the village of Essling, seeming to indicate that the French army was going to try to force a passage in the same place as a month and a half earlier. They placed cannon there to protect the bridge, and the next day, the Isle of Moulin was taken from the few Austrians who guarded it. The island was a wooded ridge near the Baillot bridge, between Lobau and the east bank. The French installed a battery on the Isle of Moulin, they built two bridges, one to link that island with Lobau and one to link it with the east bank, and then they built a redoubt to protect the head of that bridge.

The Austrians were perplexed. Was this a diversion or was the French army really going to move in the direction of Essling? Archduke Charles redeployed his soldiers. The vanguard commanded by Nordmann, and VI Corps under Klenau, positioned themselves in the north, to hold the villages of Aspern and Essling. The body of the army – made up of Bellegarde's I Corps, Hohenzollern's II Corps, Rosenberg's IV Corps and the Reserve Corps under the Prince of Liechtenstein – gathered in the north-east, six miles from Lobau. Since Archduke Charles did not know where the French were going to appear, he had arranged his army in pincer formation. If Napoleon attacked again in the north, Nordmann's vanguard and Klenau's VI Corps would have to contain him, backed up by Kolowrat's III Corps, positioned a little behind. The principal force of the Austrian army in the north-east therefore manoeuvred to wedge in the right flank of the French. But if Napoleon advanced north-east, Archduke Charles would head him off, while Nordmann, Klenau and Kolowrat would come to cut off the French left flank.

In reality Napoleon was preparing to set foot on the Austrian bank by directing his army not towards the north, nor towards the north-east, but towards the east. The Austrians thought, wrongly, that an army would not be able to pass that way because it was too marshy. In addition, they thought they would have time to react should their enemy spring up unexpectedly there. Moreover, proceeding in this way, the French would be obliged to present their left flank to the Austrians before turning north to face them.

The French army spent the day of 2 July redeploying. Divisions crossed each other to reach their allotted places. The unbelievable mass of men, bathed in the noise of the clicking and heavy hammering of the tread of men and horses, was dizzying. The cuirassiers moved in serried lines, their horses practically biting the rumps of those in front. The convoys of artillery stretched out endlessly, leaving behind here and there a carriage with a broken axle. The columns streaked the meadows with black, and numerous officers orchestrated their progress, galloping in every direction. Couriers and aides-de-camp zigzagged between the regiments, continually transmitting orders: 'Hurry up!' 'Make way for the Durutte Division!' 'Fall in behind General Piré's cavalry!' 'Clear a path!' Such was their number that, come the evening, not all the effectives had yet been able to reach their allotted position in the vast plan drawn up by the Emperor.

The soldiers tried to work out the significance of their position. They wanted to know if they would be amongst the first to mount the assault (heavy losses assured, but also better opportunities for promotion). Each time it was announced to a battalion that they would be placed at the front, some men rejoiced whilst others lamented. Each regiment was only a pawn on the chessboard, only just able to make out what was going on closest to them.

The evening brought a little cool air. The 18th of the Line was set up in a meadow. Everyone was preparing for the battle in his own way. Piquebois, his arm in a sling, devoured, all on his own, a roast chicken. Saber was seething. He had just delivered an impassioned speech to his company, evoking the glory of arms and the necessity of distinguishing oneself so as to be noticed by the Emperor. He had addressed these hundred men as though he were addressing a hundred thousand. He was practising for later on. At moments like this, he was no longer himself; ambition rendered him arrogant and inspired. He resembled a deranged gambler flinging coins on the table. He was ready, his company was ready, the army, the enemy, the world, the Emperor: they were all ready, what were they waiting for? Quick, a new map! Convinced that the war would propel him to the top of the hierarchy, he was longing for the carnage. His mind, closed off from any idea of danger, was engaged in tactical calculations that were brilliant, certainly, but which interested only him. He marched to and fro, prisoner of the interminable wait, impatient to prove himself to everyone. But prove what? Why, everything, for goodness' sake! Margont had nicknamed him 'Lieutenant Beethoven'. Like the composer, Saber had his symphonies playing constantly in his head and he avidly sought a stage and an audience.

As for Lefine, he was in quite another state of mind: he was fulminating.

'When I think of all the time we took to build our cabin on the Isle of Lobau! And now they've thrown us out! Those overpaid pigs of the Guard are now sleeping there! It's scandalous! Where is our June salary? The second of July is not June any more! Perhaps to the imperial accounting service, 2 July is 32 June. It's daylight robbery! They'll pay us after the battle, when there is no one left to receive it. That will make a nice economy, as usual! They force us to fight this war and on top of it all we have to do it on credit!'

He was talking, jabbering . . . His flood of anxiety expressed itself in an interminable commentary all telling how he was the victim of the whole world.

Stretched out on the grass, Margont, having learnt to shut himself off in order to think, reflected on the investigation. He had just had an idea.

Lefine continued his peroration: 'Do you realise that you get a salary that is almost eight times what mine is? But what would officers do without their sergeants, I ask you? Who would carry out their orders? Name me one single battle won by an army without sergeants? Hm? I'm waiting. We others, the non-commissioned officers, are the unloved of the army! Now without us, the—'

'We have to get hold of some hunting dogs,' Margont cut him off.

'Of course, dogs . . . And fish also?'

'We searched round about Teyhern's house, but we could very easily not have noticed a hiding place, a subterranean shelter. Hunting dogs would be able to sniff it out! Let's go and find Jean-Quenin. A doctor will be useful. Then we will go and find Pagin so that he can escort us with some hussars.'

CHAPTER 27

MARGONT was worried about Relmyer and he gave a sigh of relief when he saw him coming out of Teyhern's house. The young Austrian, irritated, hurried over. His drawn features gave the impression that he must have woken up several times a night, jumping at the least sound, real or imaginary.

'What are you doing here? You have to leave at once!'

The three hounds, held on a lead by a farmer, were enough to disconcert him. Margont explained his idea.

'If there is someone, pray heaven that we find him in time,' Relmyer replied. 'If there is nothing here, disappear immediately!'

The farmer let the dogs off the lead and they scattered. One ran towards the house while the others rapidly searched the area outside, their snouts to the ground, their tails wagging. Relmyer bombarded the farmer with questions. Did his animals understand what they were looking for, or were they going to pull out a hare? How long would they take to explore the area? How would they know when it was time to give up? Why was one of them barking? Could it not keep quiet?

The farmer was barely listening, merely grumbling from time to time, 'My dogs know their business: if there is anyone here, they will unearth them.' His age-weathered face brightened with pleasure, rejuvenating him. He was not worried about what these damned Frenchmen were up to, but he loved poaching. They were paying him and he was hunting with his hounds: that was enough for him.

Jean-Quenin Brémond did not like Relmyer. He was a part of the ever-growing category of those whose relations with the young hussar had been severed by his blade. However, he wanted to help Margont as best he could, even if his friend had not explained this affair except in the broadest outline. The medical officer therefore waited patiently, but stood at some distance from Relmyer. The scalpel never understands the sabre.

One of the animals disappeared into a mass of thickets, about sixty paces from the building. His two fellow hounds ran to join in, their paws flying over the ground. Everyone rushed over in their direction. Relmyer, ahead of everyone else, slowed down, and was overtaken. He had to be the first, but at the same time he was terrified of what they might find.

The dogs scraped the earth to uncover something. Lefine handed out spades and everyone began to dig. Relmyer leant against a tree. He was cursing himself and praying that there was no body. But after a while, the odour of putrefaction filled the air, coming from the ever-expanding hole. Margont thought he was going to vomit.

The farmer shrugged his shoulders. 'Your game is off . . .'

Relmyer would have liked to hit him but Margont said compassionately: 'He doesn't know about all this, Lukas. And if you take it out on him, his dogs will tear you to pieces.'

The farmer moved away. This affair was taking an unexpected turn and he wanted to avoid being too involved. A hussar went with him to keep an eye on him. Lefine kept turning his head, his mouth seeking less foul air and his eyes a less harrowing spectacle.

'It's not a hiding place, it's a tomb.'

Relmyer did not move, shrinking inside himself.

'Look at the size of the body!' exclaimed Margont. 'It's an adult, not a young boy of fifteen . . .'

Relmyer went quickly over to him.

'Who is it then?'

Margont turned to Pagin. 'Go and fetch the portrait.'

Lefine and the other hussars were moving off when Margont called them to order.

'Let's continue! We have to free the body.'

He set an example, forcing himself to ignore the sticky pestilential corpse. Lefine let his spade fall from his hands. The sight of the worms infesting that decaying carcass horrified him. Eventually Margont found himself digging on his own.

'That's enough,' Jean-Quenin intervened.

'No, I want to be sure that there is only one corpse in this grave,' said Margont obstinately.

Relmyer went to fetch sheets from the house and helped him exhume the dead man. Margont continued to dig for a while. With each spadeful, Relmyer expected to see the face of a young boy appearing, as if the earth, dark and rich, had embalmed and conserved intact the body of another victim. Relmyer then looked around him. Was he going to have to dig for the rest of his days to find all the victims?

Margont joined Jean-Quenin. 'What can you tell us about the corpse?'

In contrast to his companions, the medical officer showed little emotion. Death was an old acquaintance.

'It's an adult – I can't be sure of his age; killed with a knife, struck several times in the abdomen and chest, violently; some of his ribs were broken by the impact of the blows.'

Jean-Quenin wrapped his hand in a sheet and took hold of one of the body's arms, which he examined.

'The victim probably knew his assassin.'

'How can you say that?' asked Relmyer, crossly.

'When you're attacked, your first instinct is to protect yourself with your arms. But here, you can see there are no injuries to the arms. This man was taken by surprise by the assault and the murderer must have been standing quite close to him to be able to stab him. You only let people you trust come close to you.'

'When was he killed?' asked Margont.

'It's hard to say. The speed of decomposition varies according to numerous factors – heat, humidity, the type of soil the body is buried in . . . I would say between ten and fifteen days ago.'

Relmyer made a huge effort to control himself. He had just been shaken out of a world with one simple objective – to wait for Teyhern in his salon – into a universe of chaos where questions abounded: who was that man? Who had killed him? Why?

Margont looked at the grave.

'The body was buried very deep to prevent the smell escaping and alerting us. In addition, the tomb was well hidden: we noticed nothing when we first looked here. The assassin was very determined that we should not find his victim. Conclusion: this dead man is a major clue – may God rest his soul – and I want to know everything about him. Pagin, show the portrait to the medical officer. Jean-Quenin, can you tell us if these are the same person?'

Pagin and Relmyer looked at each other, disorientated by this question, which seemed unnecessary to them. Jean-Quenin Brémond set himself to answering the question without seeking to understand it. He was used to Margont's bizarre requests.

'No, they're two different men.'

Relmyer looked at the body, whose features had been effaced by putrefaction.

'What are you saying? You can't tell anything from that face except that it's dead! They both have approximately the same colour hair. It could be him, it could be his brother or his neighbour or half the men killed in the last two weeks.'

'Look at his cheekbones.'

But Relmyer could not bring himself to look at the cadaver. He contented himself with listening to the medical officer's explanations.

'The victim's cheekbones are more prominent than those of the man in the portrait. And the victim's lower jaw is narrower and his chin protrudes.'

'Perhaps the painting is not a good likeness—' Relmyer interrupted himself: the painting was an excellent likeness.

Jean-Quenin Brémond went on with his commentary. 'Although the nose is crushed, you can still see that it is larger and longer. And besides, it runs straight down from his forehead, what you call a Greek profile. The man in the picture has a hooked nose much more separated from the forehead. The position of his ears is also lower.'

Margont went over to the farmer with Pagin, who was still holding the picture.

He demanded, in German: 'You live near here – do you know the man in this portrait?'

'Never seen him before.'

Very reluctantly, the man followed him to the grave. As soon as he caught sight of the body, he grew agitated.

'But you do know him! Don't try to deny it!' exclaimed Margont. 'Who is he?'

'Hermann Teyhern . . .'

'What?' cried Relmyer.

The man was panic-stricken. He said desperately: 'I live peacefully at home, I didn't see anything and I don't speak French. I'll give you back the money you paid me to bring the dogs. I don't understand anything about this business and I swear I will say nothing . . .'

Margont tried in vain to question him more closely about Teyhern, then had to agree to let him depart. The farmer did not wait to be told twice and fled with his dogs. Margont went back to Relmyer.

'The assassin knows Teyhern well because he falsified the records for him. He realised that our quest would eventually lead us here, or at least he knew that Teyhern's tampering had been discovered. So he had to get rid of Teyhern. But he didn't mutilate his face: he didn't treat him the way he normally treats his victims. He took the key to the house and he put his own portrait in the salon. Then he carefully concealed the body.

We managed to find his accomplice, but our trail ends here.'

Relmyer began to rant at the corpse in German, asking it how it could have acted in that way. Pagin and another hussar stood in his path, because it really seemed as if he might fling himself on the body and beat it.

CHAPTER 28

THAT evening, everyone was back in his respective encampment. The sky was cloudy. The tension was visible on the men's faces. Soldiers were bivouacking as far as the eye could see: on the plains, in the fields, in the villages, the farms, the barns, the woods, the forest . . .

Margont paced in a circle, arms crossed, brow furrowed, as he used to do as a child in his monastic cell at Saint-Guilhem-le-Désert. He kept repeating that he refused to admit defeat, but actually, it was worse than that: he couldn't allow himself to give up.

'Did you see how badly Relmyer reacted?'

Lefine nodded, not adding that Margont was hardly taking it any better.

'He's just lucky that his major closed his eyes to his absence. It has to be said that Batichut adores Relmyer, he reminds him of himself at twenty . . . Could you stop pacing up and down?'

'No.'

'It's over,' decreed Lefine. 'The assassin beat us. He's cleverer than us, or luck gave him all the best cards, a very fine hand. Now there's only one thing we have to concentrate on: the battle to come. Let's do our work, and try to come out of it alive with all our limbs intact. I'm quite happy to fight to the death as long as it's not my death.'

'But we haven't lost yet!'

'Apparently we're lining up a hundred and ninety thousand men and six hundred cannon! And the Austrians, probably about a hundred and forty thousand and four hundred pieces of artillery. My source is reliable; it's one of my friends who serves on the general staff. But where did they find those three hundred and thirty thousand soldiers? You'd think they bought them at auction. Bids for victory, please! I have a hundred thousand men for the Austrians, a hundred thousand! A hundred and twenty thousand for Napoleon, yes I did say a hundred and twenty thousand! A hundred and forty thousand for the Archduke! Come on, Monsieur Napoleon, make an effort, damn you! A hundred and ninety thousand for the French? By thunder, he just doesn't want to lose, the bugger! Have you ever seen two such enormous armies facing each other? How many will we be next time, ten million against ten million?'

'It was all too perfect and that's what's wrong with it!' exclaimed Margont.

'It's all very well, numerical superiority, except that each time one of our regiments reaches Austrian soil, all the enemy divisions are going to converge their fire against it. The regiments will arrive one by one, in single file, so we will always find ourselves one against ten. That will mean a succession of little Battles of Essling. The Austrians will methodically crush us as we arrive. If the Emperor does not find a way of parrying their attack, we will all be massacred, even if there were to be a million of us!'

Margont stared at him long and hard.

'What are you talking about, with your millions? Are you

actually going to listen to me? The murderer was just putting us off his trail with Teyhern. But it was too perfect, too well executed to be totally false. It's in the word "too" that the solution lies. We have not stopped drawing closer to the assassin: we have discovered that the registers were tampered with, Relmyer forced him to show himself again, we know that he serves in the Viennese Volunteer regiment . . . The false trail of Teyhern worked: Relmyer believed in it, so did I . . . The man we're looking for panicked after the setback of the ambush. He had very little time to put together the scheme that made us confuse him with Teyhern. Think about the difficulties he must have overcome to set up that scenario . . . Our man had to prepare his crime rapidly because a large part of his time was taken up with the army. How could he have acted so quickly? He must have known Teyhern very well, he knew everything about him. What's more, for him to leave us such a precious clue as his portrait must mean that he's starting to lose his grip! We are so close to the real culprit! It's as if we're in the right street but we knocked at the wrong door. The assassin and Teyhern knew each other extremely well! We have to find out more about this Teyhern.'

Lefine seized a stick and shook up the fire, which was cooking the soup rather slowly.

'We have a hundred and forty thousand Austrians on one side and a murderer on the other, and you choose to worry about the murderer? We'll see to it after the battle! I know, it's possible that the man has locked up a young boy somewhere. But that's only a hypothesis.'

'I really believe it is a possibility. And that's not all. We are very close to him, he has murdered his accomplice, the Austrian army is investigating the business of the falsified records . . . For him, it's the end: he has held out a long time, but his world of hypocrisies and of manipulations is beginning to crack at the seams. If we don't name him, Relmyer will, or Luise, or the Austrian military authorities . . . He's going to flee, Fernand. He knows that someone is going to unmask him, it's no longer a question of weeks; he knows it will happen in days. The battle is keeping us here, because there are so many patrols on the lookout for deserters. But, as soon as he has the chance, he will leave the region, possibly Austria. We're running out of time to catch him.'

Margont finally stopped pacing up and down; he had just taken a decision.

'I'm going to see Luise. Only she can find out about Teyhern.'

'You're joking! What about our orders? We are not allowed to leave our regiments. The imperial police don't take it lightly when a battle is imminent.'

'Jean-Quenin can scrawl me a note. He can pretend that I've come down with typhus and they'll send me away in horror. I'll leave straight away. I'll be back before nightfall.'

Margont was too stubborn to allow anyone to change his mind. If the major wondered about his absence, Lefine, Saber and Piquebois would come up with something. They were used to doing that.

CHAPTER 29

MARGONT made his way amongst the cohorts of regiments, crossing long convoys of artillery that blocked the roads, regiments that were behind schedule, recovered invalids looking for their battalions, impatient couriers . . . In Vienna, he skirted round the large avenues, his horse splashing through the mud of the narrow streets, while the large thoroughfares rang to the sound of the hoofs of the squadrons.

Luise was watching the troop movements from her window. She was hoping to see Relmyer or Margont pass by, unlikely as that was, and she despaired at the size of the army that was about to be unleashed against her own side. She was dumbfounded when she saw Margont silhouetted against the garden gate. She hastened to go to open it for him, deaf to her mother's protestations, and led him into a back room, while Margont apologised profusely.

'How are you? Has your wound healed?' she asked immediately.

'Yes, I'm very well, completely recovered.'

'And Lukas? Has he finally found Teyhern? Did he confess?'

Margont brought Luise up to date with everything that had happened. Her face clouded. Old sorrows resurfaced, mixing with her present worry.

'This has been going on so long, and each time we think

we've got him, he disappears again. Will it never be over? It's as if we're being tortured by a ghost.'

Margont was struck by that last word.

'Luise, you're going to have to find out as much as possible about Teyhern. He's very close to the man we're after, and knows him extremely well.'

'I've already started. I knew that it might be useful to you. But it's not easy . . . Vienna is in turmoil . . . Like our lives.'

'We don't have much time. I think our man will flee as soon as he has the chance . . .'

Margont put the portrait of the culprit on a chest of drawers.

'This picture is small, so easy to carry about with you. Show it whenever possible to the people you question.'

Luise studied the face, which she was seeing for the first time. He was smiling enigmatically. She had the impression he was laughing at them. When he had posed for the painting, had he considered the possibility that one day people trying to catch him for his crimes would look at this portrait? Was that the explanation for his ironic, scornful smile?

Luise turned away and looked Margont in the eye.

'Your regiment and the 8th Hussars – will you be held in reserve or will you be first in line?'

'Only the Emperor knows that.'

'I forbid you to get yourselves killed, you and Lukas! I don't care what you have to do to stay alive.'

Madame Mitterburg called through the door, asking if everything was all right. Luise replied briefly that it was. Suddenly a dam broke inside her and she felt frail, insignificant and derisory. It was perhaps the last time she would ever see

Margont. In just a single day, the war could kill him and wipe out Lukas. So she might lose everything all over again! She had reproached Relmyer for reviving the past at the risk of committing the same errors, but now she was acting in exactly the same way by attaching herself to two people who might well be dead the next day.

'When will the war finally be over?' she murmured.

But that particular fear was only a small part of the wave of terror that submerged her. Suddenly she took Margont in her arms and held him as tight as she could. And just as suddenly she kissed him, more and more, unable to stop, fearing that when she released his mouth, he would immediately tell her that he was obliged to go. Her mother knocked at the door. Margont pulled away. Luise whispered in his ear, so softly that he almost did not hear her: 'Desert . . .'

He freed himself from her embrace, pretending that he had not heard her.

'I have to rejoin my regiment. As soon as we can, Lukas and I will come and see you and we will look together at what you have gathered about Teyhern. When the investigation and the war are over we will all be free. Then you and I will be able to—'

'No promises!' she interrupted. 'Come back safe and well, the two of you, that's all I desire at the moment. Lukas dragged you into this affair and you swore to me that you would watch over him. If one of you two dies, I will never forgive the other. So concentrate on staying alive.'

CHAPTER 30

By 3 July, the divisions were finally deployed in the correct places.

On 4 July, the army corps received precise orders about the manoeuvres they were to execute. At the same time Archduke Charles ordered his brother Archduke John to abandon his position near Pressburg in the south, because it was becoming clear that the French would not attack down there. The thirteen thousand men available to John were to join up with the left flank of the main body of the army as quickly as possible. However, torrential rain held up the transmission of the message and John's forces did not begin to move until the following morning.

Towards nine o'clock Napoleon decided to make use of the poor visibility caused by the rain. He began to send his troops across the Danube with the help of gunners, boats and barges. The French easily repulsed the little Austrian units guarding the bank. Innumerable batteries from Lobau opened fire on the villages of Aspern and Essling, immobilising the most advanced Austrian troops and creating a diversion. Napoleon sent the Legrand Division to take up position on the east bank, but at the level of the old bridgehead, to make the Austrians believe that he was going to occupy the same battlefield as in May. The Archduke fell into the trap and ordered the forces of Aspern and Essling to bombard the northern part of Lobau. He thought his round shot was causing havoc to the French and their allies, when actually they were assembling in the east of the island. Charles also released into the Danube burning boats that did not succeed this time in damaging the reinforced, protected bridges.

Towards one thirty in the morning, the French assembled the pieces of the first preconstructed bridge in order to link the east side of Lobau to the east bank. They managed it in five minutes. Two others followed. The regiments immediately began to cross *en masse*, drenched by the rain and deafened by the thunder and the bombardments.

The men advanced in serried ranks but broke rank the moment they set foot on the bridges. The officers reorganised the soldiers once they were safely on the other bank. In the pre-dawn gloom, torches provided the only light. As the hours passed, the Grande Armée formed an extremely dense unit: the army corps of Masséna, Oudinot and Davout marched at the front, supported by Montbrun's light cavalry and Grouchy's dragoons. The French were able to position themselves rapidly without losing their cohesion. When Archduke Charles finally understood what Napoleon was doing he hastily sent troops to prevent the French from advancing as they pleased. But those troops were insufficient to interrupt the march of Oudinot's and Davout's sixty thousand men. Meanwhile Masséna's IV Corps was taking the villages of Essling and Aspern from the rear.

By six o'clock that evening, Napoleon's operation had been successfully completed. His army had crossed the Danube unimpeded, manoeuvring itself with spectacular speed. The Austrians, taken unawares, had not been able to hinder their deployment. The Grande Armée occupied the immense plain of

Marchfeld, the terrain earmarked by the Emperor. It formed a convex arc backing onto the river. The centre was about six miles north-east of the bridges. The majority of the troops, the corps of Bernadotte, Macdonald, Grenier, Marmont and Oudinot, were positioned on the front line. The Imperial Guard was placed behind, with Bessière's heavy cavalry, that is to say, eight thousand cuirassiers and carabineers. The left flank, spread over six miles, was relatively weak. It consisted only of part of Bernadotte's Saxons and Masséna's IV Corps. Behind this last lay the villages of Aspern and Essling. The right wing was made up of Davout's III Corps, Montbrun's light cavalry and the dragoons of Pully and Grouchy. Napoleon had therefore constructed a strong right flank, very mobile thanks to the high preponderance of cavalry, and a powerful centre that he intended to use in a phenomenal hammer blow to smash the Austrian centre. These concentrations of soldiers had been put together to the detriment of the left flank.

The Austrians mirrored the French line, presenting a concave front stretching over twelve miles. Klenau's VI Corps and Kolowrat's III Corps assured their right flank. The élite reserve troops of the Prince of Liechtenstein joined the right flank to the extremely impressive centre. It dominated the heights of Wagram, fifty feet high and bordered by the Russbach river whose banks were extremely marshy. In the centre, Bellegarde's I Corps, Hohenzollern's II Corps and the reserve cavalry of Nostitz were stationed. Finally, their left flank was made up of Rosenberg's IV Corps and Nordmann's vanguard.

On the evening of 5 July Archduke Charles anxiously awaited the arrival of Archduke John, whose men were supposed to fall upon the French right, placing Napoleon in a very difficult situation. He did not know that his brother was still a long way off and was having no success in hurrying his troops along.

Napoleon knew that time was not on his side: he would have to act quickly in order to ensure that Charles did not receive John's reinforcements. He had no idea what Charles was planning. The Austrians had not really tried to confront him. Did Archduke Charles plan to withdraw and attack elsewhere? Until now, everything had turned out perfectly for the French. Napoleon decided to exploit the gains made during the day, contrary to his initial plan, which had not envisaged launching the principal battle until the next day. The Emperor ordered Bernadotte's Saxons to take the village of Deutsch-Wagram, to the right of the Austrian centre. Oudinot, Prince Eugène – whose army included the corps of Macdonald and Grenier – and Davout were charged with attacking the Austrian centre.

Napoleon told an aide-de-camp, 'Go and tell Oudinot that I can hear nothing at the moment, that he must march a little further and give us a little music before nightfall.'

The battle began at seven thirty. Oudinot failed in the face of the Austrians' tenacity. Prince Eugène almost broke through but Archduke Charles came in person to galvanise his men, and there also the French had to withdraw. The French Seras Division, seeing the French beat a retreat pursued by soldiers in white coats, opened fire on these last. In fact they were Saxons attached to Dupas's division, who had been caught in the cross-fire and were fleeing. These men jostled into the Lamarque, Seras and Durutte Divisions, also retreating in disarray. It took a long while for these troops to regroup. Only Davout succeeded in advancing, but as his division was isolated, he too had to retreat to his starting position.

As night fell, Bernadotte's Saxons were still wandering about on the outskirts of the village of Deutsch-Wagram. Other Saxons, the grenadiers of the Leibgarde and the von Bose and von Edigy Battalions, were sent as reinforcements, but these infantrymen did not know exactly where their compatriots were. When they arrived in the village, the gloom and the smoke of combat added to the confusion. Soldiers in white coats appeared and the reinforcements opened fire. But they were firing on the other Saxons. While the Saxons were killing each other, the Austrians counterattacked and routed their assailants.

This first attempt at an attack therefore ended in abject failure. Archduke Charles did not take action to profit from this, however; it was too hazardous to continue fighting at night.

CHAPTER 31

During the night, plans were revised on both sides.

The Emperor still intended to attack the Austrian centre. Should he succeed, the enemy army would be annihilated. Napoleon wanted to achieve total victory to force Austria to surrender and to dissuade other countries from taking up arms against him. For that he had to weaken the enemy centre. He therefore chose to keep his left flank relatively fragile. It was very extended and only defended by Masséna's IV Corps. This weakness was in reality a trap. It was designed to entice the Archduke to attack on the French left. In this way Charles would be obliged to withdraw troops from his centre to reinforce the troops on his right charged with vanquishing the French left flank. In addition Davout was to overwhelm the Austrians on their left flank, to such an extent that other enemy regiments would also have to abandon the centre, to bolster this flank. And further, this French manoeuvre would prevent Archduke John's forces from eventually joining his brother's. Napoleon would then launch his principal attack: a surge against the Austrian centre. The tactic of the weak flank had worked admirably at Austerlitz. But it was absolutely imperative that Masséna hold firm on the left flank, which would be on the receiving end of a powerful Austrian attack.

However, Napoleon underestimated yet again the fighting spirit of the Austrians. He thought that Charles would limit himself to trying to break the French left. Against all expectation, the Austrian commander-in-chief opted for a widespread offensive. He not only decided to crush the left flank of the French with Kolowrat's III Corps and Klenau's VI Corps but he also ordered Rosenberg's IV Corps to attack the French right flank while Bellegarde's I Corps and Hohenzollern's II Corps assailed the centre. The Liechtenstein reserve corps would launch the final onslaught.

On 6 July, at four in the morning, Rosenberg's IV Corps flung itself on the French right flank constituted by Davout's III Corps. Taken by surprise, Davout's men began to fall back. Napoleon hurried to the area with Nansouty and d'Arrighi's cuirassiers.

Meanwhile, Bellegarde's I Corps took over the village of Aderklaa, which marked the angle between the French centre and its left flank. Bernadotte's Saxon IX Corps, which had been severely tested by the previous evening's panic, had evacuated the village. Marshal Bernadotte had considered that he would not be able to resist the Austrians and had withdrawn. Napoleon had never imagined losing Aderklaa to the Austrians; it was crucial to the success of his scheme. If the Grande Armée were to try to crush the Austrian centre with Aderklaa still in the hands of the enemy, the Austrian I Corps under Bellegarde would be free to come to offer support to the centre. In addition, the Archduke's troops positioned on the right would be able to join the endangered centre much more rapidly, because they would not have to waste time skirting round the village. So Napoleon ordered Marshal Masséna, 'the golden boy' known for his victories, to retake Aderklaa. But this meant that several of Masséna's regiments would no longer be available to protect the left flank, which would become even more fragile.

Margont was serving in the Legrand Division of Masséna's IV Corps. Three of Masséna's divisions had massed to the north-east of the left flank, very near the centre. The Boudet Division had been left three miles from there to constitute the south-west of the left flank, with only three thousand seven hundred men facing fourteen thousand soldiers of Klenau's VI Corps, who were not yet moving from their positions.

The 18th of the Line stayed still, in battle order, under a lowering sky of massive clouds. Margont tried to work out what was planned. Thanks to the many plumes of white smoke and to the din of the cannon and the fusillades, he could tell that battle had commenced on the French right. He asked Lefine and Saber for their opinions. The former always knew everything and the latter had a particular talent for seeing through the plans of the general staff. Lefine, normally sanguine, showed increasing signs of anxiety. He kept readjusting his coat. His agitated fingers seemed to knit his worry.

'We're on the left wing! The wings are unlucky! At Austerlitz, don't you remember? Our right flank was destroyed! The Emperor adores offering up a flank, it's well known.'

Saber also seemed put out.

'There's a better chance of promotion in the centre than on the wings. How much longer am I going to languish in the role of subaltern? For pity's sake, if they would only give me a regiment, you would see what I am capable of! But no, here we are on the edge of the "Route to Glory"! What terrible luck!'

'There's something I can't grasp,' said Margont worriedly.

‘If we’re to the north-east of the left wing . . . who exactly is the left wing?’

‘Boudet,’ replied Saber.

Margont, Lefine and Piquebois looked at him in consternation.

‘Surely there must be other divisions . . .’ said Lefine.

When they looked towards the south-west they could indeed only see Boudet’s division, a minuscule dark blue rectangle surrounded by the immense golden blanket of ripe corn that no peasant had come to harvest. Whereas looking towards the centre, they could make out a stupefying conglomeration of troops. The regiments were stacked one against the other. Column succeeded column, blue rectangle succeeded blue rectangle, lines of cuirassiers glinted in the sun, batteries were positioning themselves . . . Compared to these masses, Boudet’s division appeared derisory, a little stone fallen by accident from Napoleon’s pocket.

‘It’s bait designed to attract a very large Austrian fish,’ explained Saber. ‘But if the fish is hungry and if he struggles, he will swallow everything . . .’

Should Boudet’s division get into difficulties, there was every chance that the Legrand Division, the closest unit, would be sent to help them out. Margont realised that after having been unwitting bait in Relmyer’s trap, he now found himself bait once again, this time in Napoleon’s trap . . .

Masséna was being carried in a barouche, having been injured a few days earlier in a fall from his horse. His carriage, pulled by four white horses, attracted round shot that missed the marshal but felled the members of his general staff one by one. Masséna had come to supervise the assault on the village of Aderklaa. He launched the Carra Saint-Cyr Division, which did indeed succeed in taking over the village. Bernadotte's Saxons supported it on the right. But the soldiers of Carra Saint-Cyr, galvanised by their success, passed on from Aderklaa and flung themselves on Bellegarde's Austrians, whereupon they were decimated by horrifying fire power. Archduke Charles arrived to lead a counterattack and the Austrians retook the village. The Saxons were in the process of withdrawing when the enemy light cavalry charged them. Under the nose of the appalled Marshal Bernadotte, the majority of IX Saxon Corps disintegrated into a mass of fleeing men. Napoleon, who had hurried to the right flank to try to avert disaster, crossed the battlefield in the opposite direction, trying to rally the fleeing and demoralised Saxons.

Margont was facing his company to make sure they were correctly aligned. He saw with astonishment dozens of faces registering horror. He turned round to see a knot of soldiers in flight. It was a frightening rout. Saxons, French and Hessians were running until they were out of breath, barging into each other. This wave was hurrying towards the Legrand Division. Lefine looked at this spectacle, unable to take it in, as if it were a vast optical illusion.

'Well, we're not ready to play "Victory Is Ours" . . .' he murmured.

'Don't panic! Close ranks!' exclaimed Margont.

Everywhere, officers were giving similar orders. If the Legrand Division did not manage to stay in battle order, the Austrians would attack it in its turn.

Piquebois, who considered himself rather dashing playing

the role of the wounded soldier bravely preparing to enter battle again, a role he supplemented with an entirely unnecessary cane, shouted: 'Don't worry, the 8th Hussars are in the vicinity! I was one of them; they're a fiercesome bunch! I'll break my cane over the head of the first man to run for it!'

Saber was even more vindictive.

'We don't need the Saxons! They're traitors! I'm sure they did it on purpose because they're hand in glove with the Austrians! We'll have them shot after the victory.'

But the ranks broke up anyway, undulating and fusing together . . . the formation becoming more and more confused. The recruits were no longer listening to anything. Many had practically never fought. Up until now, they had imagined that battles took place in an orderly fashion; that Napoleon understood the situation in a single glance, clicked his fingers to make the soldiers advance and a great victory was immediately won. This débâcle alarmed them. They had the impression that it was the entire Grande Armée that was fleeing and they certainly did not want to be the last to have stayed in place . . .

Margont saw his company subsiding in on itself as if squeezed by gigantic invisible hands. It was like a child curling up into a ball.

'Stay calm! Close up,' he repeated, while the first fugitives ran past him.

Major Materre suddenly appeared at full gallop, and pulled on his reins. His horse pirouetted, finally stopped, and snorted. The superior officer was outraged.

'Captain Margont, keep control of your company! You're causing chaos!'

The major immediately departed again, which worried the infantry still further. The bulk of the fleeing soldiers was now almost upon them and as they could not go round the Legrand Division, they struck through the middle, barging through the ranks, knocking over the aligned infantry, who took advantage of the chaos to join them . . . The fugitives were like a hailstorm carrying away fragments of the formation. Officers hit them with the flat of their sabres to frighten them and oblige them to stop. The entire division began to retreat in a gigantic mass, carried gradually away by the flood.

Saber hurried over to Margont. 'Has someone given the order to retreat? Must we stay in position or should we pull back?'

'What do I know?'

General Legrand's seven thousand men were moving backwards at a growing pace. Loud detonations could be heard, coming more and more quickly until they turned into a continuous roar. Bellegarde's Austrians had installed batteries in front of the village of Aderklaa and were bombarding the French at point-blank range. The round shot decimated the lines of infantry, causing horrifying gaps. Now the Legrand Division resembled a gigantic creature from which the Austrian artillery was tearing lumps of flesh. A ball ricocheted past Margont and landed on his company, scything off a series of legs. Margont froze, petrified, and then mechanically followed his retreating men.

'Close ranks!' he shouted, his mind focused on one thing: if the division did not stay packed closely together, it would be exterminated.

The left flank and the left of the French centre were on the brink of collapse. Bellegarde's I Corps and the élite Liechtenstein Corps would have been able to launch a massive attack on that weakened part of the French army. But Archduke Charles was a prudent strategist. He insisted that a corps should only advance after he was certain that it could stay linked to its neighbouring corps, so as to avoid leaving any breaches in their line. Bellegarde therefore waited for the arrival of Kolowrat's III Corps on his right, before acting. But Kolowrat still had several miles to cover because he was positioned too far west, the Archduke having thought that Napoleon would choose the same battlefield as he had used in May.

Napoleon profited from this relative respite. He went to the menaced zone and succeeded in rallying some of the fleeing soldiers. He immediately sent the remains of the Saxon regiments to the centre of his arrangement – the safest position – so that they could regain their confidence. The Legrand and Carra Saint-Cyr Divisions stopped retreating and began to re-establish themselves for battle. Nansouty's cuirassiers, come to reinforce these divisions, offered protection. Napoleon was therefore present for an impressive spectacle. The enemy right wing finally began to act, after having been delayed by the slow working of the Austrian army mechanism. Kolowrat's sixteen thousand men started to attack the north-east of the French left flank, while Klenau's fourteen thousand soldiers of VI Corps marched against the south-west, defended only by Boudet's division and the heavy artillery of the Isle of Lobau. The noise of the long, wide white columns advancing was deafening. They streaked the plain in perfectly ordered lines.

It was both good and catastrophic news for Napoleon. Good news because the Austrians were falling into his trap. Catastrophic because, with the poor state of the left flank and the left part of the centre, it could be considered that in fact it was the French who were falling into their own snare. A race against time began: Napoleon had to smash the Austrian centre before his adversaries could sweep away his left flank.

Napoleon ordered the methodical Marshal Davout, commander of the right wing, who had just repulsed the assault by Rosenberg's Austrians, to attack the enemy left flank. Davout was to take the village of Markgrafneusiedl, situated at the end of the plateau of Wagram. General Oudinot received the order to attack the enemy centre. Multitudes of blue troops surged forward while multicoloured cavalry charged. The French went at it furiously, as did the Austrians. Both front lines were constantly reinforced, devouring regiments at a pace impossible to grasp.

On the left, the danger was increasing. Boudet's division, overcome and still retreating, nevertheless tried to stem as much as possible the flow of Austrians along the bank of the Danube. General Boudet had wanted to entrench in Aspern, but Wallmoden's hussars had just massacred his gunners and had taken his fourteen cannon. He had therefore been forced to evacuate the village using sabre blows as defence . . . Instead of sending reinforcements to his left, Napoleon had chosen to save his reserve infantry to use later to exploit an eventual breach of the Austrian centre. So he improvised another solution: Masséna's IV Corps was going to form a marching column and descend to the south-west to stop Klenau's VI Corps. The problem was that in manoeuvring in this way, Masséna first had to turn his back on the Austrian I Corps under Bellegarde, and the élite Liechtenstein Corps. Then he would expose his flank to Kolowrat's III Corps before finally arriving level with the villages of Aspern and Essling, near the Danube, to confront Klenau. This five-mile march down the French left flank was likely to be extremely dangerous. To try to protect this manoeuvre Napoleon decided to use the cavalry and the artillery instead of infantry, which was most unusual in this type of movement. Lasalle's light cavalry, Nansouty's heavy cavalry and the cavalry of the Guard charged the Austrians intent on immobilising them. General Lauriston, who commanded the artillery of the Guard, was commanded to form a giant battery. He assembled all the pieces of artillery he could find – those of the Guard, of Prince Eugène and of the Bavarians under General de Wrède – and began to place the hundred and twelve cannon in a mile-long line along the north-east of the left flank, replacing Masséna's troops, who were about to depart. Over and above that, Napoleon gave the order to retake the village of Aderklaa. Molitor's division, part of Masséna's IV Corps, succeeded in taking it. But it was clear that they would not keep it because the Austrians would try everything to recapture it. Aderklaa must hold out as long as possible in order to occupy the efforts of the troops of Bellegarde and Liechtenstein. In fact that village would serve as a lightning conductor to protect the back of IV Corps.

The majority of Masséna's corps therefore formed into a column. Then the superior officers ordered, 'Column, head left.' This enormous formation of twenty thousand men began to march south-westwards. The new recruits were worried.

Margont was at the head of his company, sword in hand.

'Where are we going?' wondered Saber aloud. 'And if we leave, who will make up the north of the left wing?'

In the ranks, the infantry exchanged appalled looks or questioned the non-commissioned officers.

'Are we retreating, Sergeant?' a conscript asked Lefine.

'Everything's all right! Everything's going to plan,' Lefine assured him.

An Austrian battery thundered in the south, near the Danube.

'We're encircled!' yelled a fusilier.

'The little Corsican is defeated!' another one yelled louder.

The order of the companies changed again. The infantry speeded up; entire lines collided . . . Sergeants and captains hurried to restore cohesion. Masséna's giant column resembled a house of cards on the point of collapse.

Margont trampled the fields of golden corn, hiding his anxiety. There were Austrians massed at his back, all along his right and facing him, in the south-west. He could see enemy columns all around like giant white worms rampaging across the plain towards them to devour them. The Austrian right wing was vastly superior in number to them and they had practically not fought at all.

'Slow down, Corporal Pelain!' he exclaimed for the fifth time, for his company had a tendency to catch up the company in front.

In reply came overhead whistles, and explosions rang out on all sides. A shell exploded in the middle of his company, throwing broken bodies into the air. The round shot plundered the rows of soldiers, like black bowling balls knocking over a line of skittles . . . The survivors, spattered with human debris, stepped over mutilated bodies as they battled through the palls of smoke. Incandescent flashes ignited fires and these infernos burnt alive the wounded, unable to move. In spite of the unbearable sights around them, the formation had to stay together at all costs to intimidate the Austrians and keep them at bay.

Margont, ashen-faced, shouted: 'Close ranks! Keep in line! Realign yourselves!'

Hundreds of other voices repeated the same instructions all along the column, in an endless echo interrupted by explosions and by the cries of the wounded.

The giant battery was not yet ready to support Masséna's IV Corps. The gun carriages were hurrying to their positions where the artillery busied themselves like ants around their guns to ready them for action. There was one cannon every twenty paces, over a mile stretch. Nothing like it had ever been seen before.

Masséna decided to launch his light cavalry against the enemy, to prevent them from attacking his flank and finishing off the troops decimated by the round shot. To charge an enemy army aligned in battle order was not what hussars and mounted chasseurs usually did. Normally they were used for reconnaissance, for harassing the enemy and pursuing them when they were in retreat. But Masséna only had Lasalle and Marulaz's light cavalry at his disposal. These two thousand combatants launched themselves at the sixteen thousand men of Kolowrat's III Corps.

The cavalry set off in a cacophony of hammering hoofs, whinnying and trumpet blasts. The 8th Hussars were at their head, riding in sparse groups. Relmyer was amongst the first. Pagin and Major Batichut were slightly ahead of him, hard on the heels of General Lasalle and his escort. The hussars were yelling, their faces whipped by the wind, brandishing their sabres, drunk with the excitement of their speed and the madness of war. They saw the enemy masses rapidly grow larger. In front of their eyes, regiments hastily formed square, lines of Austrian or Hungarian fusiliers took aim, battalions of the Landwehr or of Volunteers organised themselves as well as they could, artillerymen reloaded their cannon, uhlans, dressed all in green, before charging the assailants with their lances . . . Relmyer bent low over his horse's mane, his sabre in his hand. Pagin, sitting straight in his saddle, waved his sword, shouting, 'Hurrah! Hurrah!' The Austrians disappeared in the white smoke of their gunfire. A ball to the chest felled Pagin in the full flush of youth. Hussars were slipping out of their stirrups, collapsing with their mounts, shot to pieces by balls or canister shot . . . The cavalry fought the Austrians. They sabred the artillerymen, massacred the isolated infantry, crushed the regiments . . .

Relmyer threw himself on a group of soldiers in grey coats. Suddenly he jumped. Here! Right here! He had just spotted him. It was him! The man he was hunting! Relmyer began to sabre with fury to clear a passage as far as his tormentor. But it seemed to him that the face kept moving, disappearing only to reappear elsewhere, like a reflection projected onto face after face in that crowd. Relmyer struck, slashed, struck . . . Forms collapsed, soldiers threw themselves to the ground to avoid his blade, many fled and were killed by other hussars . . .The formation finally broke up. It was a battalion of the Landwehr from Prague and not the Viennese Volunteers at all.

Finally the cavalry yielded to the superior number of their enemies and left at the gallop under a hail of Austrian bullets and round shot, taking away with them two cannon stolen from the enemy.

During this time the Great Battery had finished positioning itself. The one hundred and twelve cannon opened fire on Kolowrat's III Corps, generating a thunderous roar loud enough to drive the soldiers mad. The round shot caused chaos amongst the Austrians, flattening their ranks, destroying the lines, cutting the columns to pieces, and exploding the artillery's ammunition wagons . . . Kolowrat, stopped in his tracks by this barrage of fire, pulled his troops back to put them out of reach of the canister. He placed all his cannon in position and ordered a counterbarrage of fire. Whilst the two artilleries fought a titanic duel, pulverising each other cannon for cannon, Masséna's IV Corps pursued its course under that hail of projectiles. To encourage his soldiers, Masséna placed the musicians of one of the regiments at the head of the column to belt out military marches, the drum major, in his lace-trimmed coat, twirling his silver-topped cane . . .

The attack on the Austrian centre was starting to turn in favour of the French. In spite of the hand-to-hand conflict and the counterattacks, Charles did not succeed in checking the French advance.

Yet the French left was still in danger. To the north-west the din of the Great Battery was gradually diminishing. Austrian fire was decimating the artillerymen. Napoleon decided to hide this weakness, otherwise the Archduke would have immediately ordered his troops to attack that part of the front. He therefore called on the volunteer soldiers in the ranks of his Guard, who arrived to mingle with the surviving gunners. They manoeuvred the guns in the midst of the bodies of the artillerymen they were replacing and whom they soon joined one after the other, before being replaced themselves. The Great Battery increased the rhythm of its firing and the Austrians did not realise how much the wing was breaking up under their rain of balls.

To the south-west the situation was veering towards disaster. The poor Boudet Division was still having to withdraw and now found itself level with Lobau. The advance of Klenau's VI Corps seemed irresistible and the Austrians were nearly at the bridges, the only escape route available to the French.

Faced with the danger of the Austrians cutting off the bridges, Napoleon was forced to change his plans. Instead of keeping all his reserve troops to send in at the end against the Austrian centre, he took a large part of them – the Italian army of Prince Eugène – and directed it towards the north of the left wing. This change of plan had several consequences. It supported the left flank but also meant that not all French efforts were concentrated on the single objective of attacking the enemy centre. So the eventual breakthrough would not have the devastating results hoped for by the Emperor.

General Macdonald, serving under Prince Eugène, was assigned to lead this manoeuvre. Adhering to his convictions, he still wore his old republican general's uniform, which Napoleon did not appreciate. He formed a square, each monumental side stretching for half a mile. The survivors of a large part of the Italian army, that is to say eight thousand men, stood closely packed together to form the edges, while Macdonald and his general staff were placed in the clear space in the centre. This square began to march in the direction of Kolowrat's III Corps and the élite Liechtenstein Corps.

Macdonald had chosen this unusual formation to protect himself from the cavalry and because his troops included an enormous number of conscripts. They were too inexperienced to be able to advance in line or to change formation under fire. The formation was, however, inconvenient. It moved slowly and as the soldiers found themselves massed in a restricted space, Austrian fire power converged on them, causing carnage. As the giant square advanced, it shed, leaving behind a carpet of wounded and dead. It nevertheless succeeded in resisting attack by Scharzenberg's dragoons, helped by the support of Nansouty's four thousand cuirassiers and carabineers, and by the cavalry of the Guard, which launched repeated charges on the enemy flanks. The cavalry fell like rain under the canister shot and the bullets before being struck by Hesse-Hombourg's cuirassiers. The mounted chasseurs of the Guard harried the enemy infantry, which held firm, while the Polish Light Horse attacked Scharzenberg's uhlans. They seized the uhlans' lances, their favourite weapon, and improvised as lancers. Part of the Great Battery also helped Macdonald with their fire. Finally the Austrians began to retreat but continued to fight. In less than an hour, Macdonald's giant square had ceased to exist. Only one thousand five hundred of its soldiers survived unhurt. But the Austrians, shaken and worried about their centre and left flank, did not succeed in exploiting this success.

Napoleon then launched his last reserves, including General Wrède's Bavarians dressed up as if for a parade, the Young Guard and Marmot's XI Corps, against the centre and the north of the Austrian right flank. He kept with him only two regiments of his Old Guard. Archduke Charles, in contrast, had already used all his available soldiers.

After two hours of marching interspersed with fighting, Masséna's column finally arrived to face the troops of Klenau's VI Corps.

Three miles away, on the other side of the Danube, the Viennese were watching the battle perched on the roofs of houses, on clock towers, on ramparts and neighbouring hills. Thousands of plumes of smoke smothered the plain and the plateau of Wagram, and filled the sky. Half the world seemed to be burning. But the spectators could make out Klenau's regiments, the closest to them, and they cheered the line of white soldiers flowing along the riverbank and increasingly pushing back the astonishingly few blue troops. The flow of white was ravaging the back of the French army and playing a significant role in the outcome of the battle. Then Masséna's column appeared, sliding slowly through the fields of corn. To the Viennese it looked like a monster, a great dark blue Leviathan interspersed with the shimmering reflections of bayonets and sabres. Klenau's forces were made up of white blotches like enormous snowflakes, which moved, changed shape, regrouped or were absorbed by a village. Looked at from that distance, the war seemed unreal. The blood did not reach as far as the spectators.

The Viennese encouraged their troops by waving their hats and white favours. Their cries could not be heard above the tumult of combat. Luise's loyalties were divided. As much as she rejoiced at the advance of the Austrians she also felt they were tearing away a part of her. She did not know whether Relmyer and Margont were among the French marching on Aspern and Essling and if they might die at any minute as she watched from afar.

Masséna's giant column split into several. These branches divided up in their turn and burgeoned into regiments in battle order.

Masséna directed part of his forces to the west against Hohenfeld and Kottulinsky's divisions. The Boudet Division, having withdrawn as far as the bridges, received Marulaz's light cavalry as reinforcement. It was to retake Aspern. General Legrand meanwhile had been ordered to take Essling where Vincent's division had retrenched. The cannon on Lobau would back up these assaults.

Margont's company, a hundred soldiers strong, was arranged in a column three soldiers wide. The seventeen other companies of the 18th replicated this geometric pattern, making up blocks that together made one column of attack. The 26th Light Brigade, which was ahead of the 18th, was arranged in the same manner. This hammerhead was preparing to strike the village of Essling, swarming with Austrians.

'What's happening? Where are we? Are we losing or are we winning?' demanded a soldier, his face as white as a sheet.

Piquebois stopped in front of him.

'Well, I've just been discussing at length with the Emperor. He said: "My dear Piquebois, let me tell you my secret plans for the battle: tell our good soldiers to fire on anything that moves." '

The ruins of Essling appeared intermittently through the smoke of the cannon fire. The façades of the houses were punctured by holes made by round shot, Austrians were keeping guard on the collapsed roofs . . . There were also entrenchments. Lefine began to laugh. It was unbelievable. A month and a half earlier, he had almost been killed twice in the village of Aspern, not a mile from here. Now after six weeks of encounters, emotions and pleasure punctuated by some moments of fear, here he was again. It was a case of *déjà vu*. As if the gods or Destiny had said to themselves: 'What? They didn't all die at the Battle of Essling, these little humans? We must correct that oversight: we'll send them back there and this time we'll kill every last one of them.' Lefine was often ironic, but he was forced to admit that he had nothing on what life could offer in that respect.

With Saber, fear induced hatred. He was pacing up and down along the ranks of the company.

'Remember how we marched under the bullets. It's payback time: we'll make them dance Napoleon-style!'

He went up to Margont, who was watching the crowd of Viennese. The smoky atmosphere made it appear that they belonged to another world, floating in the clouds. Saber pointed in their direction.

'How I would love to have some cannon to point at them.

We would just need them to come a little closer . . .'

The next day he would repent of having uttered such a barbarous threat, but at that moment he meant what he said. War had changed him into a monster.

'Why don't you address our soldiers, to motivate them?' Margont suggested, to divert his attention.

Saber liked nothing better. He launched into his tenth harangue of the day, evoking heroism and the prospect of promotion.

'Our only limitation is ourselves!' he cried.

Margont, who was barely listening, suddenly looked at his friend. But Saber had nothing more to say and concluded his speech. All his speeches ended in the same way: 'What does our Emperor say about us?' he bellowed.

As always, dozens of men replied enthusiastically: '"Brave men of the 18th, I know you: the enemy will not be able to withstand your attack."'

This phrase, endlessly repeated, bolstered them like a mantra.

The village of Essling marked the most advanced point of the march of the Austrian army into the back of the French army. It was the key position in the confrontation between Masséna and Klenau. The 26th Light Division and the 18th of the Line began to make their move to the sound of beating drums.

'Forwards! Forwards!' cried the officers.

The soldiers advanced, packed so tightly one against the other that even had one of them wanted to flee they would not have been able to. The village of Essling came to life, as if the myriad Austrians occupying it had been reanimated. Plumes and plumes of white smoke were released as artillery and their hordes of gunners stormed into action, like a volcano erupting. And at the same time, there were explosions on all sides, caused by the fury of the fire from the heavy artillery on the Isle of Lobau. Buildings were blown to smithereens but their smoking debris was immediately blanketed with new soldiers defending the village. That determination impressed the French – these Austrians were not the same breed as they had fought at Austerlitz. Those Austrians had rapidly thrown in the towel under pressure. Margont did not understand their resistance – he wanted to shout that they should ally themselves with Napoleon against their oppressive monarchies. But the Austrian bullets responded to his dreams of brotherhood by storming his ranks. The drums beat out the charge, one of the few sounds distinguishable in the uproar all around.

'Long live the Emperor!' yelled the infantry.

The 26th Light Infantry and the 18th of the Line swarmed into the village and its redoubts. Saber, with sabre aloft, speeded up to overtake Margont and lead the company in a shock frontal attack on the Austrians barricading the main street. The two sides fired at point-blank range before throwing themselves at each other. Smoke drowned everything. Margont was suffocating in the blanket of fog and could recognise no one in the tumult of gesticulating figures. The flares of successive gunshots were like chaotic will-o'-the-wisps. Soldiers were firing so near to Margont that he could feel the burning wind of the guns on his face. Ghostly shadows hurried towards him, filling out and revealing themselves as enemy soldiers. A

Hungarian tried to hit him in the face with the butt of his rifle. Margont dodged but, encumbered by the soldiers around him, could only defend himself by striking his assailant on the chin with the hilt of his sword. Pain forced the Hungarian to drop his weapon. The flow of French knocked him over and trampled on him. A dismounted hussar – one of Wallmoden's cavalry – flung himself on Margont. The hussar was wounded all over and bleeding copiously, and there was a mad glint in his eye. His sabre was bent from having broken the skulls of Boudet's artillerymen. He tried to decapitate Margont, crying, 'Austria!' but Margont bent his knees just in time.

'We must save our major!' yelled a conscript, confusing Margont with his superior officer. The young soldier perforated the hussar's abdomen with his bayonet while the latter ran him through with his sword. The sappers of the 18th broke down doors with their axes and the French poured into the barricaded houses. Margont was swept forward on one of these waves; those following him were foolish enough to believe that they would find safety in there. Infantrymen were firing in a dining room and finishing their work with bayonets. In a corner of the room two Hungarians were sheltering behind a knocked over table, defending their pathetic excuse for a fortress. A lieutenant set off up the stairs, trailing grenadiers in his wake and driving back the Austrians, who defended each step. The massacre continued all the way to the first floor. Finally the building was taken. There was an exodus – soldiers running out to be sucked into the confrontations in the streets. Others lingered, pretending to be wounded or helping those who really were. Margont was about to leave when he spotted a little branch of oak on the floor. Austrians and Hungarians had a tradition of attaching a few leaves of holly, willow or poplar to their helmets or shakos . . . The tradition symbolised their desire to make peace. But these leaves were red, bathing in a pool of already coagulating blood.

Margont reached the street again. The mêlée had moved on, leaving hundreds of bodies in its wake. A captain was trying to stand up, leaning on his sabre planted in the ground. Wounded soldiers were clinging to the legs of the able-bodied, pleading for help, or at least for a drink. Others were propped against ruined walls. Margont joined the nearest French soldiers. They had crossed Essling. Austrians were fleeing before their eyes or throwing their arms on the ground and turning themselves in as prisoners.

'Victory! We've won!' cried the French.

Lefine came to join Margont, tears of joy making tracks on his cheeks blackened by gunpowder.

'We're still alive! At least I think we are . . . I have the impression that Irénée stole your campaign.'

The most advanced troops of Klenau's VI Corps were evacuating Essling in order to retrench in Aspern. But Austria's spirit was broken and Aspern also found itself under assault. This halted Klenau's spectacular progression; he was now isolated and informed Archduke Charles that he was retreating. This was very bad news for the Austrians and was rapidly followed by a series of other problems. John's thirteen thousand men, desperately needed as reinforcement, would not be there for more than two hours . . . The Austrian troops were overwhelmed and began to show signs of exhaustion when

Napoleon's fresh reserve troops assailed them. The Austrian left wing was in disarray, its right wing was drawing back and the centre was weakening by the minute. The Archduke therefore decided to order the retreat. He wanted at all costs to avoid the destruction of his army, because the fate of the Habsburg monarchy depended on it. In choosing to give in now, he was leaving himself enough healthy troops to withdraw in good order and defend themselves against the French, who would certainly pursue them.

The Austrians had lost forty-five thousand soldiers, twenty-five thousand killed or wounded and twenty thousand taken prisoner. The French and their allies, thirty-five thousand, of which two-thirds had been killed or wounded.

Napoleon declared: 'The war has never been like this before. We have neither prisoners nor enemy cannon: today we have achieved nothing lasting.'

CHAPTER 32

On 7 July Napoleon decided to let his army rest for the day. Detachments of hussars and mounted chasseurs harried the retreating Austrian army but came up against the Archduke's cavalry. The Emperor wanted to pursue the enemy army, to break it up and encircle the isolated units one by one . . . the pursuit had to be decisive in order to convert victory on the battlefield into total victory. The next day Napoleon would set all his troops to this task.

The Grande Armée was in great confusion. Everywhere, soldiers were wandering about, isolated or in little groups, looking for their battalions. It would take hours to reorganise everyone, especially as it was hard to transmit orders. Numerous officers had been killed, interrupting the chain of command. This dysfunction generated misunderstandings and rumours. It was said that Masséna's IV Corps – which had lost twenty-five per cent of its soldiers – was going to be allowed to rest in Vienna. A few minutes later an aide-de-camp announced that it was to prepare for the pursuit.

Margont was in the village of Leopoldau to the south-west of the battlefield, taking stock of the state of his company. He had sent most of his able-bodied soldiers to collect the thousands of wounded who had not yet been tended to. Lefine was in an apathetic state, amazed still to be alive. He was sitting on a heap of rubble and, at his feet, dozens of infantrymen were asleep right there on the ground – they could have been dead. Behind him the village's ruined houses threatened to collapse, so that Lefine looked like a petty king who had not yet realised that his kingdom was no more. Piquebois was supervising the distribution of cartridges. Gunners were gathered round an ammunitions wagon and were filling their cartridge pouches. The company needed an endless supply of bullets.

Saber was absolutely furious.

'Unbelievable! Unbelievable! I'm still a lieutenant – not even promoted to captain! Not even that! The Austrians were obliterating our rear, our army was lost! Who was it who re-took Essling? It was thanks to me! I led my company—'

'My company!' corrected Margont.

'I led our company in the charge that saved us all and will become legendary. I broke into Essling, and Klenau's corps crumpled like an over-extended rope when someone lets go of one end. And how am I rewarded?'

'More than thirty companies poured into Essling and its retrenchments . . .'

Saber held up a finger to correct what he considered to be an important misrepresentation.

'Ours was the first to get all the way through the village, all the others did was follow me in.'

Margont started to lose his temper. 'You couldn't see anything in all that smoke, so how can you say that?'

'Only those following behind were blinded by the smoke. It was the smoke from our company firing at the front! Since our colonel refuses to make me a major, I'll have to apply to his superior. To the general of the division. No, he would never go against the recommendations of one of his colonels. Has the Emperor been informed of my feat of arms? I demand to see the Emperor!'

After each confrontation, it was important to replace all the officers seriously wounded or killed in action as quickly as possible, so that the army could continue to function. It was traditional that heroics on the battlefield were rewarded by promotion, sometimes allowing soldiers to skip several ranks in one go. Saber would become more and more wound up as it became known that such and such had skipped captain, and so and so had skipped major . . .

Margont caught sight of Relmyer, who was trotting over to feed his horse. He waved to the hussar, who bowed in his direction. Relmyer wore a strange expression. Pagin had died right in front of him, as had his colonel, Laborde, and many other hussars of the 8th. General Lasalle had also been killed. Relmyer could not yet admit to himself that all these men were no longer there. He was riding about, a broken man, surrounded by ghosts.

'I'm delighted to see you have survived,' he told Margont and Lefine. 'Let's go immediately and see Luise to put her mind at rest. We can see how far she's got with her researches.'

He was already becoming obsessed again with the investigation . . .

'Fernand and I can only get away for the day,' replied Margont. 'Tomorrow our regiment will definitely be taking part in the pursuit.'

Relmyer nodded silently. Margont left his company in Piquebois's hands. As for Saber, he was engaged in writing his letter, failing to get past the first line, because it was rather daunting to be writing to the Emperor . . . Without him fully realising it, his letter was acting as a screen, preventing him from seeing the broken flesh all around him.

Relmyer, Margont and Lefine went off, passing lost Saxons, streams of wagons heaped up with the wounded, white lines of prisoners and repentant deserters discreetly trying to rejoin their battalions . . . All around lay corpses and the remains of horses, picked over by crows.

CHAPTER 33

THE Viennese were in mourning for Austrian hopes and asking each other what would happen now to the campaign. They questioned the French and their prisoners to try to hear news of loved ones serving in the Archduke's army.

As they went into the Mitterburgs' house, Margont, Lefine and Relmyer passed medical orderlies of the Army Medical Service. Luise had been giving them sheets to make lint, and bottles of brandy. The war was an abyss that everyone tried to fill in his or her own way. Luise stared at the three of them, motionless, incredulous. Margont had eyes only for her. Luise looked at him but Relmyer hurried to question her.

'Did anyone recognise the man in the portrait?'

'No . . .'

Luise was stupefied. After all that they had been through in the last few hours, was that all the greeting she was entitled to? Relmyer was once again a victim of his demons. Not noticing anything, he continued in the same tone.

'Were you able to find out anything about Teyhern?'

This time she went along with it. She led them into the salon. Her face was deathly pale. During the two days of battle she had not been able to stop herself imagining Relmyer and Margont dead, the one run through in a tangle of hussars, the other riddled with bullets. She had determinedly imagined the worst, as if to get used to it in preparation. She could not therefore quite believe that they were really there, and had difficulty in rejoicing fully at their return.

There were several sheets of paper on one of the tables. Some were the rough drafts that Luise had scribbled of accounts given by the servants charged with finding information. Others were more legible. Luise had cut out parts of the information and organised them logically. She had drawn up Teyhern's family tree and grouped his friends and acquaintances together in a diagram. She had worked hard and gathered many names, but on all the sheets there were question marks. Each of the lists was incomplete, there was no information at all on some people . . . It was like looking at a building under construction. Relmyer wanted to read all the papers at the same time, holding them like a fan in each hand.

'Who do you suspect the most?'

Luise took one of the papers; it was a pretext to touch Relmyer's hand.

'I don't know, Lukas . . .'

Some names were scored through, but most were still possibilities or unknowns.

'"Acquaintance", "cousin", "distant relative", "uncle", "colleague" . . .' said Relmyer in irritation, shuffling the documents clumsily.

'Let's begin at the beginning,' suggested Margont. 'Let's concentrate on Teyhern's life.'

Luise ordered the papers.

'He comes from a modest family, born in Vienna in 1773. He's always lived here or round about. His father worked for the state, for the Ministry of Finance. He was an accountant, but

I don't know much else about him. Teyhern had three brothers, Gregor, Florian and Bernhard.'

Relmyer could not keep still. He burnt with impatience. He was reading Luise's notes, anticipating what she was going to say.

'We don't know anything more about them? This one, the oldest, Gregor, serves in the Austrian army. The regular army? The Landwehr? The volunteer force?'

'I don't know . . .'

'All his brothers are suspects! But you've found out almost nothing about them! The other two aren't in Vienna any more, but where did they go? And his cousins! He has eight of them altogether . . . or perhaps he has more and you've forgotten!'

Relmyer was exhausting himself running round the labyrinth of the lists of names and the arrows linking them to indicate the nature of their relationship to Hermann Teyhern.

'Let's stick to Teyhern,' insisted Margont.

Luise's fingers were trembling. 'He never married,' she went on. 'Like his father, he worked for several years as an accountant for the Ministry of Finance. He had a lowly position and in 1801 was involved in a serious incident. Teyhern was accused of falsifying some accounts and embezzling money, quite large sums, the equivalent to fifty thousand of your francs.'

'Fifty thousand francs? Fifty thousand francs?' exclaimed Lefine, dazzled by such a sum.

'Exactly. There was even a trial. But Teyhern was found not guilty. He nevertheless wanted to change jobs and he went to the Ministry of War.'

'Not guilty?' Margont was astonished. 'Even we know that he was not exactly the most honest man . . . Besides, he owns a superb house in Leiten. And his furniture? Marquetry chests of drawers, Louis XV armchairs . . . Not to mention the porcelain, Turkish carpets . . . Yet ministry employees aren't well paid. Look at Konrad Sowsky: he was doing the same job as Teyhern but his way of life was nothing like as lavish. And from what you've told us, Luise, Teyhern did not come from a rich family.'

Luise agreed. 'A neighbour told us that Teyhern's parents died of consumption in 1800 and that they left almost nothing to their children. And most people who knew Teyhern said that he was a spendthrift. He dressed according to the latest fashion, went often to restaurants or the opera, often visited antiquarians to buy works of art . . . He was described as a misanthrope, always on his own, thinking only of himself. His work colleagues thought he came from a rich family, while his few friends imagined that he had an important post at the ministry and commanded a large salary.'

'So where did all his money come from?'

Relmyer was leaning against the table, his hands grasping the edge as if he would have liked to crush it.

'He knew what happened to those young boys whose names he added to the military registers and exacted money for that.'

'No,' Luise objected. 'He was already rich before joining the Ministry of War. He began to spend money hand over fist when he was still employed by the Ministry of Finance. After his trial many people thought he was guilty.'

'Who was his lawyer?' asked Margont.

'Rudolph Rinz. But I crossed him out because he's nearly

sixty now. The trial was short. The prosecutor complained about the verdict. But the matter never went any further.'

'What is the name of the judge?'

'Vinzenz Knerkes. But it can't be him either.'

Vinzenz Knerkes' name was crossed out on a page covered in notes.

'Why?'

'Because it's impossible.'

'Why do you say that?' Margont pressed her.

'I've often heard him spoken of, always in a positive way. He's respected by his peers. He has the reputation of judging the guilty harshly and he's particularly severe on anyone who harms children or young people.'

Margont recalled the smiles the assassin carved on the faces of his young victims. Because they had been locked away for days and deprived of food and water, they could not defend themselves. That gave their tormentor the impression that they accepted the cruelty he inflicted on them. And in a way, the mutilation also created the impression that the young men had consented to their treatment. Perhaps the murderer did feel guilt. A guilt so intense, so destructive that he tried to exorcise it with his tactic of weakening his victims and then faking their smiles?

'Perhaps the judge doubly condemns people who make young people suffer because he's punishing them for their crimes and also for his own. One culprit escapes justice but another pays double. The assassin thus tries to ease the guilt racking him.'

This remark met a lively response. Lefine shook his head,

too down to earth to accept such an abstract explanation. Luise refused to entertain the thought that a judge could be culpable. As for Relmyer, he was lost in the depths of his own reflections.

'What age is Knerkes?' asked Margont.

Luise was distraught. She had devoted so much time to her investigation and now Margont was putting his finger on one of the blanks in her research.

'I didn't find out about him . . . I thought he was above all suspicion . . . He must be more than forty. Yes, in fact he could be the right age . . .'

'A judge would be exempt from service in the Landwehr, otherwise the judicial system would not be able to function. On the other hand, as a representative of the Austrian state, he would not be able to escape joining the Viennese Volunteer regiment when the war came to the gates of the capital.'

'Our judges always come from good families,' added Luise.

'So they are all made subaltern officers, even if they do not have a military background. And a judge is a prestigious position. Knerkes would have had enough authority to convince other officers of the Landwehr and some Viennese Volunteers to organise the ambush we were victims of. Everything tallies with what we know about the murderer! Hermann Teyhern embezzled money: he was guilty. The judge certainly knew that, but against all expectation he declared him not guilty. Why? Perhaps he was paid to let him off. Then when Teyhern started working on the army registers, Knerkes decided to make him falsify them. Teyhern could not risk refusing – he was at Knerkes' mercy. At the moment I think Knerkes is the prime suspect. Let's show his portrait to someone who knows him.'

'Madame Blanken met him sometimes,' announced Luise. 'She held him in high regard because he had the reputation of championing children and young people. Lukas, I know when you said that someone had kidnapped you and Franz, Madame Blanken told Knerkes. She thought his help might be useful . . .'

Margont's expression hardened. 'So without meaning to, Madame Blanken may have caused Franz's death. Because if Knerkes is the culprit, he hurried back to Franz while Lukas and the rescue team were losing their way in the forest. It's even possible that his position helped him to sabotage the police inquiry by setting them off on a false trail. Let's go and talk to Madame Blanken.'

Madame Blanken confirmed that the portrait was of Judge Knerkes, but she refused to believe that he was responsible. She did agree, however, to give them his address. Knerkes was a widower and lived alone quite nearby in the village of Radlau, on the other side of the Danube.

CHAPTER 34

KNERKES rode alone across the fields. He smiled to himself, overjoyed still to be alive.

When the Archduke had ordered the retreat the day before, the regiments of professional soldiers had formed powerful marching columns, protected by the cavalry. But several battalions of the Landwehr and the Volunteers had dispersed, shedding deserters in droves. Knerkes had melted into the stream of the thousands fleeing.

He had hidden in a wood, waiting patiently until nightfall to let the Austrian army move far away. He had put on the civilian clothes that he had kept for this purpose. Having the rank of captain entitled him to a horse, but as he was a Volunteer the army had not yet provided him with one, as they were unable to equip such a large number of combatants. He therefore used his own mare and so there was nothing to indicate that he was an Austrian officer. From now on he would pass himself off as a civilian who had come home to collect his belongings before leaving to escape the effects of war.

At nightfall, he had cautiously set off. He had skirted north-west round the French army, watching the immense spread of the fires by their bivouacs. The wind carried snatches of the songs of the victorious soldiers. He lost time because of his wide detour and by daybreak he had still not arrived home. He knew that the hussars and chasseurs would pursue the Austrians during the day, so from dawn onwards he had been forced to move slowly. He had more or less succeeded in keeping out of the field of action of the two armies, but even so, he was careful only to move from one hiding place to the next. He hid himself in the woods, scrutinising his surroundings, looking out for the next wood, or a deserted farm . . . As soon as the coast was clear he would hurry towards his new hiding place. He had to wait a while, trapped in a thicket, as French hussars deployed in line passed in the distance. They were sweeping a meadow strewn with bodies, looking for the remains of one of their superior officers.

Finally Knerkes found himself far enough north-west of the battlefield to avoid the possibility of bumping into a platoon of cavalry, and he therefore trotted straight to Radlau.

The village was deserted. The fighting had not reached here, but Knerkes did not let down his guard. He might still come upon a deserter or thieves pillaging the evacuated houses.

He considered his position. Lukas Relmyer would never give up searching for him, and that thought appalled him. What could be worse than to have someone relentlessly tailing you? Besides, Teyhern had told him that the army had found out that he had falsified the military registers. The naïve fool had wanted to blackmail him! A few knife strokes had soon dealt with that problem. But the military investigators would never leave it there. Teyhern had sworn that he had told them nothing, but was that true? What's more, after his blackmail attempt, Teyhern had warned him that he had given his friends letters asking them to pass them on to the Ministry of War if he had not contacted them after a few weeks. Teyhern believed he was protecting himself. He had planned to leave Vienna and to take up his opulent way of life in Berlin. Unfortunately for him Knerkes had also decided to flee. He thought he would settle in Westphalia or Bavaria. People would assume he had been killed at Wagram.

Knerkes could have left immediately but he had wanted to return home for a last time. He was keen to retrieve some personal belongings as well as the money he had amassed in preparation for his final departure. He had not dared take his gold with him before the battle. Had his horse been killed or wounded, Knerkes would have had to abandon it with its saddlebags full of coins. By the same token, had he been captured, his horse and his fortune would have been seized. A new life would not be possible without money. But these were not the only factors bringing him back here. A young man, bound and gagged in the shed, awaited his attentions. Knerkes had managed to lure him to his house and overcome him just before the battle had started, interrupting him. Now that he was a widower he could use his own home for his crimes. The young man would be very weak by now: he would not be able to put up any resistance . . .

Knerkes stopped in front of his house. He felt excitement take hold of him; his face was filmed in sweat. He dismounted, hastily tied his horse to a stake and hurried over to the shed. He opened it and found himself face to face with an adult. Knerkes drew back, bewildered, as Relmyer advanced on him. Relmyer experienced a moment of total triumph. It was much more than just the feeling of confronting the criminal in order to arrest him. He was stepping out of the shadow of the shed, but he felt as though he were coming out of the cellar of the ruined farm. The prisoner, whom he had freed two hours earlier, had fled, but Relmyer imagined that there was still a young boy there and that it was Franz. His dream was coming true. In his confused state, he felt fifteen again. But he had changed into an adult skilled in combat, into an élite soldier who was easily going to floor their kidnapper. At that moment Relmyer relived his past but this time in the winning role.

Knerkes backed towards his horse. He withdrew one of his horse pistols but Relmyer was too quick for him. The point of his sabre plunged into Knerkes' wrist, forcing him to drop the weapon. Relmyer's attack had been executed to perfection. Knerkes pressed his wound with his good hand to stop the blood flowing. Margont and Lefine suddenly appeared. Margont came through one of the windows of the house while Lefine came from one of the neighbouring woods. They were quite far away. Fearing that if Knerkes noticed anything amiss he would guess that he had been set a trap, Margont, Lefine and Relmyer had hidden themselves at some distance from each other. They had formed a wide circle to ensure that they caught Knerkes in their net. They approached slowly, fearing that haste would frighten Knerkes into some desperate act. The two Frenchmen walked determinedly, pointing their pistols.

Relmyer asked Knerkes: 'What was the point of the mutilated smiles?'

Knerkes did not reply, seeing that his silence would unsettle his opponent.

'Why, why, why?' persisted Relmyer.

Knerkes had understood that he would not win a fight with Relmyer, so instinctively he attacked his weak point – his mind.

'You can't kill me,' he announced, his voice brimming with confidence. 'It's you who are my prisoner, my little Lukas.'

Relmyer had the impression that something gave way inside him. He found himself in the same situation as before; the past was consuming the present! In spite of his age, of his lieutenant of hussars uniform and his fearsome sabre, Relmyer felt frail and defenceless, just like a weakened boy.

He stared at the drops of blood dripping between Knerkes' fingers. He reminded himself that he knew more than fifty different attacks that could floor the man in a flash. But Knerkes wore the same masterful expression now as when he'd threatened Franz and him with his weapon.

'You haven't changed,' added Knerkes. 'Nothing has changed.'

At that, with the stupefying audacity of one who has nothing to lose, he turned his back on Relmyer and untied and mounted his horse. Relmyer was paralysed into inaction. Margont began to run.

'He's escaping!' yelled Lefine.

Just as Knerkes galloped off, Lefine fired, but he missed. The detonation jerked Relmyer out of his torpor. All three of them made for their horses, hidden at some distance to prevent Knerkes' horse from smelling their presence and starting to whinny. Neither Margont nor Lefine reproached Relmyer. He was in more disarray than ever. But with each step, he took hold of himself. The duellist in him, and the hussar, exhorted him to counterattack. He was the first into the saddle.

Knerkes had gained a head start. His silhouette moved speedily across the plains. He was heading west towards the Danube. He wanted to lead his pursuers into the marshy labyrinth of the river. Relmyer overtook Margont and Lefine. His horse, in harmony with its master, understood that Relmyer wanted above all to catch the fugitive and so it galloped with unusual zeal. Soon the long blue ribbon of the Danube appeared, hidden from time to time by the abundant woods.

Knerkes reached the first trees. Relmyer sheathed his sabre and took hold of one of his horse pistols. Although he was at full gallop, he aimed precisely at Knerkes' horse. The shot hit the mare's rump – it was an excellent shot, worthy of the hussar's reputation. Knerkes forced his animal forward, but now it was having difficulty trotting, its hind legs sagging. Knerkes took hold of his second horse pistol but the wound weakened his hand and he almost dropped it. He transferred it to his left hand. Relmyer fired with his other weapon and wounded Knerkes' horse again. This time the mare was immobilised. Knerkes just had time to dismount before it collapsed. He began to run through the trees and thickets. His plan had failed; he would not now be able to lose his opponents. He might be able to hide and pick them off one by one, but what were his chances of success? He could think of only one solution.

Relmyer stopped his horse and continued his pursuit on foot through the woods, so as not to offer too easy a target. He moved forward cautiously, sabre in hand, scrutinising every possible hiding place. The dense vegetation enveloped him in an oppressive green veil. The route was easy to follow: he could see drops of blood on the grass. Margont joined him, armed with a pistol and a sword. When the two men next saw Knerkes, he was wading into the Danube. The water was already up to his chest and the current was strong, swelled by the thawing snow. Margont aimed at him.

'Drop your pistol!' he commanded.

Knerkes raised his left hand and ostentatiously let his weapon drop; it sank like a stone. He did not need it any more. He smiled and continued to advance into the river. The current began to carry him off.

'He's getting away from us!' cried Relmyer. 'Fire!'

Margont could not bring himself to do it.

'He's unarmed, it would be murder,' he replied. 'Let's follow him along the riverbank.'

'If he knows how to swim, he'll find his feet on one of the little islands and we'll lose him for ever! Fire! I don't care if it's the correct procedure, fire!'

Margont was still threatening Knerkes, who was getting further and further away. Relmyer flung himself on Margont's weapon and took it from him. Margont wanted to take it back, but Relmyer stabbed him with his sabre, exactly as he had wounded Knerkes. Margont stared with disbelief at his bloody, painful wrist.

'Don't force me to kill you,' warned Relmyer. 'It would pain me immensely, but I would do it.'

Margont stood stock-still. Relmyer aimed in his turn at Knerkes. Now he was only a head moving away on the current.

He was laughing at the sight of his pursuers arguing. It was inevitable that Relmyer would fire at him. It was the last hurdle he had to cross; after that the current would carry him out of range.

To put Relmyer off, he shouted: 'Until next time, little Lukas!'

The bullet shattered his skull.

CHAPTER 35

RELMYER went back to the 8th Hussars. He had just parted from Margont and Lefine, who were on their way back to their own regiment. His profuse apologies to Margont had done little to lessen the latter's anger. Relmyer was eaten up with guilt but told himself that Margont somehow understood and would in the end forgive him. After the campaign ended, the soldiers would be given leave of absence. Relmyer would ask Luise to receive him and Margont. The Viennese, in their joy at the newfound peace, would throw balls and parties, and organise plays. Everyone would be reconciled in the sparkling of crystal glasses. Until the next outbreak of war . . .

Relmyer was radiant. He was finally free! It was only today that he was coming out of that cellar. Life would go back to normal. At the end of his period of enlistment, he would leave the army. He would work as . . . as . . . He did not know as what, but at the moment that mattered little. He would like to start a family. He would go often to Vienna. The city was no longer cursed in his eyes. He would go and work for the French administration! A former officer of the hussars would not be refused a post. In Paris! Where he would teach German to rich people. But first he was going to travel. He wanted to go to Italy. His head was buzzing with plans. Life was magnificent because everything was possible.

Relmyer floated along in such a state of happiness that he

had failed to notice the trooper who had been following him for a while now. The man attracted his attention by calling out loudly.

'Lieutenant Relmyer, it seems that you have forgotten me.'

Relmyer turned round. The man talking to him wore dark blue breeches, a scarlet dolman and a pelisse of the same blue as the breeches. His shako was decorated with a white crest. The trooper introduced himself.

'Adjutant Grendet, fencing master of the 9th Hussars. Captain Margont must have let you know previously that I was looking for you. Tomorrow the Emperor is going to send us galloping after the Austrians, and we will chase them into hell if necessary! So we don't have much time. Let's settle this now and fight our duel straight away.'

Relmyer looked at him as if he were a being from the distant past, an old ghost forgotten in a corner.

'It's just that I've given up fencing, Adjutant Grendet.'

Grendet looked askance. 'What did you say? That makes no sense to me. Can you give up your soul?'

'Please leave me alone. I wish to rejoin my regiment.'

'Good God, you will unsheathe your sword, Monsieur, or I will have your guts for garters! If you're in such a hurry, let's fight without dismounting.'

Grendet pointed his sabre, his elbow bent. His horizontal blade indicated that he wanted to run Relmyer through between the ribs and not merely to injure him lightly in a sabre contest. It signified a duel to the death.

Relmyer had no choice but to unsheathe his sabre. He had thought his past definitively dead and buried, but here was a part of it rising up again in the shape of this trooper.

The two hussars charged towards each other. Relmyer never took his eyes off Grendet's sabre while directing his own blade to the right of the adjutant's chest, covered by its blood-red dolman. Grendet was struck full in the heart by the metal flash. Relmyer also fell to the ground, his lung perforated. He took several minutes to die.

EPILOGUE

NAPOLEON expected further combat. But Austria, shaken by its defeat, capitulated. The Emperor imposed tough conditions. The Austrian Empire lost several provinces that were divided between the kingdom of Bavaria, the Grand-Duchy of Varsovia and Russia. Three and a half million people were thus forced to change nationality. What was more, Austria had to pay heavy war indemnities and its army was reduced to a hundred and fifty thousand men. It was the end of Archduke Charles's military career and his brother John was banished from political life because of his inexcusable lateness in joining the battle. Austria rapidly became a friend and ally of France, to the point that less than a year later, Napoleon divorced Josephine de Beauharnais and married Marie-Louise of Habsburg-Lorraine, Francis I's daughter. The Emperor wanted in this way to secure Austria's support definitively.

Napoleon always awarded titles linked to the arenas of battle. General Mouton was thus made Comte de Lobau, Marshal Berthier, Napoleon's confidant and chief of staff, became Prince de Wagram, and Masséna, Prince de Essling. The Emperor also promoted Macdonald, Oudinot and Marmont to the rank of marshal. This flood of rewards could not hide the fact that the campaign had been much more difficult than previous ones. However, Napoleon had triumphed again. It was the end of the European insurrection against him. Now only England, Spain and Portugal continued to be at war with him.

Luise refused to see Margont again. In her mind, Relmyer and he were indissolubly linked and as a result Margont's face would always be spattered with the blood of her dear Lukas. In a way, the death of one of them signified the death of the other.

Margont found the separation from Luise most painful.

But in one respect at least, the investigation had wrought a positive change in him. Relmyer had proved that one could triumph over one's past, even if, for him, the triumph had only lasted a couple of hours. He had finally succeeded in escaping his cellar, not only bodily but in spirit as well, and this allowed Margont to escape his own cell. It was Relmyer's deliverance that allowed Margont to free himself completely from the grip of the memories of his childhood years spent sequestered in the Abbey of Saint-Guilhem-le-Désert.

THE OFFICER'S PREY

A Grande Armée murder featuring Captain Quentin Margont

Armand Cabasson

June 1812. Napoleon begins his invasion of Russia leading to the largest army Europe has ever seen.

But amongst the troops of the Grande Armée is a savage murderer whose bloodlust is not satisfied in battle.

When an innocent Polish woman is brutally stabbed, Captain Quentin Margont of the 84th regiment is put in charge of a secret investigation to unmask the perpetrator. Armed with the sole fact that the killer is an officer, Margont knows that he faces a near-impossible task and the greatest challenge to his military career.

'Combines the suspense of a thriller with the compelling narrative of a war epic' *Le Parisian*

'Cabasson skilfully weaves an intriguing mystery into a rich historical background' *Mail on Sunday*

'. . . an enthralling and unromantic account of Napoleonic war seen from a soldier's perspective' *The Morning Star*

'. . . vivid portrayal of the Grande Armée . . .' *Literary Review*

'Cabasson's atmospheric novel makes a splendid war epic . . .' *The Sunday Telegraph*

MEMORY OF FLAMES

Armand Cabasson

March 1814. Napoleon's army is outnumbered and struggling to defend France against invasion by the European allies ranged against it. Paris itself is threatened.

When the colonel in charge of the security of Paris is found murdered at home, his face burnt and a fleur-de-lys pinned to his chest, it is clear that Napoleon's authority is being challenged by royalist plotters.

Who better to call in to uncover the plot than committed republican, Lieutenant Colonel Quentin Margont? Risking his own life, he must infiltrate the secret royalist society, the Swords of the King. But will he be able to, and why do Talleyrand's parting words as he sets off on the mission, 'Good luck, Lieutenant Colonel Margont,' have the ring of an epitaph?

Gallic Books

Paperback April 2009 £7.99

978-1-906040-84-0

THE SUN KING RISES

Yves Jégo and Denis Lépée

1661 is a year of destiny for France and its young king, Louis XIV.

Cardinal Mazarin, the prime minister who has governed throughout the king's early years, lies dying. As a fierce power struggle develops to succeed him, a religious brotherhood, guardian of a centuries-old secret, also sees its chance to influence events.

Gabriel de Pontbriand, a young actor, becomes unwittingly involved when documents stolen from Mazarin's palace fall into his hands. The coded papers will alter Gabriel's life forever, and their explosive contents have the power to change the course of history for France and Louis XIV.

Fact and fiction combine in a fast-moving story of intrigue, conspiracy and love set in seventeenth-century France.

'. . . has all the life, spirit and momentum of the best historical novels'
Le Figaro

'The heroes of the book are the stars of the era: Molière, La Fontaine, Colbert . . . a book to savour'
Paris Match

'A suspense-filled mystery, a cross between the Three Musketeers and the Da Vinci Code'
Europe 1

GALLIC BOOKS

Paperback £7.99

978-1-906040-02-4

The First Nicolas Le Floch investigation

THE CHÂTELET APPRENTICE

Jean-François Parot

Translated by Michael Glencross

France 1761. Beyond the glittering court of Louis XV and the Marquises de Pompadour at Versailles, lies Paris, a capital in the grip of crime and immorality . . .

A police officer disappears and Nicolas Le Floch, a young recruit to the force, is instructed to find him. When unidentified human remains suddenly come to light, he seems to have a murder investigation on his hands. As the city descends into Carnival debauchery, Le Floch will need all his skill, courage and integrity to unravel a mystery which threatens to implicate the highest in the land.

'A terrific debut . . . brilliantly evokes the casual brutality of life in eighteenth-century France' *Sunday Times*

'Jean-François Parot's evocation of eighteenth-century Paris is richly imagined and full of fascinating historical snippets . . .'
Mail on Sunday

'Has all the twists, turns and surprises the genre demands'
Independent of Sunday

'An engaging murder mystery that picks away at the delicate power balance between king, police and state.' *Financial Times*

GALLIC BOOKS

Paperback £7.99

978-1-906040-06-2